D0245537

Earth's Descent

Book Three: Troubled Times Series

First published in 2015 by Cherry House Publishing

Earth's Descent

ISBN: 978-0-9928389-7-3

www.cherryhousepublishing.co.uk

Other Titles:

Water's Edge (Book 1; Troubled Times Series)

Power's Out (Book 2: Troubled Times Series)

Eternal Inheritance

Cyclops (The Chronicles of Curious Creatures 1)

Thanks to Ray, Kate & Janice

ONE

"He's coming, he's coming, he's coming….." the girl whispered over and over again. "He'll find us, he's coming….." The panic in her voice was unmistakable.

Nairne placed her hand firmly over the girl's mouth and pulled her slim body in closer. She could feel the girl's breath on her hand, her head held tight against Nairne's chest, and she could feel every fibre in the girl's body shake with fear.

"Sshhh…" Nairne whispered. The boy was beside her, his face pressed against her side, his eyes tightly shut, willing himself to be invisible. They were deep in shadow, tucked tightly into the shallow alcove which formed the doorway into the tumble down shed. Ronnie stood next to her, his body tense, his arm held out across them protectively.

The footsteps moved closer. The man was no more than ten metres away, and they could hear him breathing. He stopped abruptly next to the gable end of the shed.

Ronnie glanced at Nairne and indicated that they should stay still and wait for the man to move away. She nodded in response and grasped the two children tighter. It felt as if all of them held their breath in unison as the seconds ticked by.

They could hear the sound of running water as the man urinated against the side of the building before coughing and spitting on the ground. He turned and walked back towards the camp fire. As he passed their enclosure the dogs barked loudly, throwing their bodies against the sides of their small wire prison.

"Shut up! Be quiet!" the man yelled at them, lashing out and kicking the side of the cage. The dogs yelped and moved away from him. Silence fell again.

There were about a half a dozen figures gathered

around the blazing fire, which cast dancing shadows across the ground. Nairne leaned forward and peered towards the gathering. Bright orange sparks flew up from the flames spinning into the darkness. There was no real detail, just the silhouettes of the men, and then the unmistakable shape of the woman, who cried out in terror, as she was roughly passed from one set of hands to another. She struggled and pleaded with them, her words drowned out by their shouts and laughter, but the sound was silenced by a hard slap across her face. Then she sobbed, small incoherent noises, the unmistakable sound of terror.

"We have to move now, while they're distracted," Ronnie whispered.

"We can't leave her," Nairne replied.

"There's no choice, Nairne. We can't save her. You know that. Please, this is our best chance." Nairne nodded reluctantly and pulled her gaze away from the unfolding scene. She looked down at the two children and took the boy by the hand, indicating to them to keep quiet. The boy kept his eyes tightly closed. Nairne put her other hand against his cheek and bent down and whispered in his ear. He opened his eyes and nodded solemnly.

He grasped Nairne's hand with his right hand and his sister's with his left and got ready to run. Nairne went first, with the two children close on her heels. They kept low and headed into the trees. Every breaking branch and footstep seemed to reverberate. Ronnie followed closely behind glancing back towards the camp fire. The flames showed unwelcome glimpses of the woman's fate as she began to scream for her life. The sound shattered the air, a raw, basic primal sound, as her soul raged against the injustice and brutality. The girl slowed, pulling her brother and Nairne to a standstill. She looked back, her breathing was panicked, short useless breaths interspersed with the words, 'they'll catch us, they'll catch us.....' Nairne stopped and stepped back towards the hysterical child. She grabbed her by the shoulders, pulled her head around, away from the unfolding scene and locked her gaze.

"They will not catch you, I promise! Now move!"

They began to run again. The dancing shadows from the campfire faded, but the sound of the screams still echoed both in their minds and in the air. Suddenly, the sound stopped, cut off mid scream. The silence was more frightening than the noise. At least the noise was proof of life.

The woodland was dense. The ground underfoot was uneven and they stumbled and fell frequently. Ronnie was next to them now, a small torch held in his hand, which he shone in front of them, trying to find a way through the tangled undergrowth.

The two children began to slow, their breathing ragged and laboured. Nairne and Ronnie slowed down.

"What do you reckon?" Nairne asked, glancing back towards the camp.

"We're out of earshot that's for sure, but I think we should keep moving. We need to work our way around, get back to the bikes. If they find out what we've done......" He did not finish the sentence. They both knew how serious this was. Nairne nodded.

"All right, we can rest for a few minutes, but then we need to keep moving." The girl nodded. She continued to hold onto her brother's hand, while he crouched down on the ground, catching his breath.

"I think we should go that way," said Ronnie. "I know the terrain is steep, but we have a better chance if we have the advantage of height, and we can go over the top of the hill then skirt back round, what six, maybe seven miles? It's either that, or we try and sneak back past them. The river runs to the east, but I don't fancy our chances of crossing it, certainly not in the dark."

They began to climb. The ground was steep and rocky. There was no discernible path and they had to detour around boulders and fallen trees. The tough clumps of grass were unyielding and caused them all to slip and fall.

It grew steeper, and within a short time the boy was labouring, his legs shaking and his pace slowing. Ronnie undid his rucksack and passed it to Nairne, who slung it over one shoulder, where it banged against her own. Ronnie scooped the boy up and carried him on his back. His skinny arms encircled Ronnie's neck, clinging on for all he was worth.

Suddenly and without warning the girl stopped and gasped. Her hand wrenched free from Nairne's grasp. Nairne turned.

"What is it? What's wrong?"

"Can't you hear them? It's the dogs....." the girl replied in a whisper. She was frozen to the spot. They all stopped and listened. The sound was faint but distinctive.

"It's all right. They're just barking. You saw them at the camp and they were locked up," Nairne said, reassuringly.

"No," the girl replied. "You don't understand. That's what they do. That's how they catch you. They hunt you down with dogs….."

Nairne grabbed the girl's hand and began to run.

The ground grew steeper. They were more than half way up the hill. The trees began to thin out, as the landscape became too barren and dry to support them. The rocks and hummocks of grass were interspersed with patches of scree. As their boots made contact they slipped and slid, struggling to move forward. Nairne's lungs ached from the effort and sweat ran down her back. The weight of the rucksacks and the girl dragging behind her sapped her strength. She could see Ronnie pushing ahead, like a man possessed, head down scrabbling up the slope, the small body on his back attached like a limpet to a rock.

Ronnie paused next to a large boulder. He gently lowered the boy onto the ground before scrabbling onto the boulder and looking back down into the forest below. In the distance he could see intermittent glimpses of light spread out in a semi-circular formation, moving towards them.

"Can you see anything?" Nairne asked, as she reached the boulder.

"Yes, they're definitely looking for us. They're coming this way."

"How far? Can we outrun them?" She knew the answer from the expression on Ronnie's face.

"Shit! We need to get over the top and back into the trees. We need cover!" she exclaimed.

They ran, as fast as they could manage, lungs aching, leg muscles screaming and cramping. But they kept on moving. Ronnie never looked back. He ran with his head down, his tiny passenger clinging on. Nairne held the girl's hand tightly, pulling her along. The girl's breathing was ragged, interspersed with mumbled words, 'he'll catch us….. the dogs…… he'll catch us……'

The barking grew more distinct, along with voices, the words as yet unclear, but the tone full of menace. The brow of the hill was just visible. To their left was a line of trees, Scots pine, planted in rows. They turned and headed for the cover of the trees. The ground beneath them consisted of deep furrows and ridges, forcing them to move in single file. Ronnie shone the torch ahead of them, and they could see an end to the regimented rows. Up ahead lay mixed woodland, with native deciduous trees mixed in with forestry planting.

"We're at the summit," Ronnie gasped. "Downhill from now on!"

"We're not going to outrun them."

"I know," he replied.

"Right, so plan B then?" Nairne asked.

"Plan B it is." Ronnie pulled some change from his pocket, selected a coin and tossed it in the air, caught it and waited for Nairne to choose.

"Tails," she said. He uncovered the coin.

"Tails it is. Best of three?"

"No, I won the toss, so this is how it goes, as soon as we find water we split up. You take them and keep them safe. I'll lay a false trail and meet you back at the bikes."

"Nairne, you saw what they did…… I'll go," he replied, his voice full of worry.

"No, this rescue bid was my idea." She pulled his head down and kissed him gently on the lips.

They set off again at pace into the woodland. Up ahead was a clearing and to the far side of it, the beginnings of a small stream. They headed towards it, following the water downhill as the stream grew wider. Once the flow of water was sufficient they waded into it. After fifty metres they stopped.

"Right, this is it," said Nairne. She slid Ronnie's rucksack off and gave it to the girl, helping her tighten the straps. Then she undid her own rucksack and handed that to Ronnie. He put the boy down and took the rucksack from her, strapping it to his back. He fumbled in his belt and passed Nairne the handgun he had concealed beneath his jacket. She put it into her jacket pocket and adjusted her bow, which was still slung across her back. The two children stood together, the boy grasping his sister's hand. The girl spoke.

"Where are you going?"

"I'm going to lead those men in the wrong direction while Ronnie takes the two of you to safety. Don't worry, I'll see you again soon," she replied.

"Don't go!" The girl reached out and grabbed Nairne's wrist. "Please don't go, they'll catch you…."

"They'll never catch Nairne," said Ronnie. "She's far too fast and clever. Come on, we need to get moving." With that he began to walk away downstream. The two children followed him, looking back every few seconds. Ronnie did not look back.

TWO

Nairne started back down the river retracing their route. She left the stream and she ran. Without the weight of the rucksacks and the children, she moved quickly. She needed to head straight back to their camp. She needed to lead them back there and distract them if Ronnie and the children were to have any chance.

When they had met the gang two days earlier, she had suspected that all was not as it seemed. There were about half a dozen of them. Their camp had been there for a while. The pair of articulated lorries went out each day to surrounding settlements, trading and bartering. She and Ronnie had stumbled upon them by chance, and the trading had been straightforward. The group, although heavily armed, had been friendly enough inviting them to sit down and have a drink while they discussed business. They'd agreed.

Drew, the group's leader, was a large man in his mid-thirties, with tattoos covering both arms from wrists to shoulders. His face was unshaven and his long hair was tied back in a pony-tail. He had a strong west coast accent and his manner was rough. Ronnie had done the talking. Nairne had kept her head down and her hat on. They never suspected that she was a girl. When they were out travelling she preferred that people did not realise. It was safer that way. Drew had been very curious about the community. He tried to ascertain its exact location; how many members they had and what forms of security. Ronnie remained polite but gave away nothing of any value. The fewer people who knew of its location the safer they all were.

The trade went well. They swapped some vegetable seeds for spare parts for one of the Land Rovers. Parts

7

were becoming more difficult to find. Nairne doubted Drew and his mob would use the seeds themselves but they were a valuable commodity for those who were working the land. It had been Maggie's idea to start a proper collection system. A percentage of each crop was left to ripen and go to seed, then two of the women gathered, dried, packaged and labelled the seeds, with growing instructions attached. It was like a cottage industry which had proved popular within the surrounding villages. Nairne and Ronnie had swapped the seeds for various items the community needed. They'd also explained to others how to collect their own. It was vital in the long term that as many people as possible kept and stored seeds. There could come a time, faced with a particular virus or poor harvest, when their community would need to go and source vegetable seeds from somewhere else. They were also keeping a record of who they traded with and, when possible, what varieties of foodstuffs others were growing.

Nairne had accompanied Ivan, one of Drew's men, to collect the part. He took her to one of the lorries, opened the rear door and climbed in. Nairne was amazed. It was a mobile car garage, stuffed with parts, tools, tyres; in fact everything you could need. Ivan rummaged through a couple of boxes at the front of the lorry.

"This may take a few minutes, but I know we have the part," he shouted to her.

She nodded and stood waiting. The second lorry to her left, sat with the back door open and inside a mass of tinned food and other supplies filled the cavernous space, most bearing government labels. These were official rations that had obviously been diverted and were now being sold or traded to desperate people. The rationing system had begun to fail the previous winter, deliveries had become sporadic, so Nairne felt relieved that the community did not rely on them. It was just one more sign of how bad things had become.

To her left there were two box vans and a transit van. Nairne thought she could hear something inside the transit van, a soft banging sound. She would have assumed it was a dog, but she had seen the dogs next to the camp fire, safely confined in a large sturdy cage; three bulldogs. It was difficult to be sure, certainly not family pets. The sort of dogs people were rightly scared of.

The noise grew louder; it was erratic, gentle banging sounds, faster and slower. Casually, Nairne moved towards the transit van, still keeping her eye on Ivan, who, with his back to her, pulled boxes out of the way and struggled to reach something hidden deep within the lorry's bowels. Nairne took the opportunity to steal a glance through the rear windows of the van. The glass was filthy and the interior dark. She craned her head forward, almost touching the glass, trying to see where the sound was coming from. Suddenly, a small hand slapped hard against the inside of the glass, then a face. Nairne stumbled back with fright, almost losing her footing. A girl of about nine or ten, with a dark complexion, perhaps Asian, peered out. Her long, black hair hung limply, sticking to her face. Inside the van would be hot, extremely hot, Nairne realised as she moved closer. It was a warm sunny day. The girl was speaking, her tone urgent, her voice muffled, and the words unclear. She pressed both her palms against the window. Nairne could not hear the words clearly but she could lip read enough through the glass.

"Help me, please help me....." Nairne tugged at the door to the van. It was locked. She heard Ivan moving inside the lorry. She indicated to the trapped girl to stay quiet. She mouthed the words. 'I'll come back,' before she stepped away and returned to the back of the open lorry.

"I told you! I knew we had that part. See!" beamed Ivan, handing the box down to Nairne. She put it on the floor and opened it, checking the part carefully to ensure it contained the correct model and specification for their vehicle. She nodded and closed the box again. Ivan accompanied her back to the centre of the camp where Ronnie sat chatting to Drew. Nairne held up the box to let Ronnie know the trade was done. Opening the rucksack, Ronnie removed the large parcel of seeds and handed them to Drew.

"Thanks son, good to meet you both. If you give us directions we'll stop by when we're in your area. Who knows what else we might have that your community could benefit from," Drew smiled as he spoke.

"I'll show you on the map," said Ronnie. Drew pulled out a map of the region and Ronnie selected a spot, pointing to it. "Just up here. You can't miss us."

Nairne couldn't believe he was telling them the location of the community. She shot him a warning glance, but Ronnie just smiled casually.

"Well, it's been a pleasure doing business with you, remember to keep those seeds somewhere cool or they will be no use to anyone," Ronnie remarked, getting to his feet. He could sense Nairne was keen to leave. She had that 'what are you doing?' expression on her face.

They shook hands with Drew and Ivan and headed back into the woods, taking a short cut to the bikes, which were parked about a mile away near the road. They stayed silent until they were far from the camp.

"Why did you tell him where we lived?" Nairne asked, her tone disbelieving.

"I didn't. I just chose a random spot. It seemed easier than saying we don't trust you, when we were in the middle of a deal. Anyway, they were a bit rough round the edges but they traded fairly."

"Ronnie, they have a girl back there in the camp, inside one of the vans. She can't be more than ten years old."

"What, one of their kids?"

"No. She looked……scared out of her mind. She asked me to let her out, but the van doors were locked. We need to go back and get her."

"What? You want to go back and break into one of

their vehicles. Did you see the weapons they have? You don't even know what is going on......" His words trailed off. He knew as he spoke that they couldn't just ignore this. "Right, we need to wait until it's dark then we can go back down. I should be able to open the van relatively easily, then we just need to sneak away unnoticed, but you do know if they catch us......"

"I know," she replied.

By the time darkness fell, three more men had arrived at the camp, travelling in a small box van. Nairne and Ronnie watched from the woods. Ronnie had brought the binoculars so they could see what was going on. One of the new arrivals opened the back of his van and climbed inside. Minutes later they heard screaming and shouting. A young woman was dragged from the back of the vehicle. She had her hands bound behind her back and she cried out in fear. He dragged her to one of the other vans, opened the rear door and man-handled her inside, before joining the others at the camp fire.

"What the hell is going on?" Ronnie whispered.

"It looks like they trade in everything, including people."

The men sat down to eat around a blazing fire. One of them was roasting an animal carcass. He turned it every few minutes. Once ready, he slid it from the spit and carved chunks from it, which he handed out. Bottles of beer were also passed around.

"I suggest we wait a little while, until they're totally relaxed, then we can go down to the transit van, get the girl and get back to the bikes," said Ronnie. Nairne nodded in agreement and they settled down to wait. About an hour later Ivan walked over to the box van, where the woman had been imprisoned earlier that evening. He slid open the roller door on the back and climbed in, emerging a few moments later with the bound and struggling woman in tow. He pulled her towards the camp fire.

"Oh shit," said Ronnie. "This does not look good."

"No. We need to do this now!"

They set off towards the van, keeping low, and moving quietly through the bushes and young saplings which lay between them and the campfire. The doors of the transit van were facing away from the camp fire, so the body of the vehicle obscured them from view. Ronnie shone a small hand torch at the rear lock, then he removed two small metal tools from his pocket.

"Hold the light for me," he whispered. Nairne took the torch and shone it on the lock. Ronnie inserted the implements and began to move them around, after a few tense minutes the lock clicked open. He lifted the handle and swung the door open. Nairne shone the torch inside.

The two children were huddled against the rear of the van. They were filthy, and the van stank of urine and faeces. Their clothes were torn and ragged. The girl pushed back her hair and placed her hand over her eyes to shield herself from the torchlight. The boy, who was no more than seven years old, clung to her, his face buried in her clothing. Nairne moved the torch beam back so the children could see her and Ronnie. She held out her hand.

"Come on, we need to go," she whispered urgently.

The girl began to move, pulling the boy with her. Ronnie lifted them out of the van and gently closed the door behind them.

Nairne made good time. She travelled downhill while her pursuers were still working their way up towards the summit. She slid down the scree, which had been so hard to ascend, and ran down the gentler slopes. Her knees and hips jarred with the impact, but she had to make it back to their camp with enough time.

She could see the odd flash of light above her as they swung their torches around. The dogs were barking excitedly, and she hoped they were still on their leads. The camp site was almost in view. Nairne could smell the smoke from the bonfire. As she reached the final patch of woodland, the ground evened out and her pace slowed slightly. Her chest ached from the exertion, but she kept moving. Within minutes the lorries were in view. She jogged back to the edge of the camp and paused, looking around. It was eerily quiet, too quiet. She crouched down low and covered the last fifty metres as silently as possible. Then she saw him; one lone guard, pacing up and down near the remnants of the bonfire. He stopped and rummaged in his pocket, took out a pack of cigarettes and lit one. Nairne could see his face, just for an instant, in the glow cast by his lighter. He took a long drag and exhaled slowly. A rifle hung loosely over his shoulder. Nairne swung her bow from her back and inserted an arrow. She pulled back the bow string and walked towards him. When the distance was no more than fifteen metres she spoke clearly.

"Turn around and slide that rifle to the ground."

He swung around, startled by her presence. She saw him look at the crossbow and arrow and she could almost hear him thinking, 'but I have a gun.' He pulled the rifle round, not to drop it as instructed, but to fire it. She let the arrow go. It struck him in the chest before he got the rifle raised. He fell back hitting the ground with a thud.

She ran over to his prostrate figure and kicked the rifle from his reach. Then she knelt down, there was no sign of a pulse and he did not react when she touched him. She pulled the arrow back out from his chest and put it back with the others.

Next, she looked around the camp. There were tools scattered about, one of the men must have been doing some digging. She picked up a heavy shovel and went over to the two box vans. She pushed the edge of the shovel under the roller door and used it to lever the door open. After a couple of sharp pushes the lock began to stretch until she heard it pull loose. She pushed the door up. The van was empty. She went round to the next one and forced the lock. As she opened the door she could hear muffled cries. Nairne switched on the torch and shone it into the vehicle.

The two women were huddled together at the back of the van, cowering from the light. One of them whimpered and they clung to each other. Nairne shone the torch onto her own face, pulling off her hat.

"Come on, we need to move now."

They hesitated for a moment then scrabbled towards the front of the van. She helped them out. They were both shivering.

"What about Anita, where is she?" one of them asked.

"Is that the woman they took out earlier?" Nairne enquired. The women nodded in response. "I'm sorry, she's dead. Her body is over next to the camp fire." One of the women began to sob. "Look, we don't have much time; they are on their way back. Can either of you drive?" The older of the two nodded. "We need to find the keys to the transit van and we need to get out of here." The three of them rushed over to the vehicle. The front doors were unlocked. "See if the keys are inside. I'll be back in a few minutes."

She left the two women rummaging through the glove box and side door pockets of the van. She sprinted back to the dead man and searched through his pockets. Finally she found a set of keys. 'Please, let these be the right ones,' she thought. She lifted his rifle and searched around the edge of the camp until she found some clothing. Taking a couple of tee-shirts, she went back to the box vans and removed the petrol caps, stuffing one end of the tee-shirt into each.

She threw the keys to one of the women.

"Try these." The woman caught them and climbed into the van, inserting them into the ignition.

"Yes, it is the right key," the woman replied. They all paused. They could hear barking and shouting. Nairne looked up. The men were no more than three or four minutes away.

"Right, start the van and then wait for me." The woman nodded and turned the key, the van burst into life, the engine made a throaty noise as she revved it and put the vehicle into gear. The other woman scrambled in the passenger side holding the door open. Nairne took a lighter from her pocket and lit the ends of the tee-shirt on one van and then the other, before running to the transit van. She climbed in pulling the door shut.

"Drive!"

The woman obeyed and they set off down a rough track into the trees. The vehicle bumped and rocked as it lurched over the uneven ground, gears clanking and the engine protesting at its rough treatment.

Minutes later the box van exploded as the flaming fabric made contact with the contents of the petrol tank. A giant ball of flame lit up the sky. The second explosion followed moments later.

As Ronnie reached the bikes, the two children were close behind him. They were exhausted. The boy could hardly catch his breath, while the girl slumped to the ground. Her shoulders heaved as she tried to speak.

"What...... now?" she gasped.

"We wait for Nairne. Then we get as far away from here as we can."

"What? On the motorbikes?" She looked terrified.

"That's right. Don't worry, you just have to hold on tight. It's quite safe." She did not look convinced.

"So, what are your names?" Ronnie asked.

"I am Sahasra and this is my brother, Subhash," she replied.

"Pleased to meet you both." Ronnie held out his hand which the girl shook formally. Subhash stood behind her, obviously shy.

Suddenly, the sky lit up with a dazzling ball of flame and a huge explosion. The two children cried out in panic and pressed their bodies to the ground.

"It's all right, I guess Nairne is on her way!" Ronnie grinned, unstrapping the rucksack from his back. He took the other one from Sahasra and strapped one to each bike. "We need to be ready to move. Sahasra, you can travel with Nairne and I'll take your brother with me, okay?" The girl looked up and nodded solemnly. Ronnie wheeled the first bike onto the edge of the road. The ground was rough and it was an effort to move the bike over the uneven surface. He came back and got the second one. "Come on, she'll be here shortly." The two children got to their feet and hand in hand they followed him.

The woman driving the van did not spare the vehicle. She pressed her foot hard to the floor. The headlights showed the pathway ahead and she turned and twisted the steering wheel to avoid the biggest of the potholes.

"The road is just ahead. I think the nearest town is east so turn left when we reach the road. I'll leave you the rifle, just in case they catch up with you. Do you know how to use one of these?" Nairne asked the passenger, who sat sandwiched in the middle.

"No, I've never used a gun," she replied, eyes wide with fear.

Nairne handed her the rifle.

"It's loaded, safety catch is here, that is it on, and that is it off." She flicked the catch. "When you fire there will be a kick back so brace yourself, place the butt firmly against your shoulder. And if you point it at someone, be prepared to use it. Make sure you aim to kill. Chest shots are easiest as it is a bigger target. Remember, if they catch you again, they will kill you. Don't hesitate, understand?" The woman nodded and took the rifle from her. The road came into view and the van turned left. "You can let me out here." The driver slowed down and brought the van to a stop.

"Good luck," Nairne shouted, as she opened the door.

"Where are you going?" the woman asked. "They'll

catch up with you on foot."

"Don't worry, I have my own transport." With that she slammed the van door behind her and started to run down the road in the opposite direction. Within a few minutes she could see the outline of Ronnie and the bikes on the road ahead. She waved and picked up her speed.

THREE

"I can't believe that! Who the hell do they think they are?" Voice raised, Nairne stormed down the corridor with Ronnie following close behind. "They haven't got a clue, not a clue what's happening out there. And I've tried, you know I have, but what were we supposed to do, leave those kids back there? Leave them to be used for God knows what? You saw what they did to that woman….."

"Nairne, calm down. Look, it'll be fine. You know what some of them are like. They're frightened. And when people are frightened, they say stupid things." He reached out and put his arms round her.

She pushed him away.

"No, you know it's more than that. They aren't comfortable with me. They don't approve. Ever since I dealt with Steven Mitchell, hell even before then. They think I'm some sort of monster. How could I have shot an unarmed man? But they know he deserved to die. It had to be done. We would never have been free of him, never. It's just none of them would have had the guts." She pushed open the front door of the building and rushed outside. "Not suitable people to look after children, like we'd gone out there to steal a couple of kids to look after, instant happy bloody families. I don't want to look after them, but I thought at least they'd see we had to help them."

"Nairne, stop." Ronnie grabbed her arm, holding it tightly. "Don't let them do this to you. I know how angry you are. I know you didn't want to adopt Sahasra and Subhash, and they should not have assumed, or said those things. Look, we've faced them with a problem. Someone is going to have to take responsibility for the kids, and they don't know what to do, so they lash out. Why don't we see

18

if we can solve the problem for them?"

"What? Find volunteers to adopt two children? And how the hell do we do that?"

"Trust me, I have a plan," he replied, steering Nairne towards the walled garden.

Isobel was in the greenhouse, watering the seedlings. She waved to them as they approached and came outside to greet them.

"How are you both? How was the trip? Have you seen Paul yet? He is so keen to find out how you got on." Isobel fired the questions at them, excitedly.

"We've been to his room, but there was no sign of him," said Nairne. "How has he been?" She had been reluctant to go on the trip with Ronnie, leaving Paul for two weeks. She still worried about him. His recovery had been slow. He found it difficult to walk more than a few faltering steps even with the aid of two crutches, and he spent a lot of time in the wheelchair they had found for him. Steven Mitchell's knife had damaged his spinal cord. Doc Brown said he was very lucky to have survived the attack but he remained unsure if Paul would ever walk properly again. Paul put on a brave face, as did Isobel, but Nairne knew he was depressed. He felt like a burden to the community.

"He's been good," said Isobel. "I think he finds it hard, especially when the two of you are away on a trip and he's stuck here, but he's been doing his exercises every day and taking Dog out for very slow walks. He's even mastered getting up the stairs with his crutches."

"And what about you?" Ronnie asked. He knew the strain on Isobel had been immense. She had stuck by Paul even though they had barely been an item before the attack.

"I'm fine, honestly, and we're good. It's going really well. We've moved into the same room. It seemed daft since I spend all my time there anyway and…. even dad's been cool about it. So rumour has it you came back with a surprise for everyone. What happened?"

"We acquired two small children, by accident," said Nairne. "They'd been picked up by this gang, well that's not really true. Their parents are dead, and they'd been fending for themselves and decided to try and steal some supplies from this gang. They hunted them down with dogs. When we found them they'd been left in a transit van for about four days with almost no food and barely enough water. These guys were real predators. We couldn't leave them, so we brought them back….."

"So what will happen to them?" Isobel asked.

"If you heard some of the committee members we should just drive them out into the countryside and abandon them," Nairne replied.

"Come on, that's a bit unfair. The committee weren't particularly pleased, but they'll come around. Anyway, we want to talk to you and Paul," Ronnie interjected. "Could we get together over lunch?"

"Sure, I'll just finish up here and we'll meet you in the dining hall. Give us half an hour."

Nairne and Ronnie walked back across the deer enclosure. Nairne looked at him quizzically, but he stayed silent.

"So are you going to tell me what's going on?" she asked.

"I think we may have found some temporary parents for Sahasra and Subhash."

"What, Isobel and Paul? But they're no older than us. We can't ask them to take this on…... It's ludicrous. There's no way the committee will agree to this. And Paul, he's got enough to contend with getting himself better."

"I think your underestimating them, just like the committee underestimate you. Paul can't do the things he used to, not just now. It could take months or years for him to get back to full health. So he feels he's not contributing, so he gets depressed. Well, he can contribute this way. He can give those kids something they really need, security and care. He can teach them stuff, be there if they need anything. Paul needs a reason to get better and he needs something other than himself to think about. And as for Isobel, you know she will be an absolute natural. You'll see."

"But they don't have any experience.

"Most new parents don't, but Isobel's dad is here to help, and others will show them what to do. That's what makes this a community. Don't try and find a reason why this won't work Nairne, help me persuade them that it can."

Paul and Isobel were already seated when Nairne and Ronnie entered the dining hall. Dog was sitting at the end of the table, but ran across the hall barking when he spotted Nairne. She stopped and rubbed his head. She sat down and they waited for the food to arrive. It was great to have a home cooked meal, after two weeks on the road.

"So, glad to be home?" Paul asked. "I hear you came back with some unexpected visitors."

"Yes, we did, and that's what we wanted to talk to you about," said Ronnie. "We brought back two kids, Sahasra, she's nine, and her brother Subhash has just turned seven. They have had a terrible time, no family left that they know of and four days being held by a bunch of psychotic losers. At the moment they're sleeping in Nairne's room. They are exhausted. Nairne and I met with the committee this morning, so we need to find volunteers to look after them."

"For how long?" Isobel asked.

"I suppose for good. The committee were none too pleased at us turning up with two more mouths to feed, even if they are only kids. Let's just say things got a bit heated," Ronnie replied. Paul raised his eyebrows and looked at Nairne.

"Heated is a bit of an understatement. It is the view of

several members of our esteemed committee that we were reckless to bring them back here and that we couldn't expect the community to rally round and look after them. And wait for this, that we were a totally unsuitable couple to look after children," Nairne interjected.

"Who the hell said that?" Paul's tone was angry. "What the hell do they mean?"

"I think they mean that someone who shoots an unarmed man and watches him bleed to death, and a thief, are unsuitable role models," she replied. "Basically, some of the committee don't want them to stay here. I am not sure where they would like us to take them."

"So who are you going to ask? I mean it's a huge thing to ask someone to do? What about one of the Balfour brothers? They both love kids and their wives are both pretty easy going?" Paul replied.

"But they both have a child of their own. No, we wondered about you and Isobel," said Ronnie. Paul dropped his fork onto the table. He looked shocked.

"You are kidding? How the hell could we look after two kids? Christ, I can hardly look after myself?" His tone was bitter. "We don't have any experience. And in case you'd failed to notice I can't walk properly. Honestly Ronnie, you're taking the piss. We couldn't possibly take them on, could we?" He looked at Isobel. She hesitated.

"I don't think so, no…. Paul's right, really we couldn't."

Paul pushed his wheelchair away from the table and headed towards the door. Isobel went after him.

"Brilliant, that went well," said Nairne. "I told you it was stupid."

FOUR

Sahasra and Subhash slept for most of the day and rose just before six, as hunger finally woke them. Nairne sat in the room reading, with Dog at her feet. Subhash was first to open his eyes. The movement alerted Dog who stood up and rushed to the side of the bed to greet the newcomers. Subhash squealed in panic and pressed himself against the wall, clutching at his sister, who woke with a start.

"You are all right, it's only Dog. He's one of the good guys," said Nairne. "Dog, sit." On queue Dog sat obediently at the side of the bed and rested his head on the edge of the mattress. "He's been guarding you while you were asleep. Why don't you give him a pat?"

Subhash shook his head, unconvinced. Sahasra pulled herself up away from Dog's head but reached out a hand and tentatively stroked the top of his head.

"His hair is all wiry," she said.

"That's because he is part lurcher," said Nairne. "They have wiry hair and are used for hunting. He's got other breeds in there as well; part Labrador, I'd say since he is such a greedy dog." Dog pushed his head forward demanding more attention. After a few minutes Subhash leaned over his sister and stretched his hand out gently touching the top of Dog's head.

"And he's called Dog?" Sahasra asked.

"Yes, that's right. He's just called Dog. My brother named him and I think it kind of suits him, don't you agree? Now, the pair of you must be hungry. Do you want me to fetch you some supper, maybe some soup and what about a piece of cake?" Their faces lit up and they nodded vigorously. "Don't worry, I'll be back shortly. Do you want Dog to stay and wait with you?" They both nodded again.

When Nairne returned both children were sitting at the small table in her room with Dog sandwiched between them, shifting his head from side to side to let each pat him in turn.

"You know you'll spoil him," she laughed, as she placed the tray on the table. She lifted off the two bowls of soup, two glasses of milk and two pieces of Jenny's famous carrot cake. Their eyes were like saucers.

"I can't believe you have cake. We haven't seen cake in...... I can't remember!" Sahasra declared.

"Eat your soup first. After you've eaten I'll show you where things are and then it's back to bed. You both look exhausted." While the children ate, Nairne re-made the bed. She looked out a couple of clean towels and two old tee shirts. She crossed the hall to the bathroom and ran a warm bath. When she returned the food was gone.

"First things first, you two need to get cleaned up!" She took them over to the bathroom and after discarding their filthy clothes they both climbed into the tub. The water took on a murky look almost instantly. Nairne handed them face cloths and homemade soap. Maggie, one of the older women had become quite proficient at manufacturing it. Once washed, dried and each dressed in one of Nairne's old tee shirts, they brushed their teeth before heading back to Nairne's room.

"To bed with both of you and I'll be back in the morning." They climbed into bed and Nairne pulled the covers over them. "I'll leave the door open, just slightly so you will have some light from the hallway. I'll be in Ronnie's room down the hall, the one I showed you opposite the bathroom. If you get frightened or need anything come and wake me up."

"Okay" said Sahasra and Subhash nodded. As Nairne opened the door to leave, Dog stirred and followed her. The children both leaned forward to watch him go.

"Do you want him to stay in here with you?" Nairne asked. They nodded. "Dog stay!" Dog went back to his place on the rug under the table and settled down to sleep.

Paul rose early and after dressing he sat in his wheelchair

and set out along the corridor to Nairne's room. Dog would need a walk and it had become a regular routine to take him out. Dog did most of the walking while Paul stumbled along behind on crutches, dragging his useless legs. He could go a little further every day but it was exhausting, and some days Paul could hardly face the constant struggle.

He knocked gently at Nairne's door. She would probably lie in; they had been travelling for two weeks so she would be tired. He pushed the door open gently. Dog rose from his favourite spot under the table and stretched his legs, front and back, yawning widely.

"Come on boy," Paul whispered, backing his chair out into the corridor. Then he noticed the small boy with the improbably large eyes, sitting perched on the edge of the bed. The girl remained sound asleep. The boy reached out and tentatively patted Dog's back as he passed. "I'm taking him for a walk. Do you want to come with me?"

The boy nodded solemnly and glanced at his sleeping sister.

"Don't worry, we won't be long. Do you have some clothes you can put on, it might be colder outside?"

The boy crossed over to the table and lifted up a pair of trousers and jumper which Nairne had borrowed from the clothes store. When kids grew out of stuff it was set aside for anyone else to use for their children. The trousers were too long and the jumper too big, but at least they would keep him warm. He slipped on his tattered shoes and followed Paul out of the door. When they reached the front door Paul wheeled himself outside. His crutches were slung over the back of the chair. The boy lifted them up and handed them to Paul.

"Thanks, that's much easier than me trying to struggle around there to get them." He placed a crutch under each arm and skilfully descended the stairs. They set off across the gravel driveway to the lawn at the rear of the house. "If you find a stick and throw it for Dog he'll bring it back. Look, there are some over there, under that beech tree."

The boy ran across the grass and returned with a stick more than half his height.

"Right, throw it as hard as you can," said Paul.

Subhash hurled the stick into the air and Dog charged off across the grass, returning a few moments later with his prize.

Nairne woke with a start. Sahasra shook her, panic in her voice.

"My brother is gone, he's gone!"

"Wait, let me get some clothes." Nairne rolled out of bed and fumbled with her trousers pulling them on. Ronnie stirred.

"What's wrong, what's going on?"

"It's fine. Subhash has gone walkabouts. I'll help Sahasra find him. You go back to sleep."

"No, I'll come and help," said Ronnie, prising himself out from under the warm covers. Sahasra waited impatiently at the door. Dressed in ill-fitting clothes, she looked distraught.

"Don't worry, he won't have gone far," said Nairne. She took the girl by the hand and they set off down the corridor checking her room, the bathroom, along to the end of the corridor and through to the communal areas. "We'll check the kitchen and the dining hall, maybe he got hungry and went exploring." They entered the hall. It was almost empty and there was no sign of Subhash. Nairne asked the handful of early risers, but no one had seen him.

"Do you want us to help you look?" said Alan Balfour, rising from his chair, his half eaten breakfast in front of him.

"No, no need for panic, yet. We'll have a good look around. He can't have gone far; maybe he wandered off and can't find his way back. He's not familiar with the building yet. Come on Sahasra, let's check the kitchen."

The girl trailed behind her. Nairne tried to appear as calm as possible while her mind raced, where the hell has he got to? He wouldn't have wandered outside, not by himself. There was no sign in the kitchen so they headed upstairs and started a systematic search of the building, floor by floor. It took almost twenty minutes to search every room, cupboard and bathroom in the house and still there was no sign. As they descended the main staircase Ronnie was waiting for them.

"I think you should come and see this," he said.

"What is it? Have you found him?" Nairne asked.

"Look," Ronnie pointed into the dining hall, where Subhash was sitting in Paul's wheelchair eating his breakfast, with Dog at his side. Paul and Isobel were sitting next to him. Sahasra rushed across the dining hall and grabbed her brother's arm roughly.

"Don't you ever do that again," she chided him. "Don't you ever wander off, not ever!" She looked on the verge of tears. Subhash looked up at her and tears rolled down his cheeks. He hugged her hard.

"This is my fault," said Paul. "It was stupid of me, but your brother came to help me walk Dog. As you can see," he glanced at the wheelchair, "walking is not one of my strong points at the moment so having someone to help was great. I'm sorry if we gave you a fright. We thought we would be back before anyone got up, and when we got back you were all out looking for us, I guess. Will you forgive me?"

"Yes, I just got such a fright," she said.

"Why don't you sit down here," said Isobel, "and I'll fetch you something to eat. I'm Isobel, by the way, and this is Paul."

They both shook hands with Sahasra. Ronnie and Nairne joined them at the table. After they'd eaten, Isobel offered to show the children around and take them down to see the cattle, the rabbits and the deer. Ronnie glanced at Nairne, that knowing look of I told you so. She smiled back. He was right. Paul and Isobel were great with them.

FIVE

Jack MacTaggart sat down heavily. He looked over at Isobel and Paul, who were perched on the edge of the sofa. His mind was whirring. They had been so insistent on seeing him and so reluctant to tell him what it was all about.

"Well, you've got my attention, so who is going to tell me what is wrong?"

"Dad," Isobel sighed, "nothing's wrong, we just have a favour to ask of you, that's all. We wondered if you would be willing to swap rooms. Since you have this whole place to yourself, including my old bedroom, and we are squashed together in Paul's room. We're going to need more space."

"What?" He jumped up out of the seat. "Are you telling me you're pregnant?" He looked happy about it if a bit surprised. "I had no idea you wanted to have a baby, so soon, you're just children yourselves, but if that is what you both want......."

"God's sake dad, I am *not* pregnant," Isobel laughed, embarrassed. Jack sat down again somewhat deflated. "But we do have some news. We want to take in Sahasra and Subhash. We've spent a lot of time with them over this last week, and we know you have the committee meeting tomorrow to decide what to do with them. So we're volunteering. We'll look after them. If you swapped rooms it would mean the kids could have their own room and we'd have a living room as well. You'd always be welcome to come in here. You'd be like their adopted granddad, and we might ask you to help out a bit because we have no idea what we are doing, but someone has to take them on."

Jack MacTaggart had met the children, and he'd seen the boy trailing around after Paul.

"I don't know what to say. I hope Ronnie and Nairne haven't pressured you into this. They brought the kids here so it's their responsibility. I know some people on the committee have doubts about their suitability as parents, but I think they'd do a fine job and I'm willing to argue that case."

"Jack, we have discussed it with them," said Paul. "You know Nairne and Ronnie want to do some travelling and, let's face it, they are likely to be asked to make more trips on behalf of the community. I can't do that anymore, but Isobel and I can do this. Those kids have been through some terrible experiences. I love Nairne and Ronnie, but there is no way they're ready to settle down with that sort of responsibility. I think we are. We know it is a lot to take on and I know you're going to say we have enough to contend with, with my recovery, but this gives me an added reason to want to get better. Those kids will need me to do stuff for them. It's an extra goal to aim for."

"Dad?" Isobel got up and crossed over to her father. "We know what we're doing. Will you help us?" Jack MacTaggart looked at his daughter. She was so like her mother, in so many ways. She was always taking in waifs and strays.

"Come here." He hugged her hard. "Of course I'll help you."

"No regrets?" said Ronnie, when a week later Nairne moved the kids clothes along to Isobel and Paul's new rooms.

"I'll miss them," she replied. "But the committee are right we're not ready to do this. I want to get back out there and I want to know what's happening. I feel like it's all just rumour and speculation, without proper radio broadcasts, I feel like the world is getting smaller and smaller. Who knows what's happening in Glasgow or Manchester or London, or across the Channel. I guess we used to take it all for granted; instant news, the internet, seeing things unfold across the globe and now, it is like the industrial revolution never happened."

"Where do you want to go?"

"I don't know. I just want to travel. We live here in this little idyllic world of our own, with our own food supplies, our own water, even our own electricity and yet we know that there must be people in the cities who are starving. The only real problems we face here are those caused by the weather."

"I don't think we should underestimate those," Ronnie replied. "Arthur was telling me we recorded temperatures of thirty-eight degrees last week, and it's September. We had minus seventeen in February. All we need is another winter like last year with rain almost every day and we'll have floods and God knows what to contend with."

"That's all the more reason to find out what is happening. We need to know what is going on so we can plan ahead, not hide in here hoping for the best."

"You don't need to convince me. I'm willing to go with you, if that is what you want but we need to persuade the committee."

Jack McTaggart was relieved when the committee meeting was over. He felt some of the others still had it in for Nairne. She was her own worst enemy. If she would just try and compromise a little, show some remorse for what had happened with Mitchell, but that just wasn't her style. He suspected that the killing of Mitchell had made quite an impact on the girl, but she was as defiant as ever and Jack knew, better than most of the community, that Nairne was right. Mitchell couldn't have been dealt with any other way. At least sense had prevailed and permission for their extended trip had been granted. Jack knew if she and Ronnie wanted to go travelling they would do it anyway, better to have a sanctioned trip where at least the community might benefit from what they found out and they might bring back some useful supplies.

Isobel and Paul stepping in to look after the two children had been a god-send. It had stopped some of the criticisms about Nairne and Ronnie being irresponsible and leaving others to clean up their mess. Jack had been worried about his daughter taking on two children, but it seemed to be working and the kids were settling in. The boy had not yet spoken a word to anyone, but these things took time, and who knew what they had seen out there.

He admired Nairne and Ronnie. They needed to see what was out there and information on the bigger picture could be useful. Since the power grid failure five months earlier and the cessation of government rations they all suspected that over the coming months things were going to get a lot worse. Getting a first-hand account of what was going on could prove valuable in their longer term planning.

"Two months? They sanctioned a two month trip?" Paul asked. "Are you two completely mad? Where will you go?"

"We don't know yet. We thought we'd go south. Nairne wants to go to Langholm to see Mr Cranshaw, her old neighbour, then who knows. We might travel across the border into England, if we can, and see what is going on there," Ronnie replied.

"You will be careful, won't you? Nairne's been different since, you know that business with Mitchell. She's, I don't know, reckless. You've seen it haven't you? The way she provokes people, the risks she takes. Christ, acting as a decoy to rescue the kids. What if they had caught her? It's like she just has to keep pushing the boundaries."

"I know you're right, but she is going on this trip with or without me," Ronnie replied. "At least if I go along with her then hopefully I can help her stay safe. You know I'll look out for her."

"What are you two up to?" Nairne asked, as she joined them at the dining table.

"Ronnie was just filling me in on the trip. I take it you are going on the bikes and leaving Dog here?"

"Yeah, it's the most economical way to travel, and anyway, I think Dog's camping days are behind him. He's getting on and I am sure he'd rather be here with all of you and the kids spoiling him. You are all right with that, taking care of him for me?"

"Of course we are. He's no problem and Subhash adores him. You'll give my regards to Mr Cranshaw. I'd love to come with you."

"Yes, I know. You can come next time. I'm sure you'll soon be back on your feet properly. I have to say, I am looking forward to seeing him. He was so good to me, to all of us after my dad died. I'm looking forward to seeing the new farm."

SIX

"What the hell happened here?" Ronnie wiped his forehead. It was thirty-four degrees and wearing the crash helmet was unbearable.

"I have no idea," Nairne replied, climbing off her bike. "It looks like a war zone. Everything is burnt; I've never seen anything like this. It's like someone has tried to erase the whole town from the map." She had never been to Langholm before, but she knew it would be similar to many other small settlements in the area: a main high street, some industrial buildings, a public park, a school, small housing estates; just a quiet little market town. Now all they could see were the burnt-out remains of some of the more substantial stone buildings. The industrial estate was a scene of melted and buckled steel, the bent and twisted remains barely recognisable. Street after street of houses were no more than burnt out shells. The roads were almost obliterated. The tar had been torn up and crude defences had been built from buses, trucks and cars. These were now blackened shells, tyres melted and glass shattered. The pair pushed the bikes forward, further into the settlement. There was silence. No dogs, no people, just silence.

"Where is everyone? There must have been at least a couple of thousand people living here. Where have they gone?"

"I don't know, but I hope they left before this happened," Nairne replied. "Let's get out of here. I don't feel like we should be here. The farm should be about fourteen miles west."

The road surface was too uneven to ride the bikes and the roadway was littered with debris. They circled around the barricades and burnt out vehicles, and after half a mile they reached the other end of the main street and the

33

countryside ahead. The light was beginning to fade and they were keen to reach Mr Cranshaw's before darkness.

"Oh my God," Ronnie whispered under his breath. "I think we've just found out where the people went." On the edge of the settlement, sitting on the first available patch of land were two abandoned diggers. The small field had been dug up and piles of soil marked what could only be mass graves.

They walked past in silence. There were no markers, no signs, and no explanation of what had happened. As soon as they left the settlement the road was clearer and they both mounted their bikes and set off. After another ten minutes Nairne indicated and pulled over. Ronnie pulled in behind her. She got the map out and examined it.

"The turning should be somewhere here on the right. It's an unclassified farm road so there might not be any signs." They scanned the road. There was no sign of any junctions.

"Maybe we missed it," said Ronnie, turning his bike around and heading back down the road. Nairne followed. They travelled back about two miles and turned again.

"I don't understand, we can see it on the map," said Ronnie.

"Unless it has been camouflaged. Sometimes it is safer if no one knows you are there." This time they pushed the bikes back down the road and after about twenty minutes they found the hidden entrance. The single track farm road had been obscured with tree branches and vegetation. The track on the other side was passable but getting the bikes through was a real struggle and it was dusk by the time they were safely on the other side of the makeshift barrier. They left the bikes hidden in the undergrowth and taking their rucksacks and weapons, they headed down the road.

The farm house looked deserted. There were no lights and no signs of life. Suddenly, a powerful torch beam shone in their faces and they both raised their hands to shield their eyes from the glare.

"Stop where you are!" The voice was gruff and strong. They could not see anyone. "Put your weapons down." They did as instructed and stood very still.

"Mr Cranshaw," Nairne called out.

"Do I know you?" The voice responded.

"We haven't met, I'm Nairne Grear. I used to live next door to your uncle, Robert Cranshaw, over in the Borders. I'm here to visit him. We don't mean any harm."

"Right, you can lower your hands and come on up to the house."

They picked up their weapons and walked towards the two storey rendered farmhouse that looked grey in the fading light. The windows were protected with homemade shutters which were bolted shut. It looked more like a fort than a family home.

Hugh Cranshaw gestured for them to come in, holding the door open. He was a large man, with a shock of black hair and a full beard. He towered over Ronnie and Nairne and shook each of them by the hand as they entered the cosy kitchen.

"Sorry about that, but we can't be too careful." He ushered them into the room and introduced his wife, Julia, and the two older children, Ben and Ewan.

"Our youngest, Margaret is already in bed," said Julia. "Why don't the pair of you take off your coats and come and have a seat, I'll get some supper for you and the boys can make up a bed in the spare room. You will stay over, won't you? It's not safe to be out after dark."

"Thank you," Ronnie replied. "That would be great."

"And Mr Cranshaw?" Nairne asked. She could feel them all looking at her. She knew that look. She knew he was gone. Hugh's face said it all.

"I'm sorry Nairne, he passed away in November, something to do with his lungs. We couldn't get any proper medical treatment and we looked after him as best we could but.....he just faded. He talked about you and your brother a lot. I know he was very fond of the pair of you and sad to move away. Once he found out that you had left he was so worried about what might have happened to you. I think he hoped you might turn up here. I am sorry you were too late to see him."

"So am I. He was a lovely man and he was so kind to us, to all of us." As she spoke the two boys left the room to attend to the spare room and Julia began to organise some food for them. Nairne and Ronnie sat at the generous farmhouse table with Hugh, while Nairne told him what had happened with her father's property and Steven Mitchell's takeover bid. She filled him in on the new community, and how Mitchell had pursued her and Paul and had tried to take control of the place.

"Uncle Robert wasn't keen on him, felt there was something not right, but what could he do? So, he's dead now, this Mitchell?"

"Yes, he's dead," Nairne replied.

"So what happened?" said Ronnie. "We came through town or what was left of it."

Hugh sighed and sat back in the chair, Julia stood behind him, her expression grim.

"A massacre, that's the only way to describe it. They came in January, there was thick snow and heavy frosts. The town had hunkered down waiting for the weather to break. There had been very few supplies from the government, but with crops from surrounding farms people were just getting by, those that were left. We lost a lot the previous year in the typhoid and dysentery outbreaks that swept down from the city. Anyway, we'd had problems with groups coming over the Border, off and on since the original Border conflict. Just small raiding parties, but this was different. They were well armed, military style vehicles and proper weapons against a town of unarmed people. They just rolled on through, burning and looting. It went on for about five days. We could hear the gunfire and explosions. After the first day I went into town, cross country, to see if I could help…..but it was useless. Those people didn't stand a chance. And what these guys couldn't steal they destroyed. Those who survived fled. You've seen it. There is nothing left, nothing to stay for. We went back into town a week later and helped to bury the dead. After that, I covered the end of the driveway. It's safer if people don't know we are here. Now there is just us and two other families in the farm cottages. They help out with the land for a share of the crops, but there's no long term safety here."

"There's no safety anywhere," said Julia. "The world has lost its way. Who would think we'd live to see this. Men with guns roaming the streets. Gangsters, taking what they want, killing people and nothing is done about it." Hugh clasped her hand.

"Julia lost close friends, people she had known all her life. She grew up here."

His wife excused herself and left the room.

"I'm sorry, we didn't mean to upset her," Ronnie said. "We'd just never seen anything like that."

"I hope you'll never see anything like it again, but I think there must be more of this across the country. Anyway, Nairne we have something for you. We had a visit from one of your neighbours, Jock Elliott from Kersmains. He came over to see Uncle Robert and brought a letter with him. This was about a year ago now. Hang on, I'll fetch it. Uncle Robert said we should hang onto it in case you showed up. He said no one would go to the bother of trying to send a letter unless it was something really important." He rose from the table and vanished into the living room. They could hear him rummaging in the desk drawers, searching for something.

"Found it!" He returned clutching a sealed brown envelope, with Daniel Grear and their old address on the front. "It was delivered by hand, a guy who had been paid handsomely for his trouble. When he got to the property and found it abandoned he tried the next farm along the road, Jock Elliot said he would hang on to it, in case you came back. Here." He held the envelope out and Nairne took it.

She turned it over and peeled back the sealed edge removing two sheets of paper from inside. Her eyes scanned the contents. The writing was rushed, a jagged scrawl.

"What is it?" Ronnie asked, as Nairne had turned white. "Nairne?" She held the letter out and he took the pages from her.

Hugh Cranshaw watched as Ronnie read the contents of the letter. The girl looked like she had seen a ghost. She was trembling. Ronnie handed the sheets of paper to Hugh.

"I don't understand, who is Angela?" Ronnie asked.

"My mum, she's my mother," Nairne replied.

"But I thought she was dead. You said she died in an arson attack."

"That's what the police said. They came to the door, this was way back right at the start of the troubles. She had dysentery. The block of flats in London, where she lived, was burned down and lots of people were killed. There was no body, but they said she had perished. I don't understand. How could she have let us think she was dead? How could she have done that to us?"

"And now she wants help," said Hugh. "Looking at this she is desperate and she has no idea your dad's dead, no idea at all. She must have been waiting all these months for him to get in touch or to go and get her."

"Well she can go on waiting. She was dead for me way before that fire. She was dead to me the moment she left us." Nairne stormed from the room, they heard the front door open and close.

Ronnie got up. Hugh put his hand on Ronnie's arm.

"I'd give her some time, son. That's a lot to take in. Come on. Sit back down and let's break open a bottle. I think we could all do with a drink."

SEVEN

They stayed with the Cranshaws for two more days, and Ronnie and Nairne were sad to leave. Hugh and his wife had made them so welcome, plus the kids were lovely and so keen to spend time with the visitors. Nairne put on a brave face in front of the Cranshaws, but Ronnie could see she was reeling from the news. He had tried to discuss it, to find out what she wanted to do, but his efforts were met with a stony silence.

Hugh had insisted on providing them with fresh supplies for their journey back. He walked down to the end of the driveway with them to retrieve the bikes.

"You know you're always welcome, if you pass this way again." He shook both of them by the hand.

"And you," said Ronnie." If you end up moving north, look us up. The community could do with some farming expertise, and if you can bring some assets with you......"

Hugh nodded. He watched them drive off down the roadway, then pulled the bracken and branches back across the opening.

The road was deserted and they travelled for about two hours, keeping their speed steady and avoiding any of the small settlements. Eventually Ronnie pulled over and stopped his bike. Nairne pulled in behind him. It was a relief to remove the crash helmets as the temperature was already beginning to rise and it was going to be another scorching day.

"So, how long are you going to keep this up? Are we going to get all the way home before you say what's on your mind?" Ronnie asked.

"I don't know what you mean," Nairne replied.

"Christ, Nairne, you know exactly what I mean. You are honestly going to tell me we're just going back home. You don't want to even discuss the possibility of trying to find

39

your mum. That you are happy with that. All this 'she's dead to me anyway' crap. If it means so little to you why the hell are you behaving like the world has come to an end?"

"I'm not…."

"The hell you're not! You might have put on an act with the Cranshaws but you don't fool me. It's like living next to an unexploded bomb: the great silence before the bang. You won't talk about it, you won't let me help you. I don't know what to do any more. Even before the letter from your mum, you're like some reckless child. That stunt with Sahasra and Subhash, you could have been killed and you don't seem to care."

"Of course I care. Should we have left them there? Is that it?"

"No, you know that's not what I'm saying. I just don't think it's always up to you to take the risks, always up to you to save the day. I don't want to see you get hurt."

"Well, if you want someone who hides behind the walls of the community maybe I'm the wrong person for you." Her temper was flaring, she could feel the colour in her face. They had never had a row, not like this.

"Nairne, I'm not going to let you push me away. I want to help you. I want to support you. I want you to stop pretending everything is all right."

"Fine, fine, I'll tell you what I feel then, shall I? I feel it's totally unfair that my dad knew what would happen and planned everything to keep us safe, and look what happened to him. I think it's unfair that scum like Mitchell can come along and get my brother killed. I think it's unfair that Paul can't walk. I think it's unfair that people in the community judge me for killing Mitchell. I think it's unfair that my mum can just come back into my life and back inside my head, when I've dealt with all that. How could she let us grieve for her? My brother was in pieces when she died. How could she have let us think she was dead? And now, why should I help her? She left us. She just saw something better, something more exciting, shiny and new, and she left us. And she never looked back."

"You should help her because she's your mum. It's as simple as that. Some parents are good at what they do and some are crap, but she's still your mum. What would Zane have done?"

"That's unfair; you leave him out of this. He had no idea what she was like. After his accident she wanted to leave him behind, take me and leave him behind because he was damaged and it was too much like hard work, yet he still worshipped her."

"Yes, because she was his mum and maybe he was better than her, maybe he understood how important family is. And she didn't want to leave you Nairne, she wanted to take you with her."

"Yes, she did want to take me because her other child was damaged, not because it was me. It was like being second prize in a competition. If Zane had been okay, if he hadn't had his accident she would have chosen him. I was just the consolation prize."

"You can't know that, maybe she would have taken you both."

Nairne did not respond. She knew she couldn't just go back to the community and pretend the letter had never reached her. She knew she had to do something but she hated Angela. She hated her for breaking up their family and she hated her for wanting to leave Zane behind. It didn't matter that her mum had wanted to take her, in fact that made it worse, like they were there to be bargained over. And what could they do, all they had was a scrawled letter dated a year ago with an address in London; who could say if she was still there or if that address even existed anymore. The only news they had from London came in the sporadic broadcast by pirate radio stations. You never knew if what they said was true or not.

"Nairne, if you want to try and find her I'll come with you. We'll set off now, today. Just tell me what you want me to do."

"It's too dangerous and too far, and if we find her, then what? I don't want to take her back to the community with us."

"Let's worry about that once we find her. She may not want that. She may just want help to get out of London and to get back to Scotland. Whatever the problem is, it must be serious or she wouldn't have written to your dad. From what you have said they didn't part on good terms."

"No, they certainly didn't."

"So, are we going down there, to see if we can find her? You said you wanted to travel, see what was going on and this is a perfect opportunity."

"I don't know. You remember how bad Glasgow was and that was last year. God knows how bad things have got in London. I can't ask you to take that risk for me."

"Fine, you could go on your own. I'll head back home, let everyone know where you've gone."

Nairne stared at Ronnie in disbelief.

"Got you. Of course you can ask me to go with you. You know I'd do anything for you," he laughed.

"Anything?"

"Well, maybe not anything, but yes, I'll go with you. Come on, let's turn around. We could cover a fair distance today and there's no point in delaying things." With that he slipped his crash helmet on and climbed back on the bike. Nairne followed suit.

They reached the border with Northumberland by early afternoon. The verges were littered with debris: burnt out vehicles, the remains of trees, concrete blocks, anything that would provide a useful road block. The road had been cleared, but there was plenty of evidence of conflict as a 'Welcome to Northumberland' sign came into view.

The tattered sign had been spray painted with a warning, and patches of rust were beginning to eat away at it. Crude barbed wire fences had been erected on each side of the carriageway and stretched out across the neighbouring fields into the distance.

"Perhaps we should have built a wall," Ronnie suggested, as they surveyed the surrounding scene.

"I think the Romans tried that," said Nairne. "I don't think it was very successful. What I don't get is why people were so quick to draw this line? The Border didn't mean anything before, not really, but as soon as the trouble started we all became so Scottish, so nationalistic."

"I guess it was just an easy rallying cry for those people lucky enough to be in the north. A sort of instant tribal membership. If you lived to the north of this line you should be safe and if you lived to the south, then tough. I suppose it's probably like this across Europe."

"It's crazy. How can people think we'll be safe? I don't think climate change will recognise the Border. It's just taking a bit longer for us to see some of the worst effects and I guess we were already used to colder weather in winter."

"No one plans that far ahead, they just perceive that somehow things are better further north so they try to move. Come on, let's find somewhere we can stop that is not so exposed, and we'll have some food and look at the best route." Ronnie climbed back on his bike and Nairne followed.

Within ten miles they reached the edge of Kielder forest, the regimented trees carpeted the hills on each side of the road. There were signs of tree felling on a grand scale on the lower slopes, the parts easiest to reach. There was also evidence of fires. To the east, a massive swathe of forest was burned to blackened and dead tree stumps. The fire had swept across the hillside stopping only at a break in the trees caused by a previous felling operation. There was no sign of any new planting. It looked like people were turning to this soft, quick-growing timber for fuel.

EIGHT

The afternoon bell sounded. It could be heard across the grounds: a sound from the past, a sound of old churches and schools. The two women put down their tools and began the walk back across the cricket pitches, through rows of neatly tended vegetables, past the cricket pavilion, now a store for tools and home to the livestock: chickens, geese and ducks. They walked across what had been the playing fields, which were now home to a crop of potatoes, cabbages and turnips, the winter food supply, and into the main courtyard. They did not speak. The older of the two, her face lined with worry, head down, had little to say. The younger one still wore an expression of hope, or perhaps belief.

The courtyard was grand. The red brick Victorian facade with arched windows and the impressive central bell tower dominated the site. The bell rang again, a final call to everyone to assemble in the main chapel.

"After you." The younger woman held the door open, smiling gently and let the other woman past, a sign of deference and respect for her position in the community. The older woman nodded in thanks and entered the chapel. Most people were already assembled, a murmuring of whispered exchanges continued until the doors were closed. Then silence fell.

All eyes faced the front. The large circular stained glass window, flanked by three long panels, depicted Jesus Christ's ascension into heaven, his arms outstretched, a blinding yellow light surrounding his head, his expression serene. Angels with trumpets, their robes a glowing shade of blue, lips pursed to instruments raised to the heavens above, were all testaments to the school's history and the wealth of its founders.

The position, which would until recent times, have been

occupied by the priest undertaking school services or other acts of worship was filled by a man who wore no religious regalia: his appearance was smart and simple, if somewhat conservative: a dark blue shirt, open at the neck, and black jeans. His complexion was bronzed from the sun and his thick, dark, wavy hair was cut short. His eyes, like his hair, were dark brown, but they held the light. An energy and intelligence shone through them. He was what most people would consider to be handsome with chiselled features and straight white teeth. His face was free of signs of worry or concern, and younger looking than his forty-seven years.

When he spoke, his voice was firm, the accent English with no strong regional slant. However, his tone was one of authority and as he spoke everyone listened. Afterwards the people filed from the chapel, their murmuring voices rising once more, as they made their way in smaller groups and clusters down the internal courtyard corridors and along to the dining hall. The tables and chairs were laid out in regimented rows and within minutes most people were seated, while a few of the women ferried bowls of food to each table. The hall had changed little since its days as a private school and it still performed the same function. The grand fireplace had been reopened, the chimney cleared out and it was now used as the main heat source in colder weather. One table was set apart from the others, the top table, placed at a ninety degree angle to the rest, with seats on just one side. He sat in the middle, enjoying a view across the hall and his people. To his right sat his most trusted assistant, a man with sallow skin and an angular face. He was slimly built but strong. To his left sat the older woman. Her face still showed signs of worry and tiredness making her look older than her forty-one years. The other seats were taken up, on the right by three young men and to the left two young women.

"You look tired," he spoke gently to the woman, his voice caressing and concerned. "I told you that you don't need to work outside. We have others to do that sort of work. You could spend your time indoors, take things easy."

"I'm fine, I enjoy the outdoors. The sunlight and the exercise are good for me. I'll be fine, just feeling a little run down. It's nothing to worry about," she replied, her face breaking into a smile, trying hard to look happy. "Perhaps tomorrow I will stay in, spend some time with the children…. if that is all right."

"Whatever you want. You know I only want what makes you happy." He squeezed her hand gently and then turned to talk to the young man on his right. She zoned out, not listening to their chat, not listening to any of the voices and sporadic laughter, the clatter of dishes, the sounds of the community. She listened only to her heart beating. She could feel it in her chest, hear her pulse in her eardrums: the thud, thud, thud, not too fast, not as fast as it sometimes was when it raced as though it was rushing to use up all the heartbeats she had left.

"Angela, Angela….." the young woman's voice was raised slightly as she touched the older woman's arm gently and passed her a serving bowl containing broccoli and cauliflower. "Angela, you've hardly touched your food, try some of these. They were picked freshly today." The girl used the serving spoon and placed some of the vegetables onto her plate.

"Thank you, Susan," she smiled, took the bowl and passed it along to the man.

"You were miles away, what were you thinking about?" the girl asked.

"Oh, nothing important, I was just thinking about the work we did today. The harvest has been better than expected."

The girl nodded in response but did not look convinced.

"Are you sure you are all right? You seem….I don't know, you seem like you are somewhere else. I was

46

worried it was something I had said, or done."

"I'm fine, just tired. We did a lot today. I guess more than I realised. Perhaps I'll have an early night and no Susan, it's not you. I enjoyed working together today. I don't want you to be worried about anything. You haven't done anything wrong."

After eating, people began to leave, heading for their own rooms. Angela pushed her chair back and stood up. The man leaned over and took her arm.

"Where are you going?" He gripped her forearm firmly.

"I thought I'd look in on the children and then get some rest, I feel quite tired."

"But I thought…. I was looking forward to your company," he smiled.

"I'm sorry, maybe tomorrow evening." She placed her hand over his, squeezing it gently.

He shrugged and loosened his grip. She made her way from the hall, glancing backwards as she reached the door. He was not looking at her, he was engaged in conversation with Susan, and the girl's face glowed with pleasure.

The nursery was located on the first floor; it was a spacious room with large windows. There were eight children under five, who spent most of their time here, when they were not outside playing. Their meals were served separately, earlier in the evening, and after that there was a short period of relaxation and play before bedtime. Angela stood at the doorway and peered through the glass, watching the small figures run around, playing with a selection of wooden toys, building bricks, and dolls. Two women watched over them. She did not go in, but she watched them for a few minutes, her heartbeat increasing, the thumping in her ears becoming deafening. She felt almost light headed and put one arm out against the wall to support herself. One of the women glanced up and saw her; she smiled and beckoned to her, inviting her in. Angela smiled in return but shook her head and pointed down at her watch, pretending she had somewhere else she had to be. She stood for a few seconds more, closing her eyes, fighting back the tears before walking away back to her room.

She pulled the curtains over, plunging the room into darkness, then she switched on one small light. The room was spacious and tastefully decorated, with a large, comfortable double bed, and enough space for a sofa and chair in front of the generous fireplace. It was still too warm to need a fire. The evenings were still mild for this time of year. A fire would have been good, not for the heat but for the comfort of it, watching the flames flicker, watching the glowing embers. Angela cast her mind back to the house she had lived in before, with Daniel. She had complained bitterly about having a real fire, yearning for central heating, instant warmth, no mess, no dirt, no cleaning. She took a deep breath, no point in dwelling on the past, she told herself, no point at all.

She undressed slowly. Her lower back ached, 'too much bending and lifting,' she mused. It ached a lot recently and she knew she did not have to work in the gardens, no one would say anything, no one would complain, at least not to her face. But she liked being outside, feeling the sun on her skin, feeling the breeze, feeling alive. She put on a long, plain night shirt, too large for her. It belonged to him but he never wore it and she still liked the feel of the soft fabric against her skin. She climbed into bed and switched out the light, but although exhausted, sleep evaded her, as it did so often.

"Susan, come on you know how much I want this, come on. I know you feel the same way, I can see it in your eyes, your beautiful eyes." He bent down and brushed her lips with his. Susan blushed, she could feel the colour rise up her neck and across her cheeks. She pulled her head away.

"It's all right for you, no one will think badly of you, but what if people find out? What if she finds out? I don't want to cause any upset. She has been so kind to me, like an older sister, showing me how everything works. I would feel terrible if she found out."

"So, we just need to be careful, don't we? I am not going to tell her and you aren't going to tell her so what's the problem. I know you think she's very kind, but she's no angel, despite her name. Angela can look after herself. Anyway, she has made it quite plain that I am not wanted. Always one excuse after another, too tired, and not feeling well…but if you aren't interested, if I have read this all wrong then I'm sorry." He pulled away from her and held his arms up in a gesture of apology. "I just thought…..but my mistake. It was just I have never met anyone like you before. I knew the day you arrived. I just knew it. You don't know what it is like, the burden of being responsible for all these people, for making sure everyone is looked after, and sometimes I need someone to share that with. Angela just doesn't give me that support and I hoped that maybe you…..but if you're not happy here then just say. It's not a prison. You are free to leave…."

The girl hesitated, but only for a moment.

"No, don't go, not yet." She put out her hand and took hold of his arm and led him into her room.

NINE

Ronnie had been to York with his father many years ago. He would have been about ten years old at the time. The memories were vivid: the city gates, the fortress-like walls surrounding the old town, and the narrow, twisted alleyways of medieval buildings, leaning at precarious angles, pushed tight up against one another. And at its heart, the cathedral. His dad had insisted on taking him inside, to see the splendour of it all, with its gold and finery. He wondered what state it was in now.

They were only five miles from the city, the beginning of urban sprawl lay ahead. Most of the houses still appeared to be occupied and the roadway was in reasonable condition. They had stayed overnight on the edge of Kielder forest, or what had been the forest. Much of it had been burned, and it was impossible to tell if this had been accidental or deliberate. Two scorching summers in a row and forest fires were easily started. It looked like there had also been significant recent storms. Of those trees that had survived the ravages of a forest fire many of them had blown over, their broken limbs lay rotting on the forest floor.

Nairne was in the lead, about thirty metres ahead of him. She sat comfortably on the motorbike now, as if she had been riding it for years. She glanced back at him then she began to slow down, her left indicator blinked as she pulled into the verge. Ronnie caught up with her as she pulled her helmet off and wiped the visor. Rain had been falling steadily for the last hour or so, just a gentle misty covering making the dry roads feel greasy. Ronnie pulled off his helmet.

"What's up?"

"Listen," said Nairne.

"I don't hear anything," he said, concentrating.

"No, neither do I. Nothing at all. We haven't seen anyone since we reached the edge of town. I know some of the houses look occupied, but we haven't seen or heard one other living soul. Don't you think that is strange? People must have heard us approaching, these things aren't exactly silent, but no one has come out to have a look. No one is out in any of the gardens which look like they have been recently managed."

The residential street of nineteen thirties brick red, semi-detached houses all had small front gardens. Most no longer contained flower beds or bushes or privet hedges. Instead there was evidence of productive vegetable growing.

"Maybe when people hear traffic they think it is safer to stay indoors, maybe there's been trouble, armed gangs, who knows."

"Yes, but no one at all? It just doesn't feel right."

"I know, let's just keep moving, and see if there's any sign of life up ahead."

They put their helmets back on and drove up the road slowly, both scanning the houses for any signs of life. The road curved to the right and sloped gently. At the bottom there was a junction with the all too familiar sign of a road-block. Two buses and some badly damaged cars obstructed the route. They stopped about a hundred metres before the road block and pulled the bikes over to the side of the road. Still there was silence. No voices shouted to them from the barricades, no warning shots were fired. They waited, five, ten, fifteen minutes passed and still nothing.

"I guess we are going to have to get a bit closer," said Nairne. She moved the hand gun to her front pocket, while Ronnie unslung his rifle from his back. They left the bikes propped up at the edge of the curb and moved forward cautiously. Once they were within twenty metres or so, Ronnie called out. His voice sounded unnaturally loud in the total silence.

"We just want to pass through. Going south, we don't want any trouble."

There was no response, but there was a movement, a fleeting shape just at one side of the makeshift barricade. Nairne tapped Ronnie's arm indicating that she had seen something.

"What was it?" he whispered.

"I don't know, I couldn't make it…... Ronnie, run!" Nairne tugged at his arm, pulling him towards her. Time slowed down. She felt her legs pushing hard against the ground, turning her body around a full one hundred and eighty degrees. Her thigh muscles bunched and pushed. Her strides were long and fast and yet it was as if she were running through treacle. She could feel Ronnie next to her and she could hear the sounds, the sounds of feet against the tarmac, from the left of the barricade and from the right. She could hear the breathing, the panting and then the barking, loud and low. The bikes were at least another fifty metres away. They were not going to make it. Suddenly, Ronnie was pulling her arm, dragging her towards one of the houses. The front garden was protected by a low brick wall, a metal gate in the centre. Ronnie jumped the wall in one stride and Nairne followed suit. As she landed in the garden the first of the dogs reached its target and leapt. She felt the force of its weight hit her back, large paws pressed against her shoulders and she fell forward crashing to the ground, the dog pinning her down.

She let out a scream and pulled her head down. She attempted to push herself up. Warm breath engulfed her exposed neck, while saliva dripped onto her skin. Ronnie turned and ran at the writhing forms on the ground, lashing out with his heavy boot and making contact with the underside of the dog's rib cage. The dog lost its grip and slid sideways, yelping in pain. As it regained its footing, Ronnie hit it with the butt of his rifle, cracking the weapon off the dog's muzzle. It fell to the ground, squealing; the sound piercing, its body writhing as blood poured from its head. Ronnie hauled Nairne to her feet and then he charged towards the front door of the house and kicked it hard. The door creaked as the lock strained. Ronnie kicked it again and again. The door frame splintered. Nairne was behind him now. Gun in hand, she fired at the next dog to clear the wall. The bullet hit the animal in the chest, but its momentum carried it forward and it fell only feet away. She shot it in the head.

As the door flew open Ronnie pulled her inside and slammed the door shut behind them. Three more dogs cleared the wall and threw themselves against the closed door, jumping up, their faces visible through the small frosted glass aperture. They barked as their frenzied bodies banged against one another. Ronnie pressed his whole weight against the door to hold it closed, as the lock now hung loosely from the frame.

"Get something to wedge this shut," he yelled.

Nairne dashed down the narrow hallway and passed a small book shelf. She tipped it forward spilling books onto the carpet as she shoved the shelves along the tiled floor. Together they turned them sideways and wedge them across the opening.

"Hang on, I'll get something heavier," she said, disappearing into the living room and returning a few minutes later with a second set of shelves which she hauled out into the hallway. This set they propped in front of the others, lending some extra weight to the barricade. They both slumped to the floor, breathing hard.

"Are you okay?" Ronnie asked, his hand moving up to her neck. Nairne unzipped her leather jacket and pulled the collar down.

"I think so. I don't think it managed to bite through the fabric." She was gasping for air, her heart pounding. Then she was shaking, a violent current running through her entire body that she could not stop.

"I can't see any blood," said Ronnie, the relief in his

voice all too apparent. They both knew what an infected wound could mean; with no antibiotics, injuries like that could be life threatening. He put his arms around her.

"God, I can't believe that, we were so lucky. Those dogs look well fed so they can't have been fending for themselves for long. That second one, the one I shot, had a collar on. Where do you think they've come from?"

"I reckon they probably belonged to whoever set up that road block, guard dogs probably. If this was a wild pack there would be more variety. They all look like fighting dogs to me; two Alsatians, a Rottweiler and maybe some sort of Doberman cross. They've been trained to attack," Ronnie said standing up and squinting through the small window as the dogs continued to howl and bark. His movement caused a new wave of frantic activity outside.

Nairne stood up and returned to the living room, peering out of the bay window. Within seconds the dogs were at the window ledge, their paws pressed against the glass, jaws gaping, barking and yelping. She went out into the hall.

"I guess there's no one home," she stated. "But I suppose we should have a look around just in case." Pistol in hand, she walked down the main hallway with Ronnie close behind. There was a door under the stairs. Nairne pushed it open, revealing a small bathroom. They moved on. The door at the end of the corridor was closed. Nairne indicated to Ronnie, who stepped forward and grasped the handle, pushing the door open as she pointed the gun inside. The kitchen was silent. The wooden work surfaces were strewn with the remnants of food packaging. Dirty dishes sat in the sink, piled into a heap. Plastic bottles of water stood in an orderly row on the draining board. The back blind was drawn leaving the room is semi darkness. Ronnie pulled the cord and the blind rose silently. Outside lay a typical English suburban garden, with wooden fences separating it from the adjoining neighbours. It was spacious with a brightly painted timber shed to the rear partially hidden by an old apple tree. The lawn had been dug over and the main body of the garden had been divided into regimented vegetable beds. It looked cared for, although some of the vegetables had started to go over.

Dead flies littered the kitchen window sill. Heaps of little black bodies lay desiccated by the warmth of the sunlight. Over the sink, a few survivors still buzzed around, landing on the food encrusted plates.

"We should check upstairs," said Nairne. "It looks like everyone just got up and left. See there by the back door." She pointed to the two pairs of heavy duty gardening boots which lay discarded next to the doorway. A rear porch revealed two coats, hanging on brass hooks, the cuffs dirty with traces of soil.

They headed back along the corridor and up the stairs.

"Hello, is there anyone here?" Ronnie's voice echoed. The hallway was dark. The three doors on the first floor were all tightly shut. They opened the first door revealing the main bathroom, towels still hung on the rail, and a dressing gown hung on the back of the door.

The next door swung open revealing a child's bedroom. The wallpaper, originally bright and cheerful, now faded and unloved. A pastel duvet and a scattering of stuffed toys covered the single bed, and a desk with an old computer on top, sat next to the single wardrobe.

They stood and looked at the third door.

"Here goes," said Nairne, grasping the handle. The curtains were closed, but Nairne didn't need light to know what was in there. The smell hit them both like a physical force and a low buzzing filled the room. Ronnie edged across the darkened room and pulled open the curtains. Both of them covered their faces, in a vain attempt to block out the stench of death. The bodies were at least a week old. A couple, it was impossible to tell their ages, but they were lying beside one another. She was under the covers while he lay on top, fully clothed as if he had just laid down to rest next to her and then had never got up. Next to the bed was a small table with an empty glass and a couple of pill bottles, their caps off and the contents gone.

"Oh my God," Ronnie gasped. "Let's get out of here." They both stumbled into the hall, pulling the door shut behind them. But the smell followed them; they could taste it. They rushed downstairs, gasping for fresh air.

"What do you think? Suicide?" Nairne asked.

"I don't know, maybe, but if so it doesn't explain where everyone else is. Those dogs have made so much bloody noise people right up and down the street must have heard them, and yet there is no sign of anyone out there, no one at all."

"Maybe people are too afraid to go outside, like a siege, and everyone is frightened of being attacked. We don't know how many dogs there are."

"Yeah, but surely you would try and set some sort of trap for them, get the neighbours to help and take care of it. You wouldn't just stay in and wait until you ran out of food. And talking of food, the garden is full of vegetables. These people weren't going hungry, so why kill yourself?"

"Let's have a look around. If it was suicide they might have left a note," Nairne said, going back into the living room. She looked around the room, checking all the surfaces, the obvious places you might leave something you wanted to be found. There was nothing. On the mantel piece there was a photograph of the couple from upstairs. At least she assumed it was them. They were in their forties, both smiling and in front of them a girl of about six, her hair in pigtails and her face scrunched up into a smile. The picture had been taken on some long forgotten holiday, perhaps Spain or Portugal. They were all sitting next to a swimming pool, the clear blue water was mirrored by the bright blue summer sky. They looked tanned and happy, smiling for the camera with cocktails in their hands. Nairne lifted the photograph and looked at them. She felt a lump in her throat and blinked her eyes to clear away the tears that were forming there. She hadn't known them. She didn't even know their names, but to think this is how it had ended, alone, their bodies left rotting in their own house, no-one coming to investigate. An image of Evelyn came into her mind, lying battered and bloody on her kitchen floor. She placed the frame carefully back in its original position.

"Did you find anything?" Ronnie asked as he entered the room.

"Just this," she showed him the photograph. "I guess the other room belongs to their daughter. I wonder where she is now."

"They still had food supplies, a few tins in the cupboards, plus the food they were growing outside. Why would they kill themselves? Why don't we try the next-door neighbours, see if there's anyone there."

"What about the dogs?" They could still hear them padding around outside the front of the house. There were at least three of them.

"We could go out the back door and climb the garden fence," Ronnie suggested.

"What, and just hope they can't get around to the back?"

"I'll go next door, you stay in here. Go to the window and make sure they can see you and that you keep their attention. I won't be long."

Nairne looked less than convinced, but they couldn't just sit here and wait for the dogs to go. Eventually, they would have to do something to get back to the bikes.

Nairne could hear Ronnie unlock and open the back door. He was being as quiet as possible while she was banging on the front living room window, sending the dogs into a frenzy of renewed barking and jostling. The noise was incredible and yet there were no signs of life, no twitching curtains or faces at the windows, just the empty houses with their blank interiors staring back at her.

Ronnie crept across the back garden and hauled himself over the wooden fence into the next-door neighbour's garden. It looked similar to the one he had just left: vegetable beds and fruit trees dominated the space with a large poly-tunnel to the rear, full of plants pressing against the stretched and dirty plastic. The back of the house had large patio doors with the curtains tightly drawn. Adjacent to these, and a mirror image of the other house, was the kitchen window and back door. The windows were double glazed and tightly shut, but the back door had a single glazed window divided into six panels. He tried knocking, but there was no response. He walked up the garden path and looked up at the house. All the curtains were closed. Searching around he spotted a half brick lying next to one of the vegetable beds, and returning to the back door he used it to break one of the panes of glass. The sound seemed unnaturally loud and he had visions of the dogs descending on him. Reaching through the broken window, he found the key in the lock and turned it. The door opened silently.

"Hello, is there anyone here?" he shouted into the darkened room. His voice reverberated around the small space. He closed the door behind him and walked through the kitchen. The house was similar to the one next door, the only difference was the more modern furniture and fittings. He went through to the living room and pulled back the curtains. The movement was enough to alert the dogs, one of whom rushed over, despite Nairne's activities, and began to jump up at the window. There were family photos on the wall of a younger couple, perhaps late twenties or early thirties, with two small children. He walked out into the hallway where children's toys were piled on a set of shelves next to the staircase, and coats of various sizes hung from a row of hooks on the wall. Ronnie climbed the stairs, a bad feeling coming over him. The first door he opened was a child's room, bunk beds, and wallpaper with pictures of trains and cars. The beds were neatly made, with duvet covers, the top bunk Batman and the bottom bunk continued the car theme. He closed the door behind him and opened the next door, his hands sweating as he grasped the handle, expecting the worst, but the room was empty, the bed unmade and the curtains drawn. He breathed out in relief. Ronnie searched the rest of the house, but there was no clue as to where the people had gone. There were plastic bottles filled with water on the kitchen counter, just like next door, and the cupboards revealed a few tins of food. He closed the back door behind him and walked up the garden between the rows of vegetables. The garden looked slightly more unkempt than the neighbouring one and it looked as though the plants in the poly-tunnel were running riot. He pushed open the door of the poly-tunnel. It was full of tomatoes and cucumbers, the tentacles of green pressed hard against the plastic. The hot air blasted his skin. Large ripe tomatoes, some bursting from their skins hung on desperate looking plants badly in need of water. There was a basic irrigation system. A water butt which gathered rain from the shed roof was connected by a series of plastic pipes, drip feeding water to the precious crop. It looked as though the butt had run out of water several days before as the plants were beginning to sag under the weight of the burgeoning fruit and the heat of the tunnel. He pushed his way back out of the oppressively hot space relieved to be in the cooler air once more. But there was a smell in the air of old bonfires and burning fat. It reminded him of the smell of cooking meat over an open fire.

Ronnie walked further up the garden past the poly-tunnel and found the site of a large and powerful bonfire. The area was charred black, remnants of chunky timbers lay in a pile with a thick layer of ash. Ronnie kicked at the edge of the pile. 'This must have been a real inferno,' he thought. His boots disturbed the ash and the smell of burning fat became even stronger. He could see what looked like a white sphere protruding from the ashes, about the size of a child's football. He dislodged it with his foot and jumped back as the empty eye sockets gazed up at him. The bottom jaw was no longer attached.

"Oh Christ!" he exclaimed to himself. "We need to get out of here." He climbed back over the fence into the other garden. Only now, as he was at the rear of the garden did he see the grave. A mound of earth with three paving slabs laid roughly on top was marked with a rough wooden post. The thick piece of wood had been hammered into the ground with the word 'Maddie' scrawled on it. The site was too small to contain an adult. Ronnie hurried back down the garden and let himself in through the back door.

"Nairne, we need to get out of here. They're dead, all dead."

Nairne met him in the hall.

"Dead? Are there bodies in the house?"

"No, the house is empty their bodies have been burned at the end of their garden, and the girl, the girl in the photo, there's a grave out there about the right size for a child. Whatever happened here none of the people in these two houses survived it and there is no sign of life from any of the other properties on the street."

"What do you think?"

"I don't know, some kind of disease, something in the water? Whatever it is we need to get away from here. We need to get to the bikes."

A search of the kitchen unearthed two out of date tins of meatballs. Nairne lit the small gas camping stove, the previous occupants had been using, and heated the food in a small pan. The smell was strong and meaty. Ronnie took the cooked food back to the empty house next door and emptied the contents into two bowls. He placed them on the floor in the hallway. Nairne continued to bang on the windows to keep the dogs' attention, giving Ronnie time to get in position. Then she stopped and pulled the curtains over. A few minutes later Ronnie opened the front door of the adjacent house, letting the door swing back, its hinges squeaking loudly. He ran down the hallway through the kitchen and out the back door, slamming it closed behind him. The dogs had heard the noise, sensed the movement and before he was out of the house they were in the hallway. Their feet slid and scraped on the tiled floor, and they banged against each other trying to get at the food. Nairne came round from the house next door and pulled the door shut trapping the dogs inside. They were too distracted to notice.

She had a sick feeling in her stomach, leaving them trapped in there but she pushed the thought from her mind and ran down the road towards the bikes with Ronnie close behind her.

TEN

"Get your hands up now, where we can see them. That's right. Slowly does it," the voice boomed at them through a loud hailer. The Yorkshire accent was strong and the words were distorted by the equipment. Ronnie and Nairne kept their hands up and stepped forward away from the bikes. Straight ahead were the ancient walls of York and the North gate, reinforced with hastily built barricades comprising of damaged vehicles and concrete blocks. "What do you want?"

"We're just passing through on our way south and we're looking for some supplies," Ronnie responded, his voice raised to be heard over the distance.

"No one is allowed to enter. We can't take the risk. You might be infectious."

"We're both fine. Why do you think we would be infectious? We just want to get some supplies, food and water for a couple of days, and some fuel for the bikes."

"There's some sort of sickness. Lots of people have died, so we've closed the city to visitors. No one comes in and no one goes out. We don't know what it is, but people are dying. Lots of people. It may be in the water, but we don't know for sure."

"We have stuff to trade. We don't need to come in if someone can come out with supplies, we can leave our stuff here."

"What have you got?"

"Seeds, vegetable seeds," Nairne responded. "They're fresh and from a reliable source. Our community harvested them this season and they've been carefully packed."

There was no immediate response. They could hear the crackle of radios as the unseen guard asked a superior for guidance. Minutes passed.

"Someone will be out to see you shortly. Stay there where we can see you. We have weapons aimed at you. Understand?"

"We understand, we'll unpack some seeds from our bags. We'll put our weapons on the ground, is that all right?" Ronnie asked.

"Yes, just take it slowly," the voice responded.

Ronnie and Nairne lowered their hands slowly and then each unfastened their weapons and laid them carefully on the ground to the right hand side of the bikes. Ronnie stood with his arms raised while Nairne undid one of the panniers from the side of her motorbike. Cautiously, she unzipped the top and lifted out several small plastic boxes. She checked the labels on each. Four boxes should be sufficient, she thought, as she zipped the bag back up. She stood next to Ronnie and they waited. A doorway at the bottom of the gate opened and a man came out wearing a pair of overalls, a face mask and plastic gloves. He moved towards them. He was stocky, shorter than Ronnie and was pulling a small trolley on wheels, stacked with two plastic fuel containers and some plastic bags. He stopped about five metres away.

"I've brought some fuel for the bikes and a funnel." He unloaded the containers from the trolley and threw the plastic funnel towards Ronnie, then pushed the two fuel containers forward with his foot before stepping back. "And in here are some food supplies, all in packets or tins. There's nothing fresh since we don't know what's causing the illness and we don't want to spread it to you."

"Thank you," Ronnie responded. Stepping forward, he lifted the first of the fuel containers and unscrewed the cap from the petrol tank on the bike. Placing the funnel inside, he poured in the fuel. Next he filled the tank on Nairne's bike before replacing the lids on the two containers and pushing them back towards the man.

"Here," said Nairne. She put the four boxes of seeds down on the ground and stepped back. Each box contains a list of the contents plus instructions for storage, sowing and care. We've also included details on how to harvest seed next time. If possible, the seeds should be stored somewhere cool, a refrigerator if you have one working. We've put in a number of varieties of each crop."

"Thanks," the man replied, as he bent down and retrieved the boxes placing them inside his overall pockets. "You're headed south? How far have you travelled?"

"We live up past the central belt in Scotland so a couple of hundred miles so far."

"How is it up there?" Are people getting by?"

"Yes, in the countryside it's not too bad," Nairne responded. "But the cities are pretty bleak. This summer water supplies have been a bit of an issue as there has been very little rain."

"Yeah, it's been the same here. And now this sickness."

"So what happened?" asked Ronnie. "We stopped a couple of miles back, had a run in with a pack of very hungry dogs. We went into one of the houses, but everyone was dead."

"No, the north side of the city is pretty much empty now. It started in mid-August, a few people being sick, diarrhoea, temperatures and then some of them died, but within a couple of weeks the numbers were growing and people died quickly, after one or two days. There are lots of theories; dysentery, typhoid or cholera, but no one knows for sure. The only thing we know is lots of people die. So, about two weeks ago, we closed the gates and now no one gets in. It's a temporary state of affairs as we'll run out of supplies eventually, even with the smaller number of people left, but we hope the weather will have cooled down a bit and it may help to slow it down."

"Thanks for the supplies," said Nairne.

He nodded in response and strapped the two empty fuel containers back onto the trolley before passing over the bag of provisions.

"Where are you headed exactly?"

"London," said Ronnie.

"London?"

"Yes, we're looking for someone."

"Good luck, I hear it is pretty bad down there and pretty rough. You two be careful." With that he turned and walked back over to the gate.

They rode south, skirting the city and did not stop until York was far behind them. After another seventy miles, Nairne pulled in at the side of the road. Ronnie parked behind her and they both removed their helmets.

"Are you okay?" he asked. She looked tired, her face was pale and she had dark circles beneath her eyes.

"Yeah, it's just so damned warm with all this gear on and the insects are unbelievable. I think I need wipers on my helmet to deal with the fly smears. We should check the map, try and avoid any major centres of population. If York is anything to go by it's probably safer if we avoid people altogether."

"What do you reckon it is?"

"Who knows, it could be anything, water borne, air borne or in their food. That guy could have been right though; it could be cholera or dysentery. It sounded pretty bleak in there, sitting waiting for it to pass or waiting for the food to run out." Nairne pulled the map out from the plastic carry case inside her jacket and began to unfold it. While she located their position, Ronnie opened one of the bags and removed a bottle of juice given to them as part of the earlier trade. He unscrewed the top.

"It's past its sell by date but still, it's probably safer than the nearest water supply," he said as he took a drink from the bottle and passed it to Nairne.

"I think we should go this way and avoid the main settlements. I know it's longer but we need to avoid the motorways if the ring road around York was anything to go by. We could head slightly further east, take more of a coastal route and then cut through Cambridgeshire."

The ring road around the city had been in very poor condition and as they had crossed it heading south, they had seen road blocks further along controlling access to the motorway. From a distance they looked military, but it was impossible to know if they were safe to approach. Nairne's proposed route took them over towards Hull then Lincoln and then south skirting round Cambridge and entering London from the north east. It added more miles onto their journey, but avoided contact with people as much as possible. It was already late afternoon and they were both tired.

"Let's stop at the next woodland and make camp. We can get an early start tomorrow and we should be in London by mid-afternoon. I don't want to arrive at night."

"Right, lead the way," said Ronnie, climbing back on his bike.

ELEVEN

"I'm sure. I've checked. I did the count myself, and we're definitely missing three tins. I know the harvest has been better than anticipated, but this is the third time, and I don't think it's any of the kitchen staff."

"You've done the right thing in bringing this to my attention, Don. I'll look into it. Sometimes these things need to be nipped in the bud."

Don nodded and left the room, relieved that he had not been held accountable. It was only three tins. Last time in had been a couple of boxes of crackers, of all things, but he knew Devlin would not let the matter rest, and all he could do was make sure he didn't fall under suspicion.

James Devlin considered for a moment. His two assistants were waiting anxiously for their orders, but he didn't want to rush this. Petty thieving was not new; this was the third time in as many months.

"We'll do a search, today, no notice. I want you to check every room, and I mean every single one. No exceptions. You can get started now, and you need to be finished before the end of the day shift. I don't want the culprit to have time or access to hide anything. Clear?"

The two men nodded and left the room. This was not a task they relished, but orders were orders. They began the search on the top floor. Devlin remained in his office. Turning in his chair, he gazed down out onto the cricket pitches where he could see some of the women working. Susan appeared, carrying tools out to the far corner, and behind her he saw Angela. He studied her as she bent down and carefully lifted a garden fork and spade from the pile of tools laid out for the daily shift, then she set off across the field. She turned and looked up, her eyes flicking across the windows. He stepped back instinctively although he knew she would not be able to see him up here; from down there the windows would look dark and empty. She walked slowly, stiffly, and when she reached her destination he could see her movements were awkward. Devlin continued to watch and wonder.

"Susan, are you all right? You're very quiet this morning," Angela asked, her tone one of concern. The younger woman blushed; she was flustered.

"I'm fine, honestly."

"You look tired, did you not sleep well?"

"No, really I'm fine. It looks like it's going to be another hot day," she commented.

"Yes, you need to make sure you don't overdo it, especially when it is this warm."

"I won't. It would be good if we got the rest of the carrots lifted, before the weather breaks," Susan replied.

"You're right. Why don't we make a start on that now? I was going to spend the day inside today, but once I saw the sun shining… I just wanted to be outside. I'll help you. With two of us we should be finished before noon."

"Angela, are you sure? I know you probably have much more important things to do…." Susan responded. She could certainly do with some help, but she would rather it were someone else, not Angela. She could feel the older woman watching her, and she could feel the guilt written across her own face. She put on her brightest smile. "Thanks Angela, this is very kind of you."

The carrots took up a substantial part of the bed in front of them. They were covered over in a layer of white fleece, held up on plastic hoops with the sides tightly pinned to the ground. Underneath the green feathery tops of the plants pushed against the fabric, straining to be free. The two women started at the far end of the bed, and carefully unpinned the fabric, rolling it back neatly, one on each side of the bed until they had uncovered the first section of the crop. It was an area of about two metres squared, containing eight neat rows. Between the rows were layers of old newspaper, held down with some loose compost, to suppress the weeds which would otherwise have sprung up on that empty soil and would compete with the carrots for water. Next, they lifted the plastic irrigation tubes which snaked up and down the bed between each row. Susan disconnected the pipe at the next junction and rolled it up, placing the heavy coil in the wheelbarrow.

"I'll put that back in the storeroom when we're finished," she commented. "It is such a good idea."

"Yes, it has made a big difference. Last year we were carrying water out here in buckets, it was so time consuming and wasteful. But then I don't suppose any of us had much idea what we were doing."

"So have you been here since the beginning?" Susan asked. She had only joined the community a few months ago. She had been brought back by two of Devlin's men, her and two other young women. Angela had not asked where they had come from or what had brought them to the community.

"Yes, I was here when Devlin acquired the site. There were only about twenty of us then. We'd been living in a big house past Wimbledon Common, an old ramshackle Victorian building with a reasonable garden, but it was obvious that it wasn't going to be large enough. And then this place became available, and we moved in here. It was originally a private school, quite exclusive by all accounts. Of course it had been empty for some time. I suppose after the first couple of big floods parents didn't feel quite so safe sending their kids to schools in London."

"No I guess not, but it is amazing to think this place was just lying empty."

"Yes, it was just a lucky find," said Angela. She didn't want to think about that; how they had acquired the site and how Devlin had dealt with the sitting tenants. But it had been a good move. The school site had enough productive land to provide food for all of them, at least while their numbers remained small. There were forty-two in the community now, including the children. Over the last six months there had been six new arrivals, all young women. Angela guessed it made sense. The original group had been predominantly male, with Devlin as the oldest. She was by far the oldest of the women. From the original group there had been six who had served with Devlin, before all this began. They still hovered around him like some unofficial body guard. Angela had been part of that group since its inception, since the fire, since the beginning. But still, when those six were together, with Devlin in their midst, she felt like an outsider. It was as if they all shared some secret; some past event which bound them together. Angela loved Devlin. She had done so ever since she had met him, since he had saved her, but she had also been just that little bit afraid.

"So you and Devlin, have you been together for a long time, before all this, before the floods?" Susan enquired.

"Oh, a few years now," said Angela. "Devlin saved me, literally. He saved me from a fire, a real knight in shining armour. And yes, we've been together ever since. And we have Eve, our daughter. She'll be three this year. Devlin just adores her."

"You're very lucky," Susan replied. "I'd love to have a baby. She must be the most precious thing in all the world to the two of you."

"Yes she is," Angela responded, but there was something in her tone which caused the girl to wonder.

The rest of the day passed slowly. They worked hard. The sun was hot for September and the sky remained a clear blue; a perfect summer day. There was a strong breeze from the East, and the air smelled clear and clean. On days when there was little wind, Angela could smell the stench of London around them; the smell of too many people, not enough water, no working sewage system, and almost a smell of death. The summer had been warm, too warm, and she knew from what Devlin and his men had said that things outside the confines of the school gates were getting tougher. Angela had not been out for over a year.

Sometimes she yearned to just walk out the gates, just to wander the streets, see London again, and visit the places she used to go; coffee with girlfriends in upmarket London cafes, sipping lattes and talking about nothing more important than where to shop. That was before, when she had left Daniel and moved down to London to live with Martin. He had a good job in the city, with plenty of cash, and he was fun to be with. He was not, she discovered, the most reliable guy in the world, but he knew how to have a good time. He was reckless and immature and it was like being a teenager again. He was the opposite of Daniel. Angela had thrown herself into this new life, never looking back, never pausing to think about what she had left behind. At least that is what she told everyone.

But it was a lie. Angela had made an art form out of lying to herself. She often wondered what they were doing now. Was Zane still that irrepressible boy, with the lovely smile and beautiful eyes, always wanting to please, always wanting approval? And Nairne, had she grown into a beautiful young woman? Had she lost that tomboyish awkwardness? That way she looked so serious, so challenging. And Daniel, Angela could see him coming into his own; a man who had foreseen the future, running his own little fortress, keeping his family safe, being there for them. Daniel the responsible parent, perfect at all the things Angela had so completely failed at.

She shook her head, clearing the thought from it. She needed to focus on something else. As the weeks and then months had passed she knew Daniel was not going to come or send word to her. She knew he could not and should not, forgive her.

"Angela," the girl's voice interrupted her thoughts. "Angela, I was asking about the children. Are there rules, about how many children the community can have?"

"Sorry, what do you mean?"

"For example if I, or one of the other girls got pregnant, would the community allow us to stay, I mean, we can't afford to just keep increasing the number of mouths to feed, can we?"

"No, I guess not, but I don't think there are any rules as such, after all what could we do if someone got pregnant?" As she said the words, she began to wonder, what would they do? There were eight children at present, ranging in age from two years old to eight. Most had arrived at the community with their parents. One had been born here, like her Eve. It was not something that had ever been discussed, not to Angela's knowledge anyway, but as the number of young women within the group increased it was going to be an issue for them and probably soon.

"But Susan, you are so young, you shouldn't tie yourself down. You have plenty of time to be thinking of settling down and having children. Is there someone? One of the guys you're interested in or are you seeing one of them?" Angela smiled conspiratorially.

Susan coloured, the redness rising up her neck and spreading across her face.

"No, there's no one. I was just thinking, you know day dreaming."

"What about Alex, I saw the way he was so attentive last night at supper. I think maybe he has a bit of a thing for you? I could speak to Devlin for you if you wanted...."

"No, no he's nice, but he's a bit young, a bit too.... I don't know, but no."

Alex was a shy young man, who had been with the community for the last two years. Not one of the inner circle but a kind, gentle, young man, perhaps a bit of a loner. He didn't have the same background as Devlin and his cohort. He had been taken in by the group because he was smart, good with his hands, good at fixing things, but not a fighter or a leader.

"Oh well, you shouldn't be in any rush. I am sure someone suitable will come along."

TWELVE

The road was deserted; its pitted surface uneven and in a poor state of repair. They passed empty barren fields on each side. The tide marks of earlier floods indicated how high the water had been. The soil was dead. The ground sloped downward, and both of them slowed the bikes to a halt. Ronnie was first to dismount, rummaging in his pocket for their map.

"According to the map we should be approaching Hull," he said, casting his eye down at their route. "According to the map this should be dry land."

"I guess the one thing we know for certain is that the map is useless," said Nairne, gazing out across the unexpected expanse of water. She shielded her eyes from the glare from the calm surface. She could not see across to the other side, and the road they had been travelling on just vanished into the water.

"Look at the vegetation; it's all dead, all along the edge. And the trees over there that have been submerged previously don't have a leaf left on them." Dry silvered trees jutted from the ground, their branches bare, with roots exposed, like old bones.

Nairne walked down to the edge of the water and bent down, putting her finger tips into the liquid, she tasted the water.

"Ugh, it's salty, like sea water, so this isn't a temporary flood from some heavy rain shower, this is the sea, spreading inward. No wonder all the plants are dying."

"There should be a couple of small villages up ahead, according to this." Ronnie commented. "So what now?"

"We head back the way we came and then turn east as soon as we find a road. Hopefully, we won't have to go too far."

With reluctance, they turned the bikes around. It was

not yet midday and the temperature was soaring. There was a pressure in the air and, although clouds were beginning to form, the heat did not lift. After a few miles the surrounding fields began to look greener, although there was little sign of any farming activity. The ground was baked hard. They saw no other vehicles or people. Every half mile or so there were solitary farm houses or tiny clusters of cottages. All appeared to be empty. After ten miles they reached a junction and turned eastward. The road was wider and in better condition. A few abandoned vehicles littered the verges, some looked as though they had been there for years, with tufts of grass growing up around their wheels, rust spots and dirt obscuring their windows. Some had been damaged, windscreens smashed or doors left hanging open. There was no sign of any major settlements or much evidence that anyone else had driven down this road recently. The tar was uneven and in places the grass verges had begun to encroach upon the carriageway.

The first few rain spots fell individually, large heavy drops, then a pitter patter until the individual drops were too numerous and fast to identify. Within a few minutes the rain was replaced with large hailstones that bounced off the road making a drumming sound. Nairne slowed down, the unused road surface was wet and slippery. Ronnie pulled in behind her. Nairne pushed her bike to the edge of the road. An abandoned car sat awkwardly on the grass verge. There were no trees or cover of any kind as far as they could see.

"Quick, let's wait in there," she said, shoving the bike towards the stationery vehicle. She reached the car, an old Toyota, and tugged at the rear door. It opened. Inside the car smelled musty and stale but it was dry. Nairne slid into the seat and Ronnie followed behind her. The hail stones drummed on the roof of the vehicle, the noise deafening. Within minutes the road was white. Lightning flashed overhead, illuminating the sky for just a second. Ronnie began to count.

"One, two, three….." The peel of thunder boomed. Another flash and then another. The thunder echoed more quickly and more loudly. The storm was right above them. The hail stones began to diminish replaced by sheets of heavy rain. Outside, the road was awash, large puddles began to form and the water flowed across the tarred surface from the surrounding parched earth. Within ten minutes there were several inches of water outside the vehicle, and its speed and depth seemed to increase exponentially.

"It's a flash flood," Ronnie gasped. "We need to get the bikes moved to higher ground or we could end up stranded here." He pushed open the car door and climbed out. The water on the roadway was already lapping over the top of his feet. He pushed his crash helmet onto his head and made for his bike. Nairne followed behind. Within seconds they were soaking wet, their clothes clung to them as the rain lashed down. They pushed the heavily laden bikes along the road. It was hard work, they were both hot and sweaty as the rain had done nothing to reduce the heat of the day. They reached a fork in the road and turned left. It looked drier, and the water was flowing towards them so they were definitely heading for higher ground although, with the naked eye, the level change was imperceptible. Within half a mile the road was just wet rather than treacherous, and they stopped for a rest. The rain began to ease until it was just a downpour rather than a torrent.

After a short break they set off again, driving slowly, the road covered in hazardous puddles, some hiding dangerous holes. The weather returned to clearer sky and the sun shone. They saw some objects up ahead at the side of the road. Nairne could not decide what they were, it was like a variety of bundles or sacks. She slowed down, approaching with caution, then she realised the objects were moving. One of them rose up and she could see it was a group of people, sitting on the verge, surrounded by an odd assortment of trolleys and carts which were piled high with possessions. Lots of the objects were moving now, alerted to their arrival by the sound of the bike engines, they were scrambling to their feet. Nairne could see the looks of fear and terror on the faces of the adults. They pulled the children to their feet and she could see them staring around wildly looking for somewhere to run to, somewhere to hide. She stopped her bike while they were still some distance from the nearest person. Ronnie pulled in behind her and they both took of their helmets.

Nairne placed her helmet on the seat of the bike and began to walk towards the group of people. She held her hands up in as non-threatening a way as possible.

"It's okay," she shouted to them. "We won't harm you." She stopped and waited. One of the figures broke away from the group and began to approach her, cautiously. She could hear some of the children crying and one or two of the women trying to calm them.

The figure who approached was a man in his late sixties. He walked with a slow uneven gait, limping: the walk of someone who has covered a lot of ground. He was balding, his remaining strands of white hair were unkempt and as he got closer she could see he was unshaven, his skin bronzed like worn leather from exposure to years of sunshine. His clothes were old, torn and dirty. The boots on his feet misshapen from overuse, the soles worn.

He raised a hand in greeting as he got close. Nairne stepped forward and shook his hand.

"I'm sorry, we didn't mean to frighten you," she said, smiling as she introduced herself and Ronnie, who had stayed back next to the bikes. "We're a bit lost. We were trying to get to London, but the whole area is underwater. Is there a way across?"

"Yes lass, there is. The accent, Scottish?"

"Yes that is right."

"You're a long way from home. Ernest, Ernest White, leader of this little group." He shook her hand. "You want to get to London," he mused. "Are you sure you want to do that? It's not safe to go further south. It's not safe anywhere. I'd recommend you head north, that's what we're doing."

"Why, what's wrong, you look like you've been travelling for some time."

"Yes, almost six days we've been walking. We're all from Bingham, a small settlement on the other side of Lincoln, near the river Trent. Nothing much, just a few hundred houses, a quiet little place but not much left now. No, not much left at all…"

"What happened?" Nairne asked. Mr White looked dazed, like a person in shock.

"The men came, don't know who they are. Army uniforms, said they were official, but no, nothing much left now."

"Why, what did they do?" As Nairne asked the questions she felt a cold shiver run up and down her spine. She did not know if she wanted to hear the answer.

"They took them, took all the men of working age and some of the women, just the youngsters…… just took them, we don't know where and then they set fire to the place, just burned it to the ground and told us they'd be back and any one left would be dealt with. So we took off. A sad sight I'm sure we make, but we couldn't stay…. not sure where we're going."

"Do you have any weapons or any food or water?"

"No, nothing much, just what we could save before they torched the place. That's why we were so afraid when we heard you coming, we don't have any way to defend ourselves. So far we've been lucky as the road has been pretty deserted. We've seen more, like us, on the move but that's all. We need somewhere we can settle down, houses and the like, but who's going to let us stop. I don't know, I just keep telling them North. I don't know, it could be worse there, I just don't know…." He shook his head as the words trailed off. He was weary, Nairne could see it, a man in charge of a bunch of friends and family, with no idea what to do with them, how to keep them safe.

She went back to Ronnie and gave him a quick update

on what Ernest had told her and they wheeled the two bikes down the road towards the group. Ernest walked alongside them. The group consisted of two women in their sixties, another in her late forties, another man who looked older than Ernest, and six young children. Introductions were made. Nairne and Ronnie could see the fear and strain on the adults' faces; the children, all under ten, were tired and hungry. They were not related to any of the adults, but their parents had been taken and they were left with no one. Ernest knew he could not leave them behind. They all sat back down. Nairne opened her bag and pulled out a couple of tins of food, tinned peaches. She handed them over to one of the women.

"For the kids, I'm sorry we don't have enough for all of you."

The woman took the two tins from her, clasping her hand in gratitude. She rummaged through her bundle of possessions and found a couple of plastic cups. She opened the tins and gave each of the children a cup with some slices of the fruit and the syrupy liquid.

Ronnie took out the map and with Ernest's help managed to locate their position. Ernest explained that the body of water had been there for the last two years.

"It rises and falls depending on the tidal surges but it never dries up. The land around it is dead, months of salt water have washed away the nutrients from the soil. The River Trent which connects to the Humber Estuary is also permanently flooded." Ernest said. "So large parts of the city of Lincoln are now permanently under water and the city is almost deserted." He showed Ronnie where they could get across this new waterway. "There is a ferry operating about fifteen miles further inland. It would even be possible to take your bikes across." Ernest marked the map, showing any changes he was aware of to the area in terms of roads and waterways. Ronnie thanked him.

"Can we give you some advice?" Nairne asked. She didn't want to frighten them anymore, but they needed to get organised.

"Of course. If the two of you have managed to travel all the way from Scotland we're happy to listen."

"Yesterday, we stayed in a house on the other side of York. It was in a quiet residential area, all the inhabitants were gone. There were three or four hundred houses, all of them empty. Something killed them, some sort of infection. Most likely something in the drinking water. The city of York has quarantined itself, no one in or out. However, the houses all had vegetable gardens, some of them full of produce. If you could get there you could just choose a couple of properties and move in. But don't drink the water. You need to collect fresh rain water. Wash all the food and cook it before you eat it. If it is a water borne infection it may die out once the temperature drops. At least you would have food and shelter. We can show you where the houses are."

Ronnie unfolded the map and explained the route to Ernest, telling him the landmarks to watch out for.

"And there is one more thing. There were a number of dogs," Nairne lowered her voice so the children would not overhear. "These dogs were in a pack, a hunting pack. You need to get some weapons, even if it is just sticks or clubs, and you need to be ready. It may be an isolated pack, but I'm guessing as areas become empty of people, animals are being left behind."

They shook hands and set off down the road towards the ferry. The old man stood in the road and waved to them as they vanished from sight. Then he turned back to his group.

"Come on, let's get moving. Another few days and we could be in York."

THIRTEEN

The ferry was on the far side of the water when they arrived at the crossing point. They could see it, a distant shape on the horizon, and they could hear its engine coughing and spluttering. The water was calm and flat but at least a mile or two wide. A small wooden hut, badly built but enough to offer protection from the elements stood precariously near the edge of the water. There was no-one else around so Nairne and Ronnie sat down on the rickety wooden bench and waited. A long wooden jetty jutted out into the water, the planks silver grey and weathered. The metal struts supporting it were already corroded.

"That engine doesn't sound too healthy," Nairne commented, as the vessel chugged slowly towards the shore.

"I guess they're probably making their own fuel, God knows what from," replied Ronnie, rubbing his eyes and pushing his hair back from his forehead. "I'm just glad to get off the bike for a while and get the crash helmet off. I feel like the Man in the Iron Mask. It's too hot for this."

"Yeah, we thought it was unseasonably hot back home, but this is unbearable. Looking at the ground around here they've had another dry year. I can't imagine how people are managing to feed themselves. Come to that, there are a lot fewer people than I was expecting." She sat back, leaning against the sun warmed rough planks of the hut and closed her eyes. Even in the shade the air felt oppressively hot. "If Ernest and his group are anything to go by, things are going to get a lot harder from here. Are you sure about this, about coming with me?"

Ronnie turned and squinted at her.

"No, I don't think it's a good idea. I think it would be better if I head back. You'll be so much better on your own, all alone, against the big, bad, scary world. I'll hang on here and wave you off, then I'll get back."

Nairne opened one eye and looked at him. A smile breaking out across her face.

"Fine, I'll stop going on about it. No need for the sarcasm. Thank you for coming with me."

The noise of the approaching engine was clearer now, and so was the sound of voices, passengers on the ferry. Ronnie got up and walked to the edge of the water squinting at the craft.

"It looks really low in the water, not sure I fancy this much."

"No wonder, how many people do you think are aboard that?" They could see it more clearly now; the ferry was bulging with people and possessions, every corner of the craft was weighed down with passengers. The noise was like a rumble, no words were distinct, just the sound of many voices. The craft moved slowly and steadily towards the pier. As it reached shallower waters three figures jumped from the front of the boat and onto the wooden jetty, trailing heavy ropes behind them. They began to pull the heavily laden craft alongside the pier. The ropes were tied tightly and the three men moved alongside the craft and began to help people off. The passengers were mainly women, children and older men. Each carried a bundle of possessions. There were old pushchairs, home-made trolleys stuffed with bags, boxes and an assortment of misshapen parcels. Several infants cried, fractiously, their faces red and eyes streaming as flies buzzed around the sweating mass of people.

Soon the throng were rushing down the jetty heading for solid ground. They looked weary, their clothes were dusty and dishevelled, and many were sunburnt, with scarves or old pieces of fabric made into makeshift hats. There would have been no shade on the crossing, the water exposing all to the bright burning sunshine. Several of the men had injuries to their faces, bruises, black eyes and one or two had wounds, covered in homemade bandages. They filed past Ronnie and Nairne, a few glancing curiously at them and their motorbikes.

Within ten minutes, all of the passengers and their assorted belongings were safely unloaded onto dry land. They moved as a group. Nairne reckoned there were about thirty people in total, including the children. They settled at the edge of the water, some sitting on their luggage, others sprawled on the ground. Bottles of water were passed around, along with some limited items of food. A group of the men huddled together round a map, it looked homemade, crumpled and dirty. Their voices could be heard, an argument developing about what route to take.

Ronnie and Nairne watched.

"Give me the map," said Nairne. "I'll see if this can help them, why don't you go and find out if they'll take us back across?" She looked over to the three men operating the boat. They were perched on the edge of the jetty, drinking from water bottles. The sweat was running off their faces.

Ronnie walked over to speak with them while Nairne crossed over to the group of men. They stopped speaking as she approached, turning to stare at her.

"Would this help?" She held the map out for them to see. "It only covers up to the Newcastle area, but it might be a bit more accurate than yours. We've travelled down from Scotland so I can tell you which roads were passable."

"Thank you, that would be great," the oldest of the group responded. He was at least seventy, his face was drawn and his clothes hung from him like an undernourished scarecrow.

"I'm Arnold Head, this is Eric, Ronald and William." The others nodded in greeting as Nairne shook Arnold's hand.

"Nairne Grear," she responded. "Where are you wanting to get to?"

"Anywhere that is safe," he replied. "We've been

travelling for about five days now, we don't have anywhere in mind, but we can't go south. It is too dangerous. Our village came under attack from a group of men."

"Don't tell me they took the young men and some of the women away and burned the place down," she replied.

"Yes, yes that's right! How did you know?"

"We met a group from Bingham, it's near Lincoln…"

"Yes, I know it well." Arnold replied.

"They said the same thing happened there. We met the group about fifteen miles north of here, they'd been on the road for a few days, same story," Nairne said before explaining the advice she had given to Ernest and his party.

"What do you think lads?" Arnold asked, when Nairne finished. The others nodded and murmured in agreement.

"Can you show us where this place is? It's certainly worth a go."

Nairne pointed out the location of the empty houses on the map and then Arnold pulled out a pen and drew the outline of the route on their own map. Nairne tried to remember as many landmarks as possible.

"Nairne!" Ronnie shouted over to her. "It's time to go!"

"Just coming. Good luck." Hurriedly, she folded the map and stuffed it inside her jacket. Then she dashed across to the jetty where Ronnie was already wheeling his bike towards the boat. The four men waved to her and shouted their thanks.

Ronnie introduced her to the three men on the boat. Usually there were a couple of hours between crossings, however, the captain of the vessel explained that they had been unable to fit all of the group on the boat so Arnold and the rest of them were waiting for the remainder of their party.

"Yes, there were about ten more, plus more possessions, but I was worried we'd sink if they piled on board at once. It's been like this for the last two weeks or so. Some days we just can't cope with the numbers." He sighed heavily as he unslung the last of the ropes. The engine spluttered into life, belching black smoke from the exhaust pipe which ran upwards adjacent to the small wooden cabin which afforded the crew some protection from the sun.

"Are they all like that? Refugees?" Nairne asked.

"Yeah, just about. You two are the first passengers we've had in months who have their own transport. But I'd suggest you probably don't want to take those bikes into London with you. Chances are someone will try and take them off you. You'd be better hiding them and heading in by foot. From what we hear it is a bloody nightmare down there."

"We'd been wondering about that," said Ronnie. "They are quite an attractive prize I guess, but not worth getting killed for. So what's sparked all the refugees then?"

"The Army," the captain replied, but was cut off as one of the other men interjected.

"Bloody army, my arse, they're just murdering, thieving bastards that's all they are. That uniform doesn't mean shit, not anymore…." Rage flashed across his face. Nairne looked at the Captain.

"Oh, Lennie there was a proper soldier, in the real army, you know before all this, before everything…… Anyway, he hates the way these guys strut about in their uniforms, totally undisciplined. And it's much worse now there are all sorts of factions, answerable to no–one, conducting their own little conflicts, seizing land. It's like the old feudal system with lords in their castles stealing from their subjects," the Captain laughed, but the laughter sounded almost desperate. "We just do what we can, take people across, for a price, but a fair price. There was a bridge about another seventeen miles inland but we heard that has been destroyed. So this is the only way across unless you want to swim!"

"And does everyone cross to that side?" Nairne asked, looking back at the vanishing shore, the crowd of weary travellers no more than tiny dots on the landscape.

"Yes, everyone seems to be moving north. It's a fair while since we took anyone the other way. It's too dangerous, too desperate. No one wants to go south."

Nairne and Ronnie glanced at one another, both knowing the sensible thing was to turn back and go home, to pretend they had never seen the letter; to leave Angela to whatever fate held in store for her.

"You two must have a good reason for going to London. I hope you won't be disappointed," the Captain remarked. "It should only be another ten or fifteen minutes to the shore, we travel much faster without a heavy cargo."

The shoreline came into view and, as the Captain had said, a smaller group of travelers stood waiting anxiously, some of them sheltering from the sun on the shady side of a duplicate wooden shed. The relief on their faces as they saw the returning boat was palpable. Once the craft was secured to the jetty, Nairne and Ronnie wheeled the bikes off and thanked the captain.

They set off again down the long empty road. As the light began to fade, they were keen to find somewhere safe to camp for the night.

An abandoned farmhouse seemed suitable. There were no signs of life; the land around it was scorched. The remains of the grass were burnt and yellow. The soil, no more than sand. Sheep bones and remnants of fleeces lay scattered in the corner of one of the fields; the dead animals predated and their remains cast around by foxes or dogs. The track which led to the house was rough and the ground cracked and hard as concrete. The house was a handsome two storey white rendered building, with thick stone walls and a large bay window on the front. Most of the panes of glass were missing while some of the other windows had been boarded up and a sturdy padlock had been fitted to the front door. After checking out the surrounding area and the farm buildings, Nairne managed to squeeze in through one of the back windows. Once inside, she was able to unlock the door to the dining room and let Ronnie in. They wheeled the bikes inside and looked around.

The place had been stripped bare. There were some items of furniture, but the kitchen contained no food, just crockery and pots and pans, still hanging above a fabulous range. It looked as though the previous owners had taken anything worth salvaging. Upstairs, the bedrooms were almost empty. One old mattress stood propped against the wall of what looked like a child's room. It had seen better days. In the main bedroom, there were a number of missing floor boards, which had been torn up. Splinters of wood, nails and gouges out of the adjacent boards paid testament to the violent nature of this intervention. They went from one room to another. In the bathroom, the remnants of a shower curtain hung limply from the rail above the bath. Ronnie turned one of the taps on the sink. There was nothing; not a drop of water. They returned to the ground floor. At the rear of the house was a large room which had been used as an office. One wall contained a huge set of dark oak bookshelves, the wood straining under the weight of hundreds of books, periodicals and magazines. Some lay discarded on the floor, and at one end the shelves were bare as if someone had rushed in and grabbed armfuls of the books. Several of the windows downstairs were missing and shards of glass covered the bare wooden floors.

"I guess we are not the first people to camp in here," said Nairne, examining the remains of the last fire, which had been lit in the hearth in the main living room. "Now we know what happened to the floor boards and books."

"Do you want to have a look outside, there might be stuff in some of the outbuildings or the barn," said Ronnie. Nairne nodded and followed him outside.

They crossed the yard to the two small stone outbuildings, originally used as storage for coal, logs and gardening equipment. A sit-on lawn mower stood dejected and rusting, its tyres perished and crumbling. Ronnie unscrewed the cap on the fuel tank.

"You're optimistic," Nairne laughed.

"It's always worth checking. You never know, it might have been overlooked." However, on this occasion it was completely empty.

"It probably evaporated. It looks like this place has been abandoned for some time," Nairne replied. She walked out of the outhouse and across to the corrugated barn. Inside was silent, except for the flapping of a couple of nesting pigeons, who took fright at this unexpected human intrusion. The stalls, which had once been occupied by cattle, stood empty. Some partial hay bales lay neglected in one corner. Several roofing panels had come loose allowing the infrequent rain to penetrate the building. A tractor stood at the far end, they both walked towards it.

Beneath the giant metal beast sat a bucket. The fuel tank had several holes pierced through it.

"Looks like someone beat us to that one," Ronnie sighed. "It's a pity because we could do with some spare fuel for the bikes."

"Why don't we leave one or both of them here? It would cut down on fuel. We don't have to take all our gear. I guess we could do without the tent. It's still warm enough to sleep out without one."

"That is fine as we should reach London tomorrow, so if we left one bike here and the other on the outskirts of the city, then if anything happens to one of them we could make it on foot back to here. It would only be a few days walking."

"Right, that sounds like a plan, do you want to sort out the gear. I'll see if I can catch a rabbit for dinner. I noticed there are droppings out in the yard."

They walked back to the house and Nairne left Ronnie unpacking their bags as she went out to catch dinner.

FOURTEEN

The hailstones fell like bullets, ricocheting off the ground. Susan and Angela were at the far end of the cricket pitch. There had been no warning, just the sudden noise and then the shock of being bombarded with the tiny balls of ice. A mound of freshly pulled carrots sat in two large boxes

"Quickly, get the boxes, I'll get the barrow!" Angela shrieked. They dropped the tools on the ground and Susan lifted the first of the two boxes into the wheelbarrow. Angela helped her with the second one and together they shoved the heavily laden barrow along the gravel path towards the shelter. They were both laughing with the shock of the cold wet shower, surprise giving way to amusement. They had not had rain for several weeks so any was welcome.

"We need this," Susan said. "But it would have been good if there had been some warning!"

"Yes, we are soaked through." They reached the shelter of the now converted cricket pavilion. Pushing the barrow under cover, they stood under the glass structure listening to the thundering downpour. Within a few minutes hail had turned to sheets of rain. The parched ground was hard and puddles began to develop quickly; peels of thunder rang out followed by flashes of lightning.

"It's like a proper April shower, not what you expect in September," Angela remarked.

"No, but then these last few years, who knows what to expect."

The two women watched as the rain continued to fall, turning the soil a dark shade of brown and the foliage a bright, newly washed green. Within twenty minutes it was all over, the skies returned to their predictable blue and the sun returned.

"I'll fetch the tools," said Susan. "Then I guess we better take these into the kitchen."

"I'll wait here for you. I don't think I could manage the barrow on my own."

Angela watched while Susan walked back to the discarded tools and gathered them. The rain, after the initial shock, had felt great. The atmosphere had been oppressively warm for days. The stifling heat exacerbated the stench of the surrounding city, which hung like a musty old curtain, even over this open ground.

They placed the tools on top of the barrow and together they pushed it back across the field to the courtyard. Once they reached the entrance to the kitchen area, Angela called out for some assistance and Alex appeared at the doorway. He lifted the boxes of carrots out of the barrow.

"That was some downpour," said Alex. "You two must have been soaked. If you let me get these inside, I'll put the tools away for you. You probably want to get in and get dried off." He looked at Susan as he spoke. Angela smiled to herself. He had it bad.

Susan did not respond so it was left to Angela to thank him on their behalf. She followed the younger woman into the courtyard and through into the main building.

"That was very kind of Alex, don't you think?"

"I suppose so, although we're perfectly capable of tidying up after ourselves," Susan replied, sullenly.

"I think he knows that. I think he was just trying to be kind. He obviously likes you, Susan. You don't need to be so hostile about it. I'll see you at dinner." Angela walked away. She was annoyed as Alex was such a sweet boy. She was beginning to wonder what he saw in Susan. She went up to her room and changed out of her gardening trousers, which were still wet around the ankles, then she sat down on the edge of the bed, feeling all the familiar aches and pains. Her back ached with a deep continuous pain. She had tried exercising and taking painkillers, but it made no difference, the pain was there all the time now. Five minutes rest, then she would go and see Eve.

It was tempting to spend all her time with Eve, all her precious time, but she knew that would be frowned upon. The children belonged to the community; individual parental ties were not encouraged. This was a community where everyone had their own role and job to do, based on what had been decided by Devlin. Childcare was not Angela's role. He had explained it all quite clearly at the beginning: shared responsibilities, shared ownership, which is what made a community strong. It was more efficient this way. All the children were looked after as a group, freeing up more people to work and to help keep the community on track.

Angela had been a firm believer. She had gone along with this. It was not like Eve had been planned. Angela had done the whole motherhood thing, been there got that tee shirt and she hadn't been great at it. Some people weren't designed for that sort of life. Eve had been a consequence of no access to birth control, one of the many things everyone had taken for granted previously. She remembered back to when she had first realised she was pregnant. She had been with Devlin for about six months. He had been surprised, almost disappointed in her, as if she alone had been responsible for the entire thing. He'd tried to hide his obvious irritation, and as the pregnancy developed he started to show off about it to the others. Angela had been terrified, realising that she was facing pregnancy and child birth without any medical intervention. Devlin couldn't understand it. Having children was a completely natural thing; that's what women were designed for and Angela was just being hysterical. He told her that he had seen places where women had children out in the fields where they were working and then got up and got on with their job. He'd been to so many places during his army days; the Middle East, Africa, and then he'd served back in the United Kingdom. Not that it had been very united by then. So Angela was told she had nothing to worry about. Devlin was sure of it.

None of this had stopped her from a rising sense of panic as her due day got closer. Her first two children had both been born in hospital with all the modern technology on hand. They had both been easy births, but she had been younger then. When the time finally came, one of Devlin's men had managed to find a qualified nurse who, for payment in food, had agreed to come and help at the birth. She was not a midwife but at least she had some medical training and a medical text book to refer to. There had been eight of them then, living in a three-storey Victorian villa which they had acquired a few weeks before. Angela was one of only two women in the group. Lizzie, the other woman was in her twenties. She was a flighty young girl and was the temporary companion of Devlin's right hand man, Don. She had been panic stricken when asked to help by the nurse. Lizzie had left soon afterwards. One day she was just gone. She left all her possessions, said goodbye to no one. She just disappeared. Angela wondered where she was now.

Devlin had also mysteriously disappeared on the day of Eve's birth. There was no sign of him during her five hours of labour, unlike Daniel, who had been with her for both her previous births, worried about missing it, worried about not being there to see his children born. But Devlin had been happy to return to her bedside, once all the pain and fear and mess were dealt with. She remembered how he had appeared and had been almost too afraid to pick up the tiny baby, only seven pounds in weight, a shock of dark brown hair and a tiny wrinkled face. She remembered his disappointment that Eve was female. He didn't say so but she sensed a son and heir would have been more to his liking.

Now Eve was walking and talking, ten to the dozen. She looked so much like Devlin, her dark curly hair, her deep, dark eyes and sallow complexion. She was still small for her age but she seemed to enjoy good health with nothing more serious than the odd cough or cold.

Angela was acutely aware of how precious good health was. The community had lost one child last year to whooping cough. There had been several weeks of high tension as the infection had swept through the nursery, affecting several of the children. Eve had been spared the terrible racking, wheezing cough, but not everyone had been so lucky.

She pushed herself up from the edge of the bed and wandered down the corridor to the nursery. As she opened the door, Eve looked up from her building blocks, which she had managed to balance into a tower. She struggled to her feet and charged across the room, arms held out anticipating being lifted high up into the air.

"Angel, angel," she called out to her mother, giggling and smiling.

Angela scooped her up and swung her round. Eve squealed with delight and then clung to Angela. The two young women who ran the nursery watched this display with a nervous tension. Other mothers within the community would have loved to come and spend time with their children during the working day, but that was frowned upon. The rules for Devlin's partner were however, somewhat more relaxed. Not that they disliked Angela, she was always fair to everyone and she never openly abused her position within the group.

"How are you both," Angela asked, smiling. "Susan and I got caught in that shower so we decided to call it a day as the ground is a bit wet now for lifting any more crops."

"We're fine, and so is Eve. She's been such a good girl today. We were just going to get them all ready for their dinner if you want to stay and help," replied Carron, the younger of the two women.

"Thank you. That would be good. Are you going to help us get the dinner ready?" she asked Eve, placing her back on the floor and taking her by the hand.

By the time Angela reached the dining room most of the community were already seated. Devlin glanced up as she entered the room, his expression one of annoyance. Hastily, she picked her way between the tables and sat down at his side. Alex sat next to her with Susan next to him. He nodded in greeting as Angela took her seat.

"Sorry, I got caught up with…" Angela whispered to Devlin, seeing the disapproving expression.

He raised his hand, silencing her. Angela felt her temper rise. She was not a child to be publicly reprimanded. But she sensed Devlin was not in a mood to be challenged. He looked tense, angry even, which was totally disproportionate to her misdemeanour.

Devlin paused for a moment before rising to his feet. As he stood, the noise in the room began to subside. Expectant faces turned to look at him. After a few moments there was total silence.

"It pains me to have to speak with all of you this evening," he paused. "It pains me because I have committed myself to this community, as have all of you. I have worked hard. I have struggled hard to develop a better future for us all. A future built on trust, a future where the rules are clear, where the rules are designed to help all of us!" His voice rose. "But not for the first time there are those amongst us, those you sit next to, those you trust, those you believe are part of this community. And then you discover that they do not abide by the same rules. They do not understand the difference between right and wrong. They believe the rules do not apply to them. They think they are special."

Angela could feel the colour rising in her face, surely visiting Eve, wanting to see their daughter could not have caused such rage. The rest of the room gazed on in silence, some glanced around nervously, looking for the subject of this sermon, to see if they could spot the guilt.

"When you join this community, you join our family, and families should be able to trust one another. We know what happens when some members of a society think they are better than others. We know where such greed leads us. We know, oh yes we know what such unacceptable behaviour causes. It causes the chaos, the death, the destruction of our very planet. Yes, that is what happens when the individual feels their rights and their choices are more important than the welfare of the whole." He paused as two of his men rose from their seats. He nodded to them and they walked across the dining room until they stood on either side of a young man. His name was Ralph. He was a soft, shambling boy, slightly overweight and nervous. Not much older than seventeen, his untidy hair hung around his plump face as he looked up at the two men. A look of terror flashed across his face. They pulled him to his feet and dragged him to the front of the seating area. His eyes swung madly round the room, looking for help from anyone. They pulled him round to face his accuser, Devlin. The boy was shaking. Angela could see every muscle in his body tense, as he waited to hear what his crime was, and what his fate would be.

"This boy, this upstanding member of our community who we took in off the streets, who we have looked after, has broken that trust. We have given him everything: a place to sleep, the clothes on his back, the shoes on his feet; our trust. And how does he repay us? By stealing from us, from all of us." The boy glanced at Angela and recognised the fear in her eyes. She put her hand to her mouth. She felt hot and dizzy but also relieved that it was not her flouting of the rules that had angered Devlin, that this time it was not she who stood before everyone accused and condemned.

"So do you have anything to say?" Devlin asked, placing some tins of food on the table. "Can you explain how this food came to be in your room, in your possession? Can you enlighten us all as to why you are so special?"

I didn't…. I didn't do it… I don't know, I haven't ever seen those before…." he sobbed, his words almost incomprehensible.

"So I ask all of you, what do we do with this thief? Do we deliver justice? Off with his hand so that he will not break the rules again?" Devlin placed a shiny meat cleaver on the table. The boy wailed uncontrollably and Angela felt her stomach heave. He couldn't. It was barbaric. The two men held fast onto Ralph's arms and dragged the screaming boy to the table. They held his arm out, pinning it to the wooden surface. Their fingers pressing into his flesh. He screamed and pleaded, whimpering like a small child. His body twisted this way and that, the flesh on his arm stretching painfully. His face was contorted with fear. Angela looked up at Devlin. Her head shaking, involuntarily. She couldn't sit here and watch this. She glanced to her left. Susan sat forward in her seat, her eyes wide, her breath held. The rest of the community sat frozen in fascination and horror. But no one moved. Devlin raised his hand and lifted the cleaver into the air. The entire room appeared to hold its breath. Angela began to tense her muscles, ready to stand and intervene. She placed a hand on the table to steady herself. She couldn't let him do it. As she began to move, she felt a hand on her arm, gently holding her back. She glanced around. Alex did not look at her, but she could feel him willing her to stay in the seat. His face remained impassive. Next to him, Susan leaned further forward, both hands grasping the edge of the table, and her eyes wild with excitement.

"What should I do?" Devlin held the audience captive, moving the cleaver, raising it up as he spoke. The light bounced off the blade casting dancing shapes across the walls of the room. "Should I take this hand so that we can save this boy? Or should we cast him out, cast him out into the world, back where he came from, cast him out with all that he brought to us?"

There was a murmur of approval. That was a punishment they could stomach. He had been stealing after all, and if everyone did that where would it end?

Devlin nodded in agreement and placed the meat cleaver back on top of the table. The two men pulled Ralph back onto his feet and began to drag him from the room.

"No wait!" Devlin commanded. "He should return to the streets with what he owns. Take off his shoes, take off his shirt." The two men did as they were instructed and Ralph stood before them barefoot and wearing only an ill-fitting pair of shorts. They pushed him roughly towards the exit.

Angela felt lightheaded. She had just witnessed an execution. Devlin had sentenced that boy to death. He would have little chance of survival outside with nothing, nowhere to go, no food, no water, and more importantly, no weapon.

Devlin followed as his men dragged the boy out of the room and across the courtyard. The crowd surged forward and followed their leader to watch this final humiliation.

Angela sat back in her chair. She felt sick. Susan was on her feet.

"Angela!" She tugged at her arm. "Come on or we'll miss it!" She let go of Angela and ran from the room. Angela took a deep breath. She was alone. She could hear the crowd moving across the quadrangle, their voices rising, and above it all the screams of the boy pleading for mercy.

The door of the hall opened and Alex stepped back into the room.

"You need to get out here," he whispered. "Your absence will be noticed." He looked afraid, not for himself, but for her. She nodded and got to her feet. She felt as if her legs would not be able to support her weight as she crossed the room. He held the door open for her and she paused and thanked him as she passed. He had saved her. She would have stood, she would have defied Devlin in front of everyone and there would have been consequences.

The mob, as that is what they now were, approached

the front gates. The boy was being dragged along by the two men who gripped his upper arms. He had fallen more than once and his skin was grazed, down his arms and across his face. His pale flesh looked soft and vulnerable like a baby's. He was no longer pleading. He just wailed, a continuous indecipherable assortment of sounds. Angela joined the group. She could not tear her eyes away from the boy. Around her, people shouted and jeered, people she knew and trusted, people she had grown to like and respect, but it was as if some madness had befallen them. One or two like her were silent, and some participated with less enthusiasm. Alex stayed near the back. He watched Devlin, not the boy. He watched to see what Devlin watched.

Devlin raised his hand to silence everyone. The crowd abated until the only sound was that of the boy.

"Open the gate," said Devlin, addressing the armed guard who stood to the right of the large reinforced steel gates. The guard stepped forward and with assistance lifted off the massive metal bolt which held the gates in place. He pulled the left one open, just wide enough for the two men to push the boy outside.

The crowd waited for instruction and Devlin ordered everyone back inside. They followed him. Angela tagged along at the rear, with Alex behind her. They could hear Ralph still crying and wailing as he was dragged down the road towards the jetty. Two of the men would take him across to the mainland and leave him there.

It would be dark in a few hours. Ralph needed to find somewhere safe where he could hide.

FIFTEEN

The dawn was beautiful: a red sky, light cloud and a warm breeze. Ronnie and Nairne had packed their supplies the night before and had hidden one of the bikes in the shed. After a hasty breakfast they set off. This would be the last day of the journey. They would be on the outskirts of the city within two to three hours, assuming the roads were clear.

One of the great finds in the farmhouse library had been a paper A to Z of London. It was old, battered and many years out of date, but it gave enough detail for them to be able to locate the address from the letter. The site was on the south side of the Thames, and slightly to the east. It appeared to be bounded on two sides by railway lines, and the river on the third, leaving a triangular plot of approximately five or six acres. The school was on a rise. It looked like a defensible position.

They studied the map and the route they would take.

"You look anxious," said Ronnie.

"I'm fine."

"Really?"

"I just can't understand why people would stay in the city. It must be so difficult to grow enough food, to find fuel. I don't understand why they haven't moved..... although I guess we may get there and find she's long gone."

"Is that what you want?"

"No, I don't know. I don't want to be doing this. I don't want to see her again. She always wants something. My mother never did anything unless she got something from it."

"Look, we should be there by the end of today, if all goes smoothly. You can find out what she wants and we can be gone again in a couple of days. She sounded desperate in the letter. We have no idea what's wrong, so all we can do is go there and find out. If we can help her, fine, if not then we leave again. You don't owe her anything. You don't have to do what she wants."

"I know. It just brings back all these memories, all this stuff I'd dealt with. It was exactly the same when she 'died', we had all that upset. It was like she'd left us all over again. My brother was distraught. I can't believe she let us go through that."

"Maybe she had her reasons, who knows. But we'll find out when we get there. Now are you ready?"

Nairne nodded and put her crash helmet on. Ronnie climbed onto the bike and she climbed on behind him. The countryside was deserted for the first twenty miles or so. They stuck to the back roads. The silence made the bike's engine seem unnaturally loud. It was going to be another warm day, already Nairne could feel her clothes sticking to her, her face hot inside the helmet. The roads were narrow, winding and in a treacherous condition. Pot holes and fallen branches became frequent hazards. They drove over areas of vegetation, where soil had been washed onto the tar by previous heavy rains, and weeds had taken hold. In the distance they could see smoke rising from a site to the east of them. Ronnie slowed the bike.

"What do you think?" Turning his head he mouthed to Nairne as the bike came to a halt.

"A campsite, maybe. Will we have a closer look?"

They dismounted and pushed the bike into the undergrowth and set off on foot towards the smoke. The ground sloped upwards, bare farmland now, with only the remains of some sun bleached grass, clinging hopelessly to the sandy surface. The smoke was from numerous little bonfires, and as they reached the brow of the hill, they could smell the camp before they could see it. Stretched out in the valley below them was a full sized shanty town of tents and shelters. Some horses and carts stood to one side. Small figures could be seen in the distance, tending to the fires. Children rushed about between the structures, their faint cries and laughter carried on the wind. The smell was of smoke and sweat and excrement and horses.

"How many people do you think are down there?" Nairne asked.

"I don't know, a thousand, maybe more. They look like they're travelling light."

"And they seem to be unarmed. I can't see any sign of guards or lookouts and it's not exactly the most defensible site to choose."

"Seen enough?"

"Yeah, let's get back to the bike," said Nairne.

The road, which cut through the hillside, with a steep bank to the left and a sharp fall to the right was blocked by a landslide. The perpetual rain over the previous winter, had forced water into the cracked ground and then freezing temperatures had expanded the water causing the edge to give way and cover a section of road with soil, tree roots and rocks. They got off the bike and Nairne scrambled over the loose soil and boulders to see how far the blockage stretched. She returned about ten minutes later.

"This goes on for at least fifty metres. After the next bend there are a whole line of trees down. We won't be going this way that's for sure." They got back on the bike and drove back along the road for half a mile before cutting into the field and detouring across country for a couple of miles, eventually picking the road up again.

This time the place was not so deserted. They were beginning to reach urban sprawl, London's suburbs. They could see refuse and abandoned possessions along the roadside. Remnants of lives and indications of how many people had fled along these roads. To the west, there was a patch of woodland. Ronnie cut across the road and through a couple of fields until they reached the edge of the trees.

They dismounted and pushed the bike deep into the

trees.

"I think this is as far as we take the bike," he said, undoing his helmet and placing it on the seat.

"Yeah, we're going to use up too much fuel trying to find a way through, plus I think it will draw too much attention. We haven't seen any other working vehicles for the last two days."

"Let's get some branches to hide this, and I'll disable it just in case anyone thinks of stealing it." He bent down and fiddled with the cover on the engine, removing the spark plugs and placing them inside his jacket pocket.

Nairne gathered some fallen tree branches and pushed the bike deep into a thicket of brambles, placing the branches over the top.

"You'd never notice it unless you were actually looking. We'd better check the map and pinpoint our location so we can find it on the way back," she said.

Ronnie took the map from his pocket and after some examination located their current position. He marked it with a pencil.

"I think we are about here." He showed the map to Nairne and after studying it carefully she agreed.

They set off on foot, and within the hour they were surrounded by dense housing. This far out of the city centre the houses were relatively new, built within the last twenty years or so. It appeared that some were still inhabited. Front gardens were now stripped of decoration and parking areas and instead vegetables were crammed onto the available land. They saw one or two people out tending to their gardens, but as they approached, people went indoors. At the end of the street they reached a small park. The trees, which had once ringed the edge of it, had been chopped down. There was no grass left, the whole area had been dug up and planted with potatoes and turnips. Row after row filled the small space. The aged iron railings which surrounded it had been reinforced with barbed wire along the top. The gates were securely locked and inside the space was a well-fed Alsatian dog. Alerted by their footsteps it roused itself from the ground and rushed across to the fence barking and jumping up at them.

"I guess we should move out onto the street," said Nairne.

As they stepped off the pavement and put some distance between themselves and the dog they heard a door slam and voices behind them. Ronnie turned round and glanced back. Two men had emerged from one of the houses and were walking towards them. One was armed with a baseball bat. They paused as Ronnie turned around properly raising his hand in greeting.

"Sorry, I think we gave the dog a fright. We're just passing through."

The man nodded in response and they stopped in their tracks.

"What do you think?" said Nairne. "Would it be worth trying to get some more information on what we're likely to find up ahead?"

"Maybe, but I don't want to get too close to them, just in case. You wait here while I go and speak to them."

He turned to face the two men who were some thirty or forty metres away and, taking off his rucksack, he placed his gun on the top of it, making sure they had seen he was armed. He walked back towards them.

The two men stood their ground but did not approach.

"We're heading across London to Wandsworth. Have either of you been into the city recently? Do you have any idea of what we can expect?"

"Scotch, you Scotch?" the older of the two men asked.

"Scottish, yeah, that's right."

"You've come all the way down from Scotland? What on foot?"

"No, we had transport part of the way, but yes we've been travelling for some time."

The man considered this. Pausing, he scratched his face,

which was weather worn and covered in stubble. He was in his forties, stocky, muscled and relaxed looking. The other one was just a younger version of the first, perhaps by four of five years and was fifteen or twenty pounds lighter in weight.

"No shit! That is some distance. You must have a good reason to go into the city, coming all that way."

"Especially when most people are going in the other direction," the younger man butted in. "When you get into the city you'll see why." They both nodded subconsciously, at this statement.

"Why, what's it like?" Ronnie asked again.

"It's like….." He paused considering his response. "It's difficult to describe, but the closest I can say is it's like the news footage we used to see of those other places. You know the third world, like news footage of the conditions in India or countries at war, like Syria or Iraq or…."

"It's like the wild bloody west," said the other. "The place is crawling with gangs, kill you as soon as look at you. There are armed guards protecting some parts. There's no functioning government, no schools, no proper transport or sanitation. It's just a great big slum. We don't go in there now, not for anything. If we can't find what we need out here we just do without."

"And there's the water," said the other. "The barrier is gone now. Large parts of the city are flooded on an almost permanent basis. Not too bad at this time of year but in the winter, when we get the rain, the snow, and the high tides, then it's pretty treacherous."

"So will we be able to get across the city?"

"If you've got stuff to barter with, then yeah, and your armed and know how to handle yourself, but you need to make sure you don't get caught out at night. Most areas have a curfew. Out after dark, they just shoot you down. They say it's to stop looting, but there's nothing left to steal. And what about up North, what's it like? What have you seen on your way down here?"

"It's variable," said Ronnie. "We came down past York. The city is quarantined, some kind of disease so they've closed the city, hoping it'll pass. Some places were deserted and we've seen a huge number of people on the roads moving north. Around Lincoln there seemed to be some sort of armed militia burning down whole settlements and taking away the men."

"Yes, we've heard rumours about that…." he trailed off, rubbing his face once again. "Do you know where you're going? Do you have a map?"

"Yes, we have an old A to Z. Not sure how much use it will be, but it's better than nothing."

"Show us where you're headed and we can at least tell you what we know."

"Thanks." Ronnie turned round and gave the thumbs up sign to Nairne, who picked up his bag and gun and walked over to join them.

She nodded in greeting but did not speak. Ronnie reached down and rummaged in the front pocket of his rucksack, removing the tattered book. He flicked through to the page which showed their final destination.

The older of the two men, studied the page, then flicked back to the previous section of map.

"All this," he indicated to a large area in the centre of the city. "This floods regularly. There are still bridges here and here, or there were a year ago, the last time we went into the centre, but there's also lots of boat operators, along here." He pointed to a street several hundred yards away from the river's original course. "You see, they moor the boats along here. If you can pay they'll take you across."

"So what passes for currency?"

"Food, alcohol, cigarettes, some people still accept gold and stuff like that. Do you have anything to trade?"

"We have seeds," said Ronnie. "They're light to transport and certainly around our area they've proved pretty popular." The man studied him closely then glanced at his brother. The younger one nodded, almost imperceptibly.

"What kind of seeds? We might be interested. To be honest I can't imagine you'll find many takers in the city centre. I know people grow food in the parks and what gardens there are but..... Well, as you can see we've started our own little plot in the park there, plus any empty gardens. But we've only got a few crops. No carrots or tomatoes. Haven't even seen a tomato this last year. We've got greenhouses rigged up around the back but not much to go inside."

"You're in luck then. We can give you three varieties of tomatoes and as long as you save some seeds at the end of next season you should be set. We also have carrot seeds, just one variety but they'd get you started. What can you offer in return?"

"Cigarettes and some home brewed alcohol. It's like Vodka only stronger than any of the old brands. We make it out of the potato peelings and any damaged ones that won't store, plus a few secret ingredients. It wouldn't win any prizes but it will put hairs on your chest," he laughed.

"Or make you go blind," the younger man chipped in smirking. "I'll go get our stuff." He walked back towards the house returning a few minutes later with a carrier bag containing eight boxes of cigarettes and two small bottles of alcohol.

Ronnie knelt down and opened his rucksack, removing a small parcel. He stood up and carefully opened one end of the parcel. Inside were six packets of seeds, carefully labelled.

"There are instructions inside each packet. When to sow and how to look after the plants, but remember it's much warmer down here so you could probably sow things a few weeks earlier." He handed the packet across and in exchange took the plastic bag.

They shook hands and set off down the road.

"That was useful," said Ronnie.

"Yes, they seemed like good people," said Nairne. "And it's good to think our seeds will be helping people all over the country. It really was a great idea for bartering with as we could never have carried enough in the way of food supplies."

They were in the city. It was late afternoon and the weather had held. A warm breeze did little to disguise the smell of the place.

"I guess we should find somewhere to spend the night," Ronnie suggested, stopping and removing the rucksack from his back as he stretched.

"Yes, it looks like quite a lot of the houses are empty. I suppose we could just choose one, as long as we can secure the doors behind us," said Nairne. She also felt weary, from the heat more than anything else. After some deliberation they chose an end terraced house. The street, which dated from the nineteen-forties was comprised of three-storey brick houses. A few looked occupied, smoke rose from cooking fires, however they saw no one. The property they had chosen had been vandalised. The windows downstairs were broken and the front door had been kicked in. It hung open, leaving a gaping hole leading to a dark and desolate interior. Nairne went in first, weapon in hand. Ronnie stood at the front door, an eye on the road and an ear listening out for any signs of trouble.

Downstairs, the rooms were badly damaged: graffiti covered the walls, rubbish lay strewn around, mixed with broken glass and other debris. The few remaining items of furniture were damaged. Nairne checked each of the downstairs rooms. The kitchen had been torn out, even the copper water pipes, which served the central heating, had been stolen for reuse. There was no sign of recent habitation. She peered through the back kitchen window into the concrete yard. Climbing the narrow, steep staircase to the first floor, she found the rooms were in better condition. There were two bedrooms and a small bathroom. The windows on the back of the house were broken, letting the elements in to the smaller bedroom and bathroom. There were signs of water damage and a strong odour of rot. The flight of stairs to the top floor were narrow and worn. There was a tight turn at the top and the two bedrooms up here were built in to the roof space; a roof which was leaking in several places. There were large, dark stains on the carpet. As Nairne walked across the room she could feel the floor boards shift and creak under her weight. She retreated to the doorway. The last thing she needed was to end up falling through the floor.

The first floor would be fine. The bedroom at the front was dry, and they could see the road from there.

"Ronnie, it looks good," she said, as she entered the hallway. "We'll need to rig up some sort of barricade for the front door but I think we should be safe here. There's a back door which leads out to a yard at the back. I guess there must be a lane running down behind the row. I'll check it out and make sure we have another escape route."

"No signs of anyone out here, but who knows who's watching," he replied, following her inside. "I suggest we take turns to keep watch tonight."

"Yeah. Good idea."

Darkness fell earlier here than it did at home. Nairne and Ronnie sat in the room and ate a cold dinner, opening a tin of peaches and some dried fruit they had brought with them. This was supplemented with some rabbit they had caught and cooked the day before. The place had been pretty quiet, not even any bird life, but as night fell with no streetlights or houselights the darkness became thick and impenetrable. There was silence.

They lit a candle, just one, not wanting to draw attention to their presence in the house.

"I'll take the first watch," said Nairne, rising to her feet. She used their one precious torch, to find her way to the landing. They only used the torch when they had to as batteries were a luxury. She sat at the top of the stairs, facing the front door, which they had wedged shut using a chair.

She could hear Ronnie unrolling the sleeping mat and settling down. She glanced at her watch. It was just past nine. It would be a long night. Nairne was used to keeping watch. There had been many nights when she was on the road with Paul where they had taken turns to stay up, to keep watch, to keep themselves safe. Even with Dog as a companion, sometimes it had just not been safe enough for them both to sleep at once. The hardest thing was staying awake in complete darkness, especially if you were very tired. But tonight Nairne knew nothing would make her sleep. Her brain was buzzing, full of memories and questions.

SIXTEEN

Angela woke with a start. She'd had a fitful night, tossing and turning. She had awoken during the early hours and, although she did not know why, she began to think she could hear the boy, Ralph, shouting out, crying, and pleading to be let back in. The rational part of her mind said this was impossible. She was too far from the gates, too far away to hear even if he had been there, but she couldn't get the sound out of her head.

Turning over, she looked at the pillow adjacent to her own. It was untouched. Devlin had not come to bed, or at least not to hers. She felt saddened but also relieved. Angela knew it was only a matter of time before she was publicly replaced by one of the younger women. She also knew that she was pushing him away, no longer quite so compliant, no longer quite so star struck. She'd loved being his right hand woman, enjoying all the perks that came with that position, but she knew Devlin well enough to know that once he found out her secret he would not wish to share anything with her.

Pulling herself together, Angela sat up and placed her feet on the cool wooden floor. She stood up. The pain in her back was searing. She sat back down on the bed, breathing deeply, her fists clenched into tight balls. She needed more pain killers and she needed them now.

The dining hall was already full when Angela entered. Devlin's seat was empty but Alex was still at the table. There was no sign of Susan. Angela felt the room had a different atmosphere, the others seemed subdued. She wondered how many of them were thinking about Ralph and about what they had done. She helped herself to bread and herbal tea before sitting next to Alex.

She looked at the food on the plate and felt nauseous,

but she had to eat it.

"Are you okay?" Alex asked as she took her seat. "You look very pale."

"I'm fine, I didn't sleep and my back is playing up. It hurts like hell."

"If you come down to the store room later this morning I am on duty, I'll see what I can find in the way of painkillers."

"Thank you. And thank you for yesterday."

"You're welcome. You know it would have served no purpose, standing up to him. You wouldn't have saved the boy."

"I know but…. . You know he's not a bad man, he's just…. . I think it's the responsibility for all this, for all of us. I think he feels he's got to show he's in control……" Alex looked at her as if he could see right through her, as if he knew she did not believe any of that any more than he did.

"I'd better get on," he said standing up. "I'll see you later."

It was going to be a cooler day than the last few, which was a relief. After a quick visit to the nursery to see Eve, and then to Alex to get some painkillers, Angela set off across the cricket pitch. There were some more vegetables to lift and some work was needed on the fruit trees. They had thirteen apple and six plum trees. She imagined when this had been a school that it must have been an impossible task stopping the pupils from scrumping for apples. Some of the trees produced eating varieties but most were cooking apples. The kitchen staff had developed some great recipes for using them up. She pushed the barrow down to the far end of the plot and began lifting some of the potatoes. The soil was dry and sandy and the tubers were numerous but small. It was mid-morning before Susan arrived, her face flushed.

"Morning Susan, are you all right? I made a start without you."

"I'm fine, I overslept. Is it a problem?"

"No, I just wanted to check that you were okay. I saw Alex at breakfast, he is such a kind young man."

"I'm fine. But I don't need you playing matchmaker, if you don't mind." With that Susan took her fork and pail and moved to the other end of the row of potatoes.

"Susan, have I done something to offend you?" Angela was puzzled. The girl was positively hostile. "I'm sorry, about mentioning Alex, I just thought…. Well, I think he likes you and he seems like a decent young man, but if you're not interested, I'll not mention it again."

Susan continued to work, throwing the small potatoes into her bucket and clearing the weeds to one side. Angela lifted her own fork, whatever was wrong, talking about it just seemed to be making things worse. It was going to be a long day.

It was a relief when dawn broke. Nairne and Ronnie were unused to such disruptive nights. As soon as darkness had fallen, the previously peaceful evening had been interrupted by a succession of sounds: gunfire, screaming, a couple of vehicles speeding up and down a nearby street. There was shouting and what sounded like fighting. They had remained inside the abandoned house, taking turns to keep watch, but the night had passed without incident. Studying the map over breakfast, they plotted their route.

"I reckon it will take us a couple of hours at least," said Ronnie. "And that's assuming we can get straight there with no unforeseen detours."

"Yeah, that would seem unlikely," Nairne replied, as she ate. "I was hoping if we set off early we might get through some of the city before it gets too busy."

"Good idea. I'll get the stuff together." Ronnie stood up and went over and rolled up their bedding and gathered their other possessions, stuffing clothes and cooking equipment into the rucksack. Fifteen minutes later they were walking along the street. It was deserted; no traffic and no one in sight although they could see activity in one or two of the buildings they passed. The morning was clear, and it looked like it would be another warm day. Their footsteps sounded uncomfortably loud in the unnatural quiet. Nairne was glad when they reached the end of the street and crossed over onto a wider thoroughfare. This time each side of the four lane road was lined with what had been local shops. Most were boarded up or the broken windows showed that the insides of the buildings had been thoroughly ransacked. A couple of properties had survived more or less intact, heavy steel shutters in place and warning signs painted across the front, 'Looters will be shot!' and 'Keep Out!'

They kept moving, both aware that they had no idea how dangerous this was going to get. Ronnie had his gun inside his jacket pocket and Nairne held the bow in one hand, hanging at her side but ready for use, should the need arise. Black refuse sacks, tattered and torn spilled their rotting contents onto the pavement. Piled high into miniature mountains, the decomposing waste was a feast to the rats, which could be seen scurrying around. Up ahead, the road had been barricaded with a number of vehicles, the defensive position long since abandoned. The vehicles had been left to rust. Soon they both became aware of the smell. As the temperature rose the air became increasingly stagnant: a mixture of rotting waste, excrement and death.

To their left were signs for Finchley Park. The park gates were padlocked shut and inside the entire area had been dug up and was now being used to grow food. The trees, which had once lined the edges of the park, had been chopped down for fuel here as well. The road ahead forked and they turned left.

"We should be coming up for Hampstead Heath soon. I guess that will be agricultural land as well" Nairne said. "I am amazed at how quiet it is."

"Yeah, but it is still early, only seven thirty. I'm sure it will get busy soon enough."

They passed the remnants of a supermarket, the windows caved in, the interior damaged by a fire, long since extinguished.

The rest of the row of shops were in a similar state. There was graffiti along the walls, protest messages, scrawled in angry crude letters. Nairne remembered, back at the beginning when the crisis started to bite, seeing the riots on the television, the crowds of angry protestors demanding action when faced with no electricity, no running water and the threat of disease.

"There are people up ahead," said Ronnie, slowing down. He pointed and Nairne could see a large cart, overburdened and unsteady on its wheels, being pulled by two people from the front while another figure shoved the heavy load from behind. Nairne and Ronnie walked towards them. Ronnie hailed them. It seemed safer to announce your presence than to appear to have sneaked up on someone. The people stopped and looked towards them. The figure from behind the cart raised a hand in greeting as Ronnie walked forward. Nairne dropped back slightly, her hand gripping the bow, just in case.

"Morning," Ronnie shouted to them.

The figure at the rear responded. They were close enough now to see the contents of the cart. It was a homemade affair with a couple of wheels taken from a bicycle, a plywood trailer and two poles at the front to pull it along. Piled on top were bundles of fabric, tied with twine. Two women were at the front, one in her late thirties, the other no more than a girl. The man at the rear looked slightly older. He was thick set, with dark hair and a round, boyish face.

"You're the first people we've seen this morning," said Ronnie, coming to a stop some twenty metres from the group. "We're on our way to Wandsworth."

"That's a fair walk ahead of you. Have you been in the city before?" the man asked, his accent strong.

"No, never, not even before all this…. but we have a map. Can you tell us what it is like further in?"

"Desperate in places. We try and stay as far out as possible. My advice would be stay on the main thoroughfares, avoid any of the housing complexes, high rises, places like that. They're gang areas now, almost impassable. But if you stick to the main roads you should be able to walk most of the way there. Just keep your wits about you. And if you have weapons keep them handy. Most important of all, don't be caught outside at night. Make sure you are somewhere secure when darkness falls. The city becomes a different place after dark."

Nairne caught up with Ronnie. The two women were watching the unfolding conversation and they looked frightened.

"Where are you going?" Nairne asked.

"To the Heath. It's market day today. I wanted to get there early. It's safer to transport the goods before the place gets busy."

"A market, what sort of things?"

"The Heath is one of the main growing areas for this part of the city. All the grass is just about gone now, and they grow a range of vegetables. There are also some livestock plots with pigs, goats, chickens and the like. So it has become a bit of a centre. People come to sell all sorts of things. We've got some good winter clothing here. It's taken us a few weeks to gather it so we're going to stock up on some foodstuffs for the next few weeks. But we better get moving. It's not safe to stop out here in the open for too long."

"Can I ask, where do you get all this stuff?" She indicated to the heavy cargo on the cart.

"We salvage it from empty buildings. There are a lot of empty homes, some deserted, and more where the inhabitants have died. We salvage what we can."

"Thanks for your advice," said Ronnie. "We'll let you get on." The man nodded and began to put his weight behind the cart as the two women pulled.

Ronnie and Nairne continued down the road.

"I wonder how many people have died," said Nairne. "And how many unburied bodies are lying rotting in the houses?"

"Quite a few I imagine. A couple of bad winters with no proper heating would have finished off a lot of people, plus illness or disease. We've seen plenty of evidence of rats. But it's good to know there are people growing food and it looks like some people are managing to get by."

They passed more and more people as the morning wore on, many of them heading to or from the Heath.

"It would be interesting to go and have a look," said Nairne. "But I guess we want to get across the city and make sure we find the address while it is still light."

"Yeah, we can always stop on the way home," Ronnie replied.

As they got closer to the heart of the city there were more people and a few vehicles, mainly trucks and vans, ferrying goods around. Most of the shops were closed or burnt out but there were people selling all manner of goods. The currency appeared, on the whole, to be food. And people were bartering for all sorts of items.

They entered Kensington, passing Bayswater tube station. The sign outside the now abandoned station lay broken on the pavement. Up ahead were street signs for Kensington Palace. The surrounding buildings were grand, evidence of a time now gone. Many of the houses were burnt out, black soot covering the once pale masonry. Windows were broken and graffiti covered the ground floor walls of many properties. The gates to the park were securely locked and armed men stood outside them. Through the railings they could glimpse signs of crops growing. Two homemade flags flew from the flagpole at the edge of the park. A large sign warned trespassers that they would be shot. Towers had been erected at each corner of the parkland and these contained armed guards.

Between the towers, constructed right on the edge of the parkland, was a wooden structure. There were three bodies hanging from it. From the level of decay it looked as though they had been there for some time. It was impossible to identify them as either men or women, but each one wore a sign with 'looter' scrawled across it. Nairne and Ronnie skirted around the park as quickly as they could. They turned into Camden Hill Road. Each side was lined with brick built, low rise housing. The ground floor properties were mainly boarded up, but there were signs of habitation in the flats on the higher floors. There were rows of brick Victorian town houses with small front gardens, and between the properties on the pavements were tree stumps of what had probably been an avenue of plane trees. The street narrowed slightly before widening out and joining with Kensington High Street. They could see the boarded up entrance to the Underground station, with a large warning sign which read 'Caution: Tunnels Flooded. Keep Out.' They turned left and walked down the high street, once the home of many expensive shops, it was now relatively quiet. To their left was the edge of Kensington Gardens. The original low brick wall and railings had been replaced by heavy duty concrete barricades topped with rows of razor wire. The trees in the park were all gone and the grass had been replaced by vegetables. They continued down towards Piccadilly. It was busier here, with people trading and carts and trolleys being pushed along heading to or from markets. The smell here was different, sewage mixed with a smell of the sea, a saltiness in the air. The rats were also more numerous and unperturbed by the human traffic which passed nearby.

"What is that up ahead?" asked Ronnie, stopping in his tracks.

"Water," said Nairne. "It's water." The gently sloping street just vanished underneath the water. A small wooden jetty, roughly built from reclaimed timbers, had been crudely attached to a nearby building and several small

116

boats were moored there. They could see other boats coming along what should have been Piccadilly.

"I guess this is where we find a boat," said Ronnie. They walked down to the edge of the water. The smell was overpowering as the water gently lapped against the edges of the surrounding buildings. It barely moved. Rubbish, raw sewage and debris bobbed about on the surface. Flies buzzed around their heads. A group of men perched on a collection of old rickety plastic and wooden chairs stopped talking as Ronnie and Nairne approached. One of the men rose to his feet.

"Are you looking to go across?" he asked.

"Yes, we want to get to Battersea Rise. Can we do that from here or do we need to walk further in?" Nairne asked.

"I can take you across. The nearest you'll get is maybe within a mile of your destination. Have you got a map?"

"Yes." She turned to Ronnie, who pulled the battered A to Z from his jacket pocket and handed it to her. Nairne opened it at the correct page. "We want to get here," she said pointing to the cross they had marked on the map.

The man studied it, drawing in his breath.

"Yeah, well most of Wandsworth Common is underwater or floods as soon as we get a high tide, but there are some areas around there, higher ground that are still being used. I can take you to here." He indicated a spot about half a mile from their destination. "I can drop you there. It's a fair distance, maybe four miles. That will take me some time. The boat has no engine as fuel is too difficult to get so it's all rowing power," he laughed showing a mouth almost bereft of teeth.

"It won't be cheap. It'll take me most of the afternoon to get you across...." he paused, rubbing his face. "Have you got anything to pay me with?"

"We have some tins of food," said Ronnie. "Some boxes of cigarettes and matches. They are dry and useable and also some vegetable seeds. We also have some homemade vodka."

"Not much use for the seeds, no garden," he laughed. "But the rest will do if you help with the rowing."

"That's fine," said Nairne. "We'll both take turns."

They climbed into the small rowing boat and sat facing the jetty. The man insisted on payment up front. Ronnie handed the items over and the man passed them to one of his friends before climbing into the boat. A bulldog stood up and emerged from underneath the chairs, stretching its back legs and yawning. It considered them for a few moments then trotted along the jetty and jumped down into the boat.

"I hope you don't mind dogs," the man grinned. "This is Jack. My bodyguard you could say. Can't be too careful, but any problems on board this boat and he'll tear your throat out soon as look at you."

"No problem," said Nairne. "We both like dogs," she replied, not altogether convincingly. Jack turned himself around a few times and then settled down next to their feet.

SEVENTEEN

It was quite surreal to see a familiar landscape so utterly transformed. Although neither of them had ever visited the city before they had seen footage on the news and in films. The landmarks were still there; Parliament, Big Ben, the London Eye, the Tate Modern Gallery but they were surrounded by water. There were still bridges across the original route of the Thames, but getting to them was near impossible as the surrounding roads were completely submerged.

Their progress was reasonably swift to begin with as their boat made its way through numerous streets and alleys. The buildings, their feet now submerged, sat rotting in the water. Ground floor windows had become gaping holes and inside flood water wreaked havoc.

"It's like Venice but with more atmosphere," said Ronnie, grimacing at the terrible stench which rose from the water. With each pull of the oars more unpleasant objects were revealed and the smell was overpowering.

"I'll need your help when we get out into the river proper," said the man. "There's still a current there, and if we're not careful you'll be miles downstream by the time we cross." As they progressed the water became deeper and the buildings were almost completely submerged.

"That's fine just tell me when, and let Jack know I'm here to help," Ronnie replied, casting his glance down at the watchful dog. As they emerged onto what had been the river bank they were both amazed to see the number and variety of boats crossing backwards and forwards. Sailing boats, barges, rowing boats and some badly built rafts ferried people across the water.

Ronnie got up cautiously and sat next to their oarsman. Taking an oar each, they quickly got into a regular rhythm as they moved clear of the buildings and out onto the open river. They could feel the pull of the current, trying to sweep them down river. Nairne could see the strain on their faces as the two men worked as one, pulling together, cutting their way through the water. Along with the tide, they had to dodge the other craft, some of which were travelling up or downstream rather than across.

"It's amazing, I can't believe how many boats there are," she said, gazing up and down the river. "And look at the bridge, all the people crossing on foot."

"Yes, the bridge is fine if you can afford it," the man remarked. "But it still takes a boat ride at each end to get you to the bridge. Only those really afraid of the water and with the funds to pay use it now. When the tide's high it's the safer way to cross. But we've got a few hours until we get the tidal surge. Enough time for me to get back across."

Nairne gazed at the approaching southern shore. Once they reached it, she swapped places with the man, and she and Ronnie rowed for a while. As they got deeper into the labyrinth of flooded streets he told them to stop and they swapped back.

"It can get tricky once the water gets shallower, there are all sorts of obstacles underneath: road signs, railings, bollards, abandoned cars and God knows what else. I'll take us in the last section. It'll be safer for us and the boat."

He appeared to know his way around and he guided them to a small wooden jetty attached to a block of nineteen fifties concrete flats. Nairne and Ronnie stepped onto dry land once again.

"So how are you going to get back onto the mainland?" their boat owner enquired.

"I guess we'll have to get a lift from the people we've come to see. They must have boats to get back and forwards."

"Fair enough, if you're sure. Good luck. I hope you find whatever it is you're looking for."

He pushed off from the jetty and waved to them as they headed down the street.

The ground rose steeply, and soon they were on Battersea Rise. Ronnie got the map out and they began to look for landmarks or road signs to help narrow their location. But there was no need.

To their left they saw a pair of heavily fortified gates. Next to which was the sign for St Augustine's Secondary School for Girls. They walked past on the other side of the road and round the side of the site. They appeared to be on a large wedge shaped piece of land, with the school campus in the centre, and from what they could see there was water behind them and water to their sides.

"It's like a little island." Nairne said.

"Yes, a very defensible position. That road we came up seems to be the only access, and it looks like those gates we passed are the only entrance, unless you want to try and scale the walls and the razor wire."

"No I suppose we should probably go to the gates. Let's hope the island's inhabitants are friendly," she said, but her tone was apprehensive.

They walked back along the road, but their presence had not gone unnoticed, and as they approached the gates a voice hailed them through a loudspeaker.

"Stay where you are. We have weapons trained on you." The voice was neutral not angry or threatening, just very definite.

Nairne and Ronnie looked at one another and then complied.

"Keep your hands up where we can see them. What do you want?"

"We're here to see someone: Angela Grear. Does she live here?" Ronnie shouted back in response. "We've travelled a long way, all the way from Scotland. We just want to speak with her. We don't want any trouble. Is she here?"

There was silence.

"Look, we're family, we just want to talk to her."

"Stay there. Put your weapons on the ground and stand back."

Nairne placed the bow on the ground and Ronnie put down his gun then they both stepped back. They heard the familiar sound of bolts being drawn back and one of the gates opened slightly. Two armed young men emerged, dressed in army fatigues and carrying rifles.

One indicated for them to go across and inside, the gun never wavering from them. The other picked up their weapons and followed behind. A third guard waited inside. Once inside they could see they were in what had been extensive school grounds where trees lined each side of a grand drive, leading up a steep hill to a complex of buildings at the top.

The young man who had picked up their weapons ordered that they both be searched.

"Do you have any other weapons?" he asked.

"Yes, we both have knives, strapped to our belts," said Ronnie, pulling back his jacket to reveal the sheath. He stepped forward and removed the knife, then did the same for Nairne.

"And in your bags?"

"No weapons, just clothes, some cooking equipment and some stuff to barter with. No weapons." The man nodded in response.

"Right, we'll take you up to the house."

"So is she here? Angela Grear?" Ronnie repeated.

"Yes, she's here. Come on."

Nairne and Ronnie walked forward followed by the two armed men. The guard radioed ahead and asked for two replacements to be dispatched to the front gate.

"Get Devlin and Angela, they're here to see Angela. Yes, two civilians." There was a burst of static and then a reply.

"Okay, Roger that, we'll be there to meet you."

"Angela," Alex's voice carried across the open ground. Angela glanced up, resting on her fork and waved to him. He came running towards her.

"Angela, you have to come, quickly!" he said excitedly. Susan stopped her work and looked over as Alex reached them.

"What is it? Is it Eve?" Angela felt her stomach lurch. Alex looked excited, out of breath and flustered.

"No, she's fine. You have visitors. Two young men, they came to the gate. They asked for you by name. Come on! They've sent for Devlin, but I said I'd come and get you."

"Sorry Susan, I'll be back, sorry," said Angela as she put down her fork and wiped her hands on her shirt front. Susan remained silent and watched as the two of them hurried across the grounds.

"So who are they?" Angela asked.

"I don't know. I just caught a glimpse. One of them, the tall one has very blonde hair. They've come all the way from Scotland, at least that's what they said. They said they're family."

EIGHTEEN

Nairne and Ronnie stood outside the front entrance to the building. A few of the residents had stopped to take a look at them. Their armed guard had remained behind them, silent while the other one had gone inside to find Devlin and Angela. Nairne guessed Devlin was the man in charge, as they all said his name with an air of respect. Minutes ticked past. Nairne could feel her stomach churning. She felt sick, almost light headed.

"Are you all right?" Ronnie glanced at her. He could see all the colour leave her face. He couldn't imagine how she was feeling, coming down here to see Angela had seemed like an adventure, but they had not given any real consideration to what they would find.

The front door of the building swung open. A figure appeared and flew down the front steps.

"Oh my God, I can't believe it, Zane! Oh my God!"

The woman rushed towards Ronnie, her face a mixture of joy and disbelief. She held her arms out to embrace him, but then she caught the confused expression on his face. She came to a halt, right in front of him.

"Zane, my beautiful boy." She reached out a hand to touch his face. As she did so Nairne pulled off her hat and spoke.

"Hi, Angela. It's me, Nairne."

Angela froze, her eyes switched from Ronnie to Nairne, who stood there without her hat, her head shaved. Angela gasped, her hands clasped in front of her face.

"Oh my God, Nairne, oh my God I can't believe it," She rushed forward and hugged Nairne, holding her tight. "Oh my God, I just…… I can't believe it." But she could feel Nairne tense and unresponsive, her body rigid. Angela let go and stepped back slightly, her hands still resting on Nairne's arms.

"This is Ronnie," said Nairne.

Angela looked back at him.

"I thought......the blonde hair.... I thought it was your brother......I'm sorry, you must think I'm completely mad, but when they said two young men were here and I saw your hair I just...."

"It's fine," said Ronnie, holding out his hand. "Don't worry about it, Angela. It's good to meet you."

Angela shook his hand in a mechanical way, her eyes darting back to Nairne's.

"How did you find me? How did you get here? Where's your father? I can't believe he let you travel all the way down here on your own. What was he thinking? Anything could have happened."

"Angela, can they be left with you?" the guard interrupted.

"Yes, of course, yes, thank you. We'll be fine."

He nodded and lowered his gun. Slinging it back over his shoulder, he headed off down the drive. Alex appeared behind Angela.

"Angela, why don't you bring them inside? I'll get some refreshments. It looks like they've travelled a long way."

"Yes, of course, yes, come on let's get you both inside and you can tell me everything." She looked positively ecstatic, glowing even. She smiled and Nairne was immediately right back there, right back on that sunny day with Zane and their mum. The day of his accident. Angela had smiled at her then, before she ruffled Zane's hair and left them both outside playing.

It was a relief to get indoors, into the shade. Angela showed them through to the dining room. It looked out over the courtyard, and they could see two women hanging up washing from lines stretched across the enclosure.

"Please sit, I'll just give Alex a hand, are you hungry? God, what am I saying of course you'll be hungry...?" She rushed from the room.

Nairne breathed out, the sound rushing from her lungs. She sat down at one of the tables, her body sagging.

"Are you okay?" Ronnie sat next to her and placed his hand on her back rubbing it gently. Nairne nodded unconvincingly. "Well, she's not what I was expecting, Angela. She's much younger than I imagined."

"She's just as I remember," said Nairne. "The drama queen. I can't believe she thought you were Zane….. Christ's sake, you'd think she'd know her own child." She sounded angry.

"Come on, it's not that farfetched. You said your brother had fair hair and it's been a long time. I did say to the guy that we were family, maybe she just assumed."

Angela and Alex returned each carrying a tray. Alex placed his on the table first, a pot of herbal tea and cups. Angela had some bread and fruit.

"This is Alex. Alex this is Ronnie and my daughter Nairne."

"Your daughter? I can't believe you have a grown up daughter," said Alex. "It's great to meet you both." He shook hands with each of them. "I'll leave you to catch up." He left the room closing the door behind him.

"He's such a lovely young man. I couldn't believe it when he came out and said I had visitors." Angela poured them both drinks and put the food onto plates for each of them. "Please help yourselves." She sat down opposite them.

"I still can't believe it, I would never have recognised you…. with your beautiful hair so short, and you're all grown up…." She reached out as if to touch Nairne's face then pulled her hand back, realising the gesture would not have been appreciated.

"So, you're not dead then." Nairne made the statement in a tone so unforgiving that Ronnie was sure he could see Angela flinch, but before she could reply Nairne continued.

"We got your letter, the one you sent to dad. It took some time to get to us. You said you needed help, but it looks to me like you've landed on your feet, as always. So what did you want?"

Angela sighed, giving Ronnie an almost apologetic look.

"There's plenty of time for all that, I just.... I can't believe you're here. I can't believe your father let you come all the way down here on your own. God knows what could have happened to you. It's so dangerous now to travel. What was he thinking?"

Ronnie could see Nairne's temper flair. He butted in before Nairne could say anything.

"She wasn't on her own, Mrs Grear, I was with her. We got by just fine."

"Angela, please call me Angela, Mrs Grear makes me sound likes someone's mother," she laughed nervously. "You know what I mean, it makes me sound so old." She flashed a fabulous smile at Ronnie. "I have so much to catch up on. So many questions, I don't know where to start."

"They're dead," said Nairne. The words just came out. The words which had been filling her mind for the last few days, for the last few hours. She would have to tell Angela. She would have to say it. She'd rehearsed the moment in her mind so many times, but now, it just came out.

"Sorry, Nairne, who's dead? What do you mean?"

"Dad and Zane, they're dead. Just like we all thought you were only, they really are dead, both of them."

Angela gaped at her. She looked like someone had just slapped her. She sat absolutely rigid and then she began gasping for breath, struggling to fill her lungs as if there was no oxygen in the atmosphere. Finally, she let out a long low wail. The sound ripped through Nairne's head and she got up and rushed from the room.

"No, my poor boy, no …….. It's not true…. no…" she began to weep, her body folding in on itself. Ronnie rushed to the other side of the table and took her in his arms. She collapsed against him, pressing herself against his chest

"No, tell me it's not true, my beautiful boy……." Her breathing came in great waves, interspersed with sobs and cries.

Nairne stood outside the dining room door with her heart pounding. She could still hear the screams of anguish. The noise was loud enough to attract the attention of other people, who began to enter the hallway, concerned. Alex came over to Nairne.

"Whatever is the matter? Is that Angela? What's happened?" He went to open the door to the dining room. Nairne reached out and put her hand on his arm.

"No, please, don't. I just had to give her some bad news. She'll be fine. Ronnie is with her."

"Bad news? What sort of news?" His face was full of concern. Nairne could see he was obviously very fond of Angela.

"I had to tell her that my father and my brother are both dead."

Alex looked at her aghast.

"Oh my God, poor Angela……She'll be devastated." Nairne stayed silent.

"Don't you want to go back in and comfort her?" Alex asked.

"No, I think it's better if I give her some time. Ronnie's with her."

"I'll go and fetch some brandy. I'm sure we still have some for medicinal purposes. It will help with the shock." Alex rushed off to the kitchen, leaving Nairne standing in the hallway. The others, who had gathered at the distraught sounds of Angela's weeping, dispersed back to their tasks.

Alex returned a few minutes later with a bottle of brandy and a glass. He held them out to Nairne. She did not take them, but instead opened the door to let him in to the dining room. She closed it behind him. When the door reopened a few minutes later, Ronnie emerged.

"God, that was…… hard. She is in pieces," he sighed and put his arms around Nairne.

Nairne looked up at him; her expression cold.

"Nairne, what's the matter?"

"Now she knows how it feels. Now she knows what it was like for Zane when she was reported dead. Now she knows what it was like for me when I saw my dad dragged from the river."

"Nairne, don't. Don't try and blame her for everything that's happened. She didn't cause it."

"No, but she didn't care. She never did. She just walked away and left us because it was inconvenient. She gave up her right to do the grieving mother act when she chose some bloke over her own son."

Alex reappeared, closing the door softly behind him.

"I'll get someone to take her upstairs. I think it would be best if she had a lie down. It has been a terrible shock. I assume the two of you will be staying with us for a while so I'll also get a room made up for you. You must be tired after your journey. Come on, I'll show you where you can put your stuff and get a wash. Dinner will be served at about six. Devlin will be back by then. He'll want to meet you both."

"Thanks, I take it Devlin is the guy in charge?" Ronnie asked.

"Yes, Devlin and the committee. Devlin's also…. your mother, Angela's partner."

NINETEEN

"They're in Ralph's room on the second floor. And I spoke with Alex, he seemed to know what was going on. Apparently, it's Angela's teenage daughter and a young guy, I assume her boyfriend. They claim that they have travelled all the way down from Scotland looking for her," said Don.

"Hmm, that's interesting. I wonder how they found us. And Angela, where is she?" Devlin asked.

"She's having a lie down, apparently they brought some bad news about her son and her ex-husband. They're both dead. Alex said she was pretty shaken up. They gave her something to relax her and she went up to your room."

"And these two visitors, they didn't say what they wanted?"

"No, maybe it was just to let her know what had happened…."

"Hmm maybe. That's fine. I'll meet them after dinner. I'll eat in here this evening. You can bring them in to see me after they've eaten."

"And Angela?"

"Just leave her be. I'll speak with her later."

Dinner was a quiet affair. Ronnie and Nairne were given two seats at one of the side tables. The top table had two empty places, one belonging to Angela and the adjacent one to Devlin. Alex looked after them both, fetching their food and sitting with them. He was a very pleasant young man, softly spoken, nervous even. It was obvious he thought a great deal of Angela and was still very concerned about her.

"Your poor mother, I have never seen her like that….. it's terrible. She must be devastated. I had no idea she had grown up children."

Nairne did not respond, and Ronnie could sense her discomfort at the direction of the conversation and did his best to change the subject.

"It's like a medieval banqueting hall," Ronnie remarked as they took their seats. Although the set up was similar to their own community, the differences were also marked. The top table, for the important members of the community, was not a concept they could imagine Arthur and the rest of their council being comfortable with. The people at the tables, who appeared to number about thirty or so, were very reserved, and no one other than Alex spoke to them.

"Yes, the top table is for committee members and invited guests. The rest of us take turns to sit there. Devlin likes it like that, as he can see everyone, and when he has things to tell us it makes it easier."

Ronnie and Nairne glanced at each other.

"Is everyone shy around here?" Nairne asked, in as light a tone as she could manage.

"People are not used to outsiders, and until Devlin has interviewed you both, there is probably a bit of reluctance in getting too involved. We don't usually permit visitors into the community, for security reasons."

"And the room you put us in. It looks like it belongs to someone."

"Yes, it does….. Sorry, did. The occupant of the room is no longer with us."

"Where did he go?"

"Oh, he left, quite recently."

"Interview? You said Devlin would interview us. What do you mean?" Nairne asked.

"Well, he'll want to know why you came all this way, and I am sure he'll want to know what other parts of the country are like. It's always useful to have news of what is going on."

"Yes, you're right there," said Ronnie. He reached over and took another piece of bread. "So have you been living here for a long time?"

"About two years. The community was already established when I joined. There were only about fifteen people then, obviously your mother Angela, Devlin, Don and some of the other committee members. It was so lucky for me that I was able to join them, as things were beginning to get pretty difficult outside."

"Outside, you mean in the rest of the city?"

"Yes, this place is a like a little private island. You will have seen on the way here, you have to reach us by boat for a large part of the year."

"A good defensible position," said Nairne. "I don't suppose Devlin has a military background by any chance?"

Alex was about to answer when he caught the eye of one of the top table occupants. Nairne and Ronnie both saw the change in his expression. Ronnie turned around and looked at the source of Alex's discomfort. It was a man sitting next to the two empty seats. He was in his mid-thirties, tanned and powerfully built, with a soldier's bearing. He was watching the three of them, intently. His hair was shorn to the bone, his face angular and clean shaven. He was wearing a khaki coloured shirt, the fabric stretched tight across over developed muscles.

"Sorry, I had better get on. I have duties to perform this evening." With that, Alex got up and left them at the table.

So, what do you make of that then?" Ronnie asked in a hushed tone.

"I'm not sure, they're rather secretive. I suppose we would be quite canny if we had visitors within our community but….."

"What?"

"I'm not sure, it's more like Alex was afraid to say anything. Did you see his expression when that gorilla up there was looking over at him? He looked scared."

"Yes, maybe or perhaps it's just against their rules to tell people from outside too much about the place. I can understand that. Plus Alex does seem like quite a nervy sort of a bloke."

A few minutes later, the gorilla approached them.

"Are you finished eating?" His tone was challenging.

"Yes, thanks, it was great," Ronnie responded, getting to his feet.

"Devlin will see you now. This way." The man turned and indicated to the main doorway of the dining hall. They followed him.

Devlin's office was on the second floor. It was a grand room with a great view over the grounds. A large desk dominated the space, along with a huge set of bookshelves full with text books on a variety of subjects from agriculture to medicine.

Devlin was sitting behind the desk as they entered. He rose to greet them, indicating to their guide that he should leave them. Don shut the door quietly on his way out.

"Please, both of you, come in and sit. I'm James Devlin, but everyone just calls me Devlin." He held out his hand to Ronnie, who shook it and introduced himself before nodding towards Nairne.

"And this is Nairne Grear, Angela's daughter."

"Nairne," Devlin said her name as if they were old friends. "Please come on in." He shook hands with Nairne.

"Please sit here. Angela's daughter, you know your mother has told me so much about you. It's great to finally meet you."

"Really? So what has she said?" Nairne fired the question back with an ungracious tone. Devlin paused, momentarily surprised by the directness of her response.

"Fair enough, no bullshit then. You're right, your mother has barely ever mentioned you. I knew she had two other children and that your dad, what was his name?"

"Daniel. My father's name was Daniel Grear."

"Yes, Daniel... that he was a bit of a.... how shall I put it?" He was watching Nairne as he spoke, trying to gauge how far he could go.

"I'd put it carefully, if I were you," she responded.

Devlin laughed.

"I was going to say, a bit of a forward thinker, planned ahead, and got ready for all this..." He waved his arm across the room. "Yes, a man who saw the end of things. I understand that condolences are in order, for your father and your brother."

"Yes, thank you." Nairne replied, her tone steady.

"I still can't believe it, Angela's daughter, all grown up. You don't look much like her, and you certainly don't seem to have taken after her, personality wise."

"I guess I didn't spend that much time with her," Nairne replied coldly.

"How is she?" Ronnie asked.

"Angela?" Devlin responded.

"Yes, I assumed that you would have been up to see her. Alex said you two were a couple."

"She'll be fine," said Devlin, dismissively. "I'm told you travelled all the way from Scotland, that's a long way to come. A dangerous journey no doubt. All this way to tell her about the rest of the family?"

"Yes, that's right," Nairne replied. "I thought she had a right to know.... After all, Daniel was her husband and Zane was her only son."

"It must have been difficult to track her down."

"Yes, it was, but we've done what we came to do so if it's okay with you, we'd like to stay here for a couple of days and then we'll be on our way. It's a long journey and we want to get back home before the weather changes."

"Of course, of course you can stay. I'm sure Angela will want to spend some time with you, catching up. And I can't imagine you will be in that much of a rush to get back home, certainly not once you've seen the set-up we have here. We're doing pretty well for ourselves. There are not many people living as comfortably as this. Have a look around, see what you think. I think you'll be pretty impressed with what we have achieved. It's just a pity that we have to limit numbers. I'm sure you understand."

"Yes, we understand completely," said Ronnie, cutting in before Nairne could speak. She had that look that he knew so well, the one where she was about to speak her mind.

"Right, I'll ask Alex to show you around tomorrow, I understand he has already been very helpful."

"Yes, he has," Nairne replied. "Thanks, if he can spare the time that would be great."

"I'm sure you must both be tired so I'll not detain you, but I hope we will have a chance to get to know each other a bit while you're here," Devlin responded, the statement addressed solely to Nairne. He smiled at her. "After all, I suppose I'm your sort of stepfather," he laughed.

Nairne glanced at Ronnie and they both rose and left his office. Their guide, from the dining hall, was waiting for them outside the office door.

"I'll show you to your quarters, if you'll just follow me."

TWENTY

"So what did you make of him then, Devlin, your *stepfather*?"

"Priceless, wasn't it. My stepfather. Christ, he's just the last in a line of men that Angela's hooked up with. He certainly isn't the one she left my dad for, or the one she was screwing when Zane had his accident," she paused and sat down heavily on the edge of the single bed. "To be completely honest, I didn't like him."

"Really?" Ronnie replied, sarcastically. "Look, we will only be here a couple of days, so don't let him niggle you, just relax and go with the flow."

"God, you are so annoying when you do that whole laid back thing…. You know I never go with the flow."

"I know, but maybe sometimes you should, especially when it gets you so worked up. Your mum obviously thinks he's great, and you don't have to bond with him, so just spend the few days catching up with your mum, having a rest and then we'll be on our way."

"But we still don't know what she wants."

"Maybe she just wanted to see your dad again, maybe she regrets leaving the three of you. Who knows, but I am sure tomorrow, when she's got over the shock she'll tell you what she wants. But for now, I think it's time for bed. Yes, bed, not a tent or the floor or the bloody woods, but a real bed."

They lay together on the narrow mattress, darkness had fallen and the school building was quiet. In the distance there were gun shots, across the water, but here everything was peaceful.

"Don't you think it is a bit strange to put us in a room full of someone else's possessions?" Nairne remarked. Although the bed had been changed and the room was relatively tidy the wardrobe still held the clothes of the previous occupant. There were photographs pinned to the wall and a few books piled in one corner. "It's as if the person just didn't come back one day."

"Maybe that's what happened. Alex didn't seem keen to share, so maybe the guy got ill, or had an accident or just left."

Angela lay in darkness, her breathing steady now. The grief still came over her in waves, an uncontrollable feeling which sprang from her very core. How could they be dead? She had thought about them often, the three of them in their little fortress; Daniel with his pronouncements about the end of the world, and how she had mocked him. He must have been so pleased when it turned out that he was right. Angela checked that thought. It was unfair, she knew Daniel would have wished to be wrong about what would happen. Blaming him for being prepared was stupid. But that was just it; Daniel was prepared and she had left him with their children, to look after them, how could he have let Zane die? Angela needed to know everything, every detail: when had they died, how, why? All this time she had hoped that maybe Daniel would come for her and Eve, and all this time he was already dead.

Tomorrow she would find out from Nairne, if Nairne would even speak with her. Angela had seen the hatred in her eyes, the way she had told her about them; the coldness of it. Angela could barely reconcile the young woman she had met today with the little girl she had left behind. She seemed so angry, so hard. How could she have become so damaged?

Angela heard the bedroom door open. She could sense the presence in the room moving towards the bed. She knew it was Devlin. She kept her eyes closed and her breathing steady. She did not want to speak to him; she didn't want to try and explain why she had sent the letter. She knew no explanation would be acceptable, and she did not have the strength to fight with him over this. Tomorrow, she would have to face it, but tonight she just wanted to lie here in peace and think about Zane and Daniel and what could have been.

Devlin stood beside the bed and watched her sleep, her chest rising and falling. He had not wanted to come in here and speak with her. He did not like to deal with raw emotion and there would have been an expectation that he would have been supportive, said the right thing, been a shoulder to cry on, but Devlin knew this was his weakness. He could be charming and sociable, make people like him and trust him, but he had never been good at dealing with the reality of emotions. That was one of the reasons he had chosen Angela. He remembered when he had first seen her. She'd lived in the block. He'd not long been back from active duty, still finding his feet when he got the job of building supervisor. It was just a temporary thing, but he'd been lucky to get that. Fighting men returning home, especially damaged ones, were not valued. She'd lived on the twelfth floor with some yuppie. She hadn't noticed him, but he'd seen her, the way she walked, the way her hair would swing gently backwards and forwards. She didn't appear to work however, like most of the residents she had a routine and Devlin followed that routine religiously, catching sight of her whenever possible. A couple of times she had taken the lift with him. But she hadn't even glanced at him in his uniform of navy blue overalls. He was just another one of the faceless people who helped to make her life more comfortable.

When the disease sprang up, like a punishment from God himself, Devlin knew then why he had been placed there, in that building. He knew that he had a job to do.

After the rescue and her recovery, Angela had noticed him. In fact she had been very grateful, and Devlin knew that they were meant to be together, that in saving her had done the right thing. There had been moments of doubt, after all she was sick, as sick as the others, but he couldn't let her burn, despite the risks, and despite his convictions he could not let her burn. But things had changed recently. He still loved her, but he was beginning to doubt that she felt the same. He couldn't really explain it; something in her had changed. Devlin was sure it was her that had changed, not him. He had always had the same vision, the same belief in a community of the righteous, a place where people worked together to strive for a common goal. And yes, sometimes people found that difficult. But Devlin knew in his heart that it was his responsibility to keep everyone on the right path, God's path.

He'd wondered about Angela's loyalty. He had noticed it the day before, when he had been called upon to act in judgement on the boy. He'd seen the looks she exchanged with Alex and Devlin had wondered, just how close they were? Alex had not been one of his men, not a fighting man. He'd been introduced to the group through a friend of Don's, and on that recommendation they'd taken him into the community, but he was too soft, too emotional for Devlin's tastes, and he'd seen the way the young man was so attentive to Angela. Perhaps it would soon be time to test her loyalty. He gazed down at her sleeping form. She was still beautiful but without trust what was there? He stepped back from the edge of the bed and silently left the room. Tomorrow, he would get to the bottom of this family visit.

"I guess we should get up and go and get breakfast," said Nairne stretching and yawning.

"Another five minutes," Ronnie murmured, his eyes still shut. "Just another five minutes." Nairne slid out from under the covers and pulled on her trousers and jumper. Then she left the room as quietly as possible and headed for the bathroom at the end of the corridor. The building was almost silent. She checked her watch. It was just after seven-thirty and she guessed most people would already be down in the hall enjoying breakfast. Once washed, she returned to their temporary room and woke Ronnie up.

"Come on, time to get up. We don't want to miss breakfast and it looks rude if we are the last ones down there."

"I'll be down in a few minutes, promise….."

Nairne pulled back the curtains letting the early morning light flood into the room.

"Oh Nairne," Ronnie moaned, as he stuck his head under the pillow. She laughed and set off down stairs.

The dining room was busy, and Nairne felt a definite quietening of voices as she entered the room. She had no doubt that word of their arrival and her news would have spread throughout the group. If it were anything like their community no one could keep a secret for very long, and visitors were an unusual occurrence. She spotted Alex over at the far side of the room, helping himself to some food from the counter. It was good to see a familiar face and she walked over to join him.

"Nairne, good morning, I hope you slept. It's always strange sleeping in a new place," he smiled.

"When you've been out on the road travelling as much as we have you can sleep anywhere. It was a luxury to have a proper bed. Hence Ronnie is taking full advantage of it. He did say he would be down shortly, but I wouldn't hold my breath."

"No matter, I can get one of the kitchen staff to fix him something if he misses breakfast. "Here." He reached over and took an extra plate, handing it to Nairne. "Just help yourself."

She looked at the food laid out before her, boiled eggs, some sort of bread, it was dark and coarse and smelled of fermentation. There were some plums and apples, tomatoes and a large urn full of hot water. Beside it stood three tea pots.

"I'm afraid it is all herbal teas now, there's chamomile,

nettle and mint this morning."

Nairne helped herself to the chamomile and took a piece of bread plus an egg. She sat next to Alex. Other people sat further down the same table but no one came close.

"So what are your plans for today?" asked Alex.

"We thought we'd take it easy, catch up on some sleep and start planning our return trip. We are happy to help out with any work that needs doing. We wouldn't want people to think we were free loaders, and I guess I'll need to spend some time with Angela."

"Yes, of course, you must have so much to catch up on I'm sure. I still can't believe Angela has a grown up daughter."

"And a son," Nairne replied.

"Yes, of course, but I always thought she only had the one child. I guess lots of people had whole different lives before the change."

"The change?"

"Sorry the climate change it's what we all call it. I had just started at university, had my life all mapped out, then suddenly it's chaos, there are riots in the street, people killing one another over food and water. And then one major catastrophic weather event after another. I just feel so lucky to have ended up here and to have found this new family."

"So, how do you manage for food?"

"We have the school grounds, now used as productive gardens, the cricket pitch and the football pitch. We also do a fair bit of trading. You may see Devlin and the guards setting off on trips. They take a boat across to the mainland regularly and bring back supplies."

"Yes, but what do you trade with? Money has no value, and I can't imagine you grow enough food to be bartering with?"

"Oh, I don't really know all the details, you'd have to discuss that with Devlin. I just do my duties and keep my head down. Speaking of which, I guess I'd better get on. Why don't I meet you and Ronnie back here at eleven o'clock, and I'll show you around. Your mum might be up and about by then and she could come with us. I don't imagine she will be doing any work today."

After finishing her food, Nairne went back upstairs. Ronnie was up and dressed and just about to head downstairs when she entered the room.

"There might be some food left if you hurry," she said. "Plus Alex has offered to show us around later. I'll wait here for you. I don't think it's the kind of place where we should just wander about and have a look. Everyone seems a bit edgy."

Ronnie was almost last to enter the dining room. He collected some food and found himself a seat at one of the tables. The place was almost deserted. Most people had finished breakfast and were taking their dirty plates back to the serving hatch. One or two said good morning, but no-one engaged in a conversation with him. Ronnie felt it was a bit strange. If they had visitors people generally asked about what was happening in other places. News was so hard to get nowadays that anyone who had been anywhere else, was of interest. He heard the other plate being placed down and glanced up.

Devlin sat down opposite him.

"Morning, I thought I would be last to get down here for breakfast," Ronnie laughed.

"And Nairne?" Devlin's tone was cold.

"Oh she's already eaten. Nairne is always an early riser, but I tell you it was such a luxury to have a real bed to sleep in. I was reluctant to get up."

Devlin did not respond. His expression was blank, like a mask. Ronnie continued to eat. He felt distinctly uncomfortable, as if Devlin were attempting to make him uneasy. Without warning, Devlin smiled.

"Glad you are finding our home so comfortable,

Ronnie. We always like to make visitors welcome. Especially as you and Angela are practically family. A son in law, perhaps?" he grinned.

"Not sure Nairne would be up for that," Ronnie replied. "I don't think she's the marrying kind."

"Oh nonsense, anyone can see you are a pretty solid couple. After all, it must be serious for you to risk your life bringing her all the way down here, through God only knows what dangers, just to reunite Nairne with her mum. Anyway, sometimes my lad, you need to seize the initiative. Women want the man to take control, make the decisions, especially in such difficult and dangerous times. It makes them feel secure. Trust me, she may say that's not what she wants, but she's young. She just needs taking in hand."

"I don't think that would work with Nairne, and anyway it's not really my scene. And I didn't bring Nairne down here. I just came with her. She would have made the trip alone if I had said I didn't want to come. Nairne is a very independent person."

"It's an act, I tell you all my experience of women, they may pretend to be tough but it's just an act. Anyway, I am curious about one thing."

"What's that?"

"The reason for the visit, after all this time, and how did you find us?"

"As you said, Angela and Nairne are family. I guess since her brother and father are both gone maybe Nairne felt she should see her mum, make up for lost time. But really, I think you'd need to discuss that with Nairne. She told me she wanted to come down here and I just offered to come with her."

"So do you always do what Nairne wants?" Devlin asked, the challenge in his statement obvious from the tone. They were alone in the dining area now, everyone else had set off for their day's work. Ronnie was finished eating.

"Pretty much. I guess, I better get back upstairs, Nairne

will be wondering where I've got to."

Devlin did not respond as Ronnie got to his feet and took his plate over to the serving hatch. He said thank you to the two women who were working away in the kitchen cleaning up, and then set off upstairs to find Nairne.

"The sooner we leave the better," said Ronnie, sitting down on the edge of the bed.

"You've changed your tune," Nairne replied. She was leafing through the small pile of books and personal items stacked up on the table in the corner of their room. "So what's brought about this change of view?"

"Ten minutes with your stepfather."

"Ha ha, don't tell me you've decided you don't really like him."

"No, I've decided I dislike him intensely. He goes from to rude to friendly and back again in the space of a few minutes and wait for it. I should tell you what to do because that is what all women really want."

"You have got to be kidding. Really? Bloody hell, what was my mother thinking about?"

"Perhaps she wanted to be looked after, apparently that is what all women need, especially in such dangerous times. He was also wanting to know why we are here and how we found them."

"What did you say?"

"That he would need to ask you. I just do what I'm told. Honestly though, the guy is just downright weird. I think we should speak to your mum, find out what she wants, and then get out of here."

TWENTY ONE

Nairne knocked at the door gently, almost hoping that there would be no answer. She waited, listening intently; there was no sound and she had just started to walk away when she heard the voice inside.

"Come in."

Reluctantly, she grasped the door handle and slowly opened the door. The room was spacious. Sunlight filtered through a gap in the heavy velvet curtains which covered the vast bay window. The rays of bright light highlighted slivers of the room's contents; the large solid bed and the gilt mirror above the fire place. Angela was sitting on the edge of the bed, she was dressed, but her hair needed combed, and even in this half-light Nairne could see her complexion was pale while her eyes were red rimmed and swollen.

"Angela, it's me, Nairne." She walked into the room, letting the door close behind her.

Angela looked up and smiled weakly.

"Is it too hard to call me mum?" she asked, her voice cracking. "Or maybe you have a new one, did your dad ever remarry? I always thought he would, that he'd make some other woman a good catch."

"No, there was no one. He didn't have much time for all that. He had us to look after."

"Oh Nairne, come and sit with me." She indicated to the space next to her on the edge of the bed." Nairne didn't move. She felt so tense, every part of her wanted to shout out in rage at this woman, all the anger she had felt for all these years was bubbling to the surface.

"You know I don't even have any photographs of you, nothing at all. Everything was lost in the fire, everything."

Nairne reached into her back pocket and pulled out a soft leather wallet. It had been her father's. There was no need for money, or credit cards, or identification cards of any sort, but she still carried it and inside was a small tattered picture of the four of them taken back on Zane's birthday, before his accident, when they had been a proper family. Nairne had found it in her father's possessions when she had cleared out his room. It was no longer in the album with the others. She assumed he had removed it to keep it with him when they had heard about Angela's death. So, Nairne had taken it and kept it with her. She pulled it out from between the folds of the wallet, unfolded it, and passed it to Angela.

Her mother grasped the photograph and then clasped it to her lips, tears streaming down her face.

"You can keep it. I have others back at home. You can keep that one."

"Thank you Nairne, that's so kind of you."

"What do you want? Why did you want dad to come down here? Have you decided Devlin's not the one after all, maybe thought you could pick up where you left off with dad?"

"No, I needed help with something, and I couldn't think who else to ask. I know it was wrong of me to send it, but I didn't know what else to do."

"But you've got Devlin, why can't he help you with whatever crisis you have?"

"Have you met him yet?" Angela asked.

"Yes, last night and Ronnie had a chat with him this morning. He was pretty keen to know why we are here."

"Did you tell him about the letter?"

"No, why, would that be a problem?"

Angela let out a sigh of relief.

"It would be better if he didn't know about that. Maybe you could just say you tracked me down. That you wanted to let me know about your dad and Zane. There was a girl who stayed with us not long after the fire, her name was Lizzie. You could say you met her on your travels and she remembered me, and that's what prompted you to try and find me. That you had assumed I was dead, but that she had told you I survived the fire. I can tell you the places we stayed, you could just say you went from place to place and eventually tracked us down to here." Her tone was excited, the plan unfolding in front of her. "Firstly it was a sort of Victorian house in Brixton and then there was a couple of terraced houses in....."

"Stop it! Before you start giving me lots of lies to tell, how about telling me what happened. How about explaining to me why you let us think you were dead? How could you do that to us? Zane was distraught, he never got over it..... How could you do that to him?"

"I didn't mean to, it was ..... It was all so difficult...... You know I was ill, and the place was in chaos. We had armed soldiers on the streets, looting and rioting. It was terrible – you have no idea. I was so ill, they thought I would die. Martin left me, just left me in his flat and took off. He was such a selfish, useless.... Anyway, the building caught fire. It was arson. People were scared. They thought they'd get infected. It was madness. Devlin rescued me from the fire. He saved my life. He lived nearby, and when the fire started he rushed into the building to try and save people. He was so brave. He took me away, looked after me and nursed me back to health...... I don't remember much about those first few weeks and by the time I was well enough to do anything about it I realised you would all have been told I was already dead. I didn't want to cause any more upset... Devlin said.... He said it was like a second chance, a fresh start, just him and me. He said it would be better for everyone that you would all have become used to the idea and if I got in touch it would just cause more upset. He said ...... he said since we weren't close, that I hadn't seen you for such a long time that it was better to let sleeping dogs lie... he said...."

"And what about you? What did you say?"

"Oh Nairne, I'm sorry it just seemed at the time... it seemed like the right thing to do."

"The right thing to do? That would be a bloody first! In fact, that would be a miracle. Angela Grear, my selfish, wayward, unreliable mother does the right thing. But yet again you got it so wrong."

"Nairne, I'm sorry. I don't know what else to say to you…. I know I've let you down, all of you. I know it was wrong but I can't change it." Tears began to fill Angela's eyes. "I wish I could, but I can't. And I need your help….. I know I don't deserve it but please……."

"So what do you want?" Nairne replied.

"When you leave I need you to take someone with you, to somewhere safe."

"But surely here is safe? You have Devlin to look after you. What makes you think you'd be safer going with us?"

"It's not me. It's someone else. Look, I'll show you." Angela stood up and held out her hand. Nairne didn't take it but she followed her mother out of the door and along the corridor. They went through a set of fire doors and down the corridor. They reached the doors of a large, bright, airy room, where the walls were painted a sunny yellow and adorned with children's artwork. Inside were two women and a collection of small children. Nairne and Angela stood at the glass doors peering through.

"See the little girl with the lovely dark curls?" Angela pointed to a child of about three years old who was sitting on the carpet with her back to them struggling with a set of wooden building blocks. "That's Eve, your sister."

"My what?"

"Your sister. She's my daughter, mine and Devlin's. I need you to take her with you. Please Nairne, I need you to take her back where she will be safe." Angela sounded desperate. Nairne could see the fear in her eyes. "Come on, let me introduce you. You'll love her, everyone does. She's such a lovely little girl, smart, funny……. She reminds me of you when you were that age. Come on…" Her tone was forced, trying to convey a lightness. She put her hand on the door and began to open it. Nairne backed away from her, shaking her head in disbelief, then she turned and ran up the corridor. She could hear Angela calling after her, but she didn't look back.

Ronnie stood in the hallway with Alex. He looked at his watch. It was almost twenty past.

"I'm sorry Alex, I don't know where she's got to. It's not like Nairne. She is usually so punctual, she hates it when people are late. Maybe she's still chatting to her mum."

"Yes, you're probably right. They must have so much to catch up on. Why don't I show you around, if you still want to."

"Thank you that would be great. It's always interesting to see how other people are managing. It may give me some ideas to take back with me." They set off out of the main door and headed towards the playing fields. Ronnie could see the area covered in vegetables, row upon row of potato shaws, then what looked like carrots, covered in fleece. On the far side, some areas had already been cleared, the crops lifted and eaten. Next to the main building was a paved area which had probably been the staff car park. Now it contained six commercial sized poly tunnels. Through the plastic, he could see the lush greenery pressed against the sides.

"The tunnels have been great. We can extend the season and increase the range of crops we grow. Come on." Alex opened the door of one of the poly tunnels and inside was a jungle. The air was hot and dry. Large cucumbers hung from tired looking plants, which were reaching the end of their useful life. Further along the tunnel were sparse tomato plants, bearing large fruits, some a deep, ripe red and others in varying shades of green and orange. "Once these crops are cleared up over the next two weeks we'll re-sow with some winter greens. Last year we didn't have much success as the weather was pretty severe down here but if we're lucky…."

"So how many people are you feeding on this lot?"

"There are thirty-two adults in the community, plus of course a number of kids, so all in all say forty. But we have the playing fields, the cricket pitch and what were the gardens along the main drive. It is quite an extensive site, and obviously we also get some food from the outside."

"What about fish, I mean you're just about on an island here?"

"The water is too polluted. All the waste from the city ends up there since there is no proper sewage treatment works. I guess the Thames is probably getting back to the way it was in previous centuries. Some people in the city do fish and even eat what they catch, but I'm not sure how safe it would be. We still get some tinned foods, when the guys come back from their excursions, but there has been a lot less this year than last."

"So are you self-sufficient? If you didn't get anything from outside, could you all live on this?" Ronnie asked the question already knowing the answer. There was no way the piece of land was large enough to sustain them all, especially if they had to deal with difficult and unpredictable weather conditions.

"I don't know. We haven't had to put that to the test yet. But Devlin will have worked all that out. He knows what he's doing. The guy managed to get all this organised, and we're doing fine so far. What about your place?"

"Well, it's kind of similar to this, an old school with some surrounding land. There are thirty-seven of us at the last count, and we get by. There have been no official food rations for the last eight months so we've been relying on what we can grow and trade. We have substantially more ground than you seem to have here and we have the advantage of some more livestock: a few cattle, deer, pigs, goats, chickens, geese, pheasants, rabbits and bees. The bees are new for us, but we're hopeful we can manage to increase the number of hives over the next few years. On the land we don't use for food we grow willow for burning as fuel, it is quick and easy. We also have a couple of small wind turbines and, like you, some solar panels so we generate just about enough power for lighting, refrigeration and stuff like that. The site also has a small stream running through it, so we have access to clean water which we pump into a water tank."

"Yes, water has been a bit of an issue for us, ironic when you consider we are surrounded by the stuff, but clean water is in short supply. We have a massive rainwater collection system which we store and use, and we add sterilising fluid before we use it for cooking, but it is always a constant worry. Come on, I'll show you the other crops and the animals."

They headed across to the cricket pavilion, where the chicken coop was sited. Ronnie could see a number of birds running around pecking the ground on an area which was almost bereft of greenery. The cricket pavilion housed an assortment of agricultural tools and he could see a couple of people out working in the garden.

"Come on and I'll introduce you to Susan. She's a good friend of Angela's. They work out here together most days."

Susan was facing away from them as they approached and Alex called to her.

"Susan, good morning. I'd like to introduce you to Ronnie, one of our visitors. Ronnie is Nairne's…." he paused. "Boyfriend?"

"Yes, that's right," Ronnie confirmed. "It's good to meet you."

Susan had turned to face them. Her cheeks were flushed from the exertion of the work. She shook Ronnie's hand and smiled.

"Good to meet you Ronnie. I just love that accent."

"So how are you getting on today," Alex asked.

"Slower than I'd like, but as I am out here on my own again…. sorry I know, poor Angela, such terrible news, really terrible. I had no idea she had two other children.

She doesn't look old enough. I'd better get on. I need to get all of this lot lifted before the weather turns."

"Look, I'm happy to come out and give you a hand this afternoon." Ronnie volunteered.

"That is so sweet of you," Susan replied. "But no, really I'm sure you and Nairne will have lots to do, catching up with Angela. But thank you for the offer," she laughed.

She turned and started digging again. Alex and Ronnie headed back up to the main building.

"Come on, I'll show you around the buildings."

The main building was a fine brick structure. Ronnie could picture it as an exclusive private school. There were a couple of large halls, one used for dining and another, which had been for sports, had been subdivided into a large living area and some internal workshop spaces. The classrooms were now converted into individual bedrooms. They walked along the main first floor corridor.

"Up here on the left is the nursery, and then the next room is the class for the older kids." Ronnie peered into the first of the two rooms, where the smaller children were playing. Alex pushed open the door and indicated for him to go in. As they entered the room a number of small faces turned to see.

"Alex, Alex," a chorus of small voices sang out and a couple of children rushed across the room. Alex picked up the first one to reach him and swung the child high up into the air, laughing as he did so.

"You'll get them all over excited," said one of the women from the corner of the room where she was preparing lunch for the children. She was friendly and jovial and Alex just continued to laugh, putting down the first child and picking up the second.

"This is Ronnie everyone, he's come to visit."

Ronnie stood nervously; the ways of small children a bit of a mystery to him. The kids giggled shyly and mumbled hello.

"This is Nathaniel, that one is Adam, then there is Rosy

and of course Eve," Alex informed him. Ronnie said hello to each of them.

"We'll let you get on with your lunch. See you all later."

The children called out their goodbyes as Ronnie and Alex headed back into the corridor.

"You are great with them," Ronnie said. "You should have a job in there looking after them."

"No, that wouldn't be allowed. That is not a designated job for men."

"What do you mean? You mean men and women can only do certain jobs?"

"Yes, Devlin is very clear about that. The roles are divided up. That's why Susan said no to your offer of help. That job is designated for women, and women and men never work together. Devlin says it is much better for everyone if the roles are clearly laid out, and he says that the sexes working together only causes inappropriate behaviour and over familiarity."

"But you are all adults, surely it's up to you who you get over familiar with. What's it got to do with Devlin?"

"In order for the community to work efficiently, Devlin needs to make some of the key decisions, such as who does what job, who can have relationships with whom, all those things which can cause friction and strife... You don't understand."

"You're right, I don't," Ronnie responded slightly more aggressively than intended. "Alex, I'm sorry, I know we are visitors here, but it just seems..... It's like a feudal lord deciding what his peasants can and can't do."

"Devlin has kept us safe, in here, all of us. You don't know what it's been like out there. You don't know how lucky we are. All he asks in return is loyalty, hard work and following the rules."

"Yes, but if the rules include who can have sex with whom and what jobs you all do doesn't that strike you as unnecessary? What would be so wrong with all of you making those decisions?"

"There might be conflict. We couldn't cope if everyone had as many children as they wanted, if people got together then fell out. Devlin says that too much freedom is what brought the country to its knees. He says that without those liberal attitudes we would have been better prepared for what happened. If two people wish to get married then they can ask his permission, and if he thinks it is in the best interests of everyone then he will grant that. Don and Lisa got married almost two years ago."

"Right, so what about you? What if you wanted to get married and he said no?"

"But I don't want to. I don't think I'd ever like to do that, so it's fine."

"But that's not the point. Devlin and Angela are a couple, right?"

"Yes."

"And he didn't need to ask anyone's permission for that, did he? So why should the rest of you? Who died and put Devlin in charge?" Ronnie could sense Alex's discomfort at the way the conversation was going. He sighed. "Look, Alex, I'm sorry it is none of my business, if you are all happy living like this then it's got nothing to do with me. Thank you for showing me the place. I really appreciate it. And as I said earlier, I'm happy to help out with some work this afternoon, if there is a designated task you can point me at."

"Thank you, I'll speak to Don and I am sure we can find an appropriate task for you to do if you want to. I know it may all seem a bit strange. I found it strange to begin with, but it works."

"Thanks, I do appreciate your time. I'd better go and see if I can track Nairne down. Maybe we'll see you in the dining hall for lunch?"

TWENTY TWO

When Ronnie returned to their room he found Nairne there. She was sorting through their rucksacks, folding clothes and stuffing them into the bags.

"What happened to you? Alex and I waited for you downstairs. Remember he was going to show us around the place? I assumed you and your mum had got talking….. You will never believe what he told me about the way this place is run. It's like something from the middle ages….." he paused, Nairne was still cramming items into their bags. "Nairne, what are you doing?"

"I'm packing our stuff because we are leaving."

"But what about your mum? I thought we'd agreed we'd spend a few days so you could catch up with her, find out what she wants."

"Oh, I know what she wants. If you think you had an interesting chat this morning, this one is absolutely priceless. Angela wants us to take her two year old child, her and Devlin's child, back to Scotland."

"Your mum has another child?"

"I know, it's unbelievable. She didn't give a damn about the first two, you think she'd have learned that motherhood didn't suit her, but no, she and Devlin had a baby together and now she is sick of looking after this one. So can we step in and take it off her hands?"

"So which one is it? Alex took me up to the nursery, which one is Angela's?"

"Eve, her name is Eve, dark hair, like Devlin's."

"And your mum doesn't want her? Are you sure about this? She didn't want to come with us, just for us to take the child?"

"And what about Devlin, what does he say?"

"I don't know. I didn't stick around to ask. I can't believe she thought it was acceptable to ask my dad to

155

come down here and take some other man's child away to look after. She is completely mad. We should never have come here."

"Nairne." Ronnie's tone was as level as he could make it. He could see how angry she was and how hurt. "Nairne, stop, sit down a moment. We can't just leave."

"Why the hell not?"

"For one thing we're on an island, so we need them to take us back across the water, and for another thing, this is probably the last time you will ever see your mum. You can't leave it like this. Did she say why she wants you to take Eve?"

"She said it would be safer. Safer than here, but she seems to be doing just fine, so I think that was just an excuse. She doesn't want the hassle of another kid cramping her style."

"I'm not so sure."

"But you don't know her like I do."

"Nairne, you haven't seen her in years. You were just a child when she left, so she may have changed."

"You know the first thing she asked me to do today before she dropped the "you have a little sister bombshell", she asked me to lie to Devlin. Tell him we tracked her down, and promise not to tell him about her letter. The first thing she asks is for me to start lying to everyone, just like always has."

"Why? Did she say why she didn't want him to know?"

"No, but Angela will have some reason. She always has some plot or scheme." Nairne sat down on the edge of the bed, exhaling heavily. The tee shirt she had been folding now scrunched up in her hands. "Why does she have to be like this?"

Ronnie sat next to her and put his arms round her.

"Come on, we'll figure this out. I think there's more to this. Why don't you go and give your face a wash. Then we'll go down and have lunch like everything is fine. I think I need to have a proper chat with your mum, while you need to volunteer to do some work in the garden. Women's work!"

Nairne looked at him questioningly.

"You'll see. I met a girl called Susan. She and your mum are friends, and I think it would be useful if you were to help her with her chores this afternoon, see what you can find out about this place."

Angela entered the dining hall, her face full of concern. She spotted Ronnie and Nairne sitting over to the left with Alex. She hesitated. There was no sign of Devlin or his guard. Ronnie stood up and waved to her.

"Angela, come and join us. Let me get your lunch."

He could see the relief spread across her face, as she made her way through the rows of tables and benches to reach them, as if she were the visitor. Ronnie murmured in Nairne's ear.

"No scenes for the community, just be nice."

Alex shifted along in his seat to make space for Angela while Ronnie went over and fetched an extra bowl of vegetable soup which he placed in front of her. Close up she looked terrible. No longer the bright smile that had greeted them both yesterday. Her eyes were swollen, red rimmed and raw from the many hours of tears. She looked as though she had not slept and her complexion was pale.

"Thank you Ronnie," her voiced cracked as she spoke.

"You're welcome. I thought, after lunch, maybe you and I could have a catch up. I'd love to hear all about Nairne when she was little, she never tells me much about it. Nairne was going to go and give Susan a hand outside."

"Really?" Alex asked, the surprise in his tone unmistakable. "There's no need. I am sure Susan can manage for one day."

"I'd like to," said Nairne. "Growing vegetables and working outside is one of my favourite pastimes, and I've missed it this year, since we've been on the road so much. Plus, I'd like to learn how the place works and what better way than to join in."

"I remember that first year at the cottage you and your dad were obsessed with the vegetables. I'd get her all ready for school, clean shoes and white socks, and before you know it she'd have been outside to check on the plants, covered in mud, her and the dog. We'd only just got him and he'd leap about the place, muddy footprints all through the house. And your dad would just laugh and say it was good to see you taking such a keen interest," Angela smiled at the memory, but Ronnie could see Nairne tensing, trying not to react.

"I bet she was a real handful," he said teasingly. "And Dog still jumps about all the time."

"I am sitting here," said Nairne. "Maybe it would be better if the two of you continued this discussion without me."

"You still have the dog, Zane's puppy dog? I can't believe it."

"Oh yes, he's fine, getting on. He usually travels with us, but this was a long trip and I think he's earned a rest. We left him with friends," Ronnie replied.

They chatted over the rest of the meal about the community and the school which had operated from the site before. It had been one of London's most exclusive private schools, then it had been used by the army as a base camp. But once the third flood came the area became cut off. Even this summer when drought had been an issue the area had remained an island. The crossing was not far to the nearest point of land, perhaps a hundred and fifty metres, but that was far enough to put most people off and they rarely had visitors.

"So how many boats do you have?" Ronnie enquired.

"Eight in total, four small rowing boats, two canoes and two home-made rafts. We use those for transporting supplies. They're not bad, not exactly stylish to look at but they float, and that's what matters," Alex replied. "Devlin and the guard usually go across most days to fetch supplies. Anyway I'd better get on with my work. I've still got to catch up on this morning's tasks, and Devlin and the guard will be back by four. I want to have everything done before they bring in more stuff."

Alex cleared the empty plates from the table and headed out of the door and across the courtyard.

"So what does he do all day, these tasks?" Ronnie asked.

"Alex is in charge of the supply room. He checks in all the new supplies and all the food we grow and checks out what is used. Devlin says it is vital we keep track of everything to make sure we don't run out of things and that we are not wasteful. Devlin hates waste," Angela replied.

Ronnie and Nairne glanced at each other. Their own community kept records of food and supplies but not like this. They trusted one another.

"I'll see you later. I'll go and give Susan a hand. Where was she exactly?" Nairne asked.

"She was down at the far end of the cricket pitch, lifting some vegetables. You can't miss her, she's about your height, thicker set, rosy complexion and long strawberry blonde hair." Ronnie replied.

"Was she sitting at the top table yesterday?" Nairne asked.

"Yes, I think so."

"Fine, I'll see you later." Nairne headed outside.

"So now it's just you and me," Ronnie said to Angela. "Is there somewhere we can have a chat, somewhere a bit more private perhaps?"

"We could take a walk around the grounds, I can't take you up to my room. It wouldn't be considered…. proper."

"A walk would be fine. After you."

Angela led him out of the side door of the hall and out through the front door of the building. One or two people greeted them as they passed and within a few minutes they were walking up along the driveway towards the entrance gates.

"So, you want to know all about Nairne do you?" Angela asked.

"Yes, but that's not why I wanted to talk to you. She told me what you wanted, about us taking your daughter back with us. Nairne thinks it is because you can't be bothered looking after her. She says you have form and that you are just trying to dump your responsibilities onto someone else like always."

"She doesn't think very highly of me, does she?" Angela responded.

"Can you blame her?"

"No, I don't suppose I can. She just seems so bitter and angry. I don't understand, she was such a lovely little girl. I know it must have been hard for her losing her father and brother but….. I don't know. I feel like she hates me."

"Did she tell you what happened to them? To Daniel and Zane? Did she tell you about Steven Mitchell?"

"No, I tried to ask, but she got into such a state when I told her about Eve. She just ran off. She wouldn't even let me explain."

"I think there are some things you need to know about Nairne and what has happened to her. And then, I think you need to level with me and explain exactly why you want us to take Eve with us."

By the time Nairne reached Susan she had just started work on a large bed of potatoes. The girl was kneeling down cutting down the potatoes and putting the greenery into a plastic bucket. She was using a pair of garden sheers, cutting half a dozen stalks at once, then stopping to pick them up.

"Susan?" The girl turned and looked up at Nairne, shielding her eyes from the sun.

"Hi, I'm Nairne, Angela's daughter. I thought I'd come and give you a hand since my mum isn't really up to working today."

"Really, there is no need," the girl responded coldly. She

was a couple of years older than Nairne, well built, with a pretty face and beautiful hair. "I'm used to this sort of work. I can manage without Angela for another day."

Nairne sensed a certain attitude in the statement. Ronnie had said Susan and her mother were friends, but her tone was far from friendly.

"Really, you'd be doing me a favour. I love working outside and it's such a lovely day. Angela and Ronnie are spending some time together, so I'm at a loose end. Why don't you do the cutting, and I'll pick up after you then I can help you lift some of these."

"If you want," Susan replied.

They worked in silence for a while, Nairne collecting all the cuttings and cramming them into the bucket until it was full.

"What do you do with these?" she asked.

"If you tip them into the wheel barrow and once that is full take them down to the end of the bed, over there. We have a bonfire pile. Most stuff gets composted but we've noticed the first signs of blight on these, so I've been instructed to put them aside for burning."

"Yes, you can see the foliage starting to turn. It's such a problem this year. I guess the plants are under a bit of strain since the weather has been so erratic," Nairne replied, emptying the bucket into the barrow and bending down to collect the next pile. "So do you always work out here?"

"Yes, most days."

"And have you been here long?"

"Long enough, must be nearly six months now."

"And before that?"

"I was on the mainland."

It was obvious this was not something she wanted to talk about.

"Do you like it here then?"

"Yes, it's good. I feel very lucky to have been chosen. Very lucky indeed. Devlin looks after us all very well. It is like being part of a proper family."

"Chosen?"

"Yes, people are invited to join the community. Devlin has to be very selective. Otherwise we would end up with all sorts of people here."

"Right, I guess that's true," Nairne replied. "So you must know my mum quite well then."

"I thought I did, but I never knew about you. She never mentioned she had another child. Sorry, two children. I heard about your brother."

"That's right, he was a couple of years older than me. He died a while ago."

"I am sorry to hear that. Your mum must be very upset. I take it that is why you came."

"Yes, I thought she should know what had happened, and although it was a while ago this was the first opportunity we had to come down."

Susan did not respond.

"We'll not be staying long, just a few days and then we're heading back home. We want to get back before the weather breaks."

"And your mum, is she going back with you?"

"No, she's got Devlin, Eve and all of you. I don't think she'd like to come back to Scotland. Her life is here now." Nairne was surprised at the question.

"I suppose you're right. It's just that she hasn't seemed herself over the last few months. I thought maybe she was missing home."

"I think this is her home now," Nairne replied. "And what about you Susan, do you have anyone special here?"

"God, you sound just like your mum. She's always trying to fix me up with Alex."

"He seems nice, don't you think?"

"Yes, but he's just a boy. I prefer older men, with more experience. And anyway, I have my eye on someone else. But these things aren't for me to decide. It is up to Devlin who marries who."

"Sorry, what do you mean?"

"Devlin decides who matches up. He decides on who is best suited. You can make a request, but he has the final word."

"You are making this up, aren't you?" Nairne was incredulous. "There's no way you'd all let someone make those sort of decisions for you, that is so wrong."

"Devlin says that the community must come first before our individual wishes. He has to be able to make the key decisions otherwise we will just end up back in the chaos we are all trying to get away from. If you saw what it was like out there, on the mainland, the way people behave, you would see that what Devlin says is the best way. People need to be taken care of. They need to belong to a family and that is what he has built here. I mean, it's not like he makes us all do things we don't want to, but if, for example, you and Ronnie stayed here for good and you wanted to get married you would go and ask his permission, just like men used to ask the father of the bride. Devlin would decide if you were well suited and would make sure there was no reason why the match was not appropriate. Then if he agreed, you would get married and you would be able to have children together."

"And if Devlin said no, then what?"

"Well then, you would not be allowed to. I'm not aware of him saying no to anyone so far, but I suppose it is possible, if the match was unsuitable."

"And who defines what is suitable?"

"Devlin does, because he is in charge. But he doesn't try and impose these rules on everyone, after all, he has not complained about you and Ronnie sharing a room when you are not married to one another. He accepts that you are only visitors so the rules do not need to be adhered to."

"So you are telling me none of you are allowed to have sex outwith marriage? Really?"

"Devlin has said we need to ensure that children are

brought into this world with care and consideration. You know what it was like before, girls younger than you having children with no thought for how they would look after them or concern about the burden they were placing on society. The community's children are planned and wanted and are looked after collectively, we are all responsible for them. We are all their parents. Each adult is responsible for setting a good example by the way we act."

"I guess Devlin has got everything figured out then." Nairne replied, trying to restrain the tone of sarcasm. Devlin was sounding more and more like the kind of guy you would not wish to put in charge of anyone.

TWENTY THREE

It was surreal to walk around the edge of the island. On the other side of the water Ronnie could see the city sprawled out in all directions. The water was a dirty brown, full of rubbish and waste, and as they got closer to it he could smell it. Angela had listened in silence as he had given her a brief run down on what had happened to her family, her children and her husband, over the last few years. She sobbed, struggling to hold it together as he recounted how Daniel had died and how Nairne had witnessed it. Then as he explained how Zane had been shot and his body dumped, she just cried. He explained how Steven Mitchell had pursued Nairne and Paul, and how eventually Nairne had killed him.

"You can see, Angela, she is not the little girl you left behind. Nairne is an adult. She has experienced more danger and hardship than most people do in their entire lives. She is very single minded and determined. She's loyal and strong and fair, but she is also unforgiving. If you want her help you are going to need to be honest with her."

"I can see you are very fond of her," Angela said. "You seem well suited, you are so considered, laid back even."

"Yeah, well not always, but I guess I tend to go with the flow a bit more easily than Nairne. And yes, she is very important to me. I know she is really angry with you for so many reasons, and she doesn't think you have the right to ask for her help."

"I don't," said Angela. "And if I could think of any other way I wouldn't ask. Believe me. Remember when I wrote that letter I thought Daniel might come down here. I never imagined I would be dragging Nairne into all of this."

"Okay, so what is this? Why do you want us to take your daughter away?"

"You've met Devlin. What do you make of him?"

Ronnie paused, this was Angela's partner, the father of her child. He was not sure how honest to be.

"I can't say I know him well enough to judge, but on first impressions he strikes me as a man who likes to get his own way and who thrives on being in charge."

"That's very diplomatic," Angela replied. "Go on, what else?"

"Well, he seems to have some pretty old fashioned views on women, for example, he told me to take Nairne in hand, like that would ever happen. As for the rest of the people here, they seem to look up to him, so I am guessing he has his good side."

"You're right. He does have his good side. He is brave. He can be very generous. He has saved all of us. He looks after us."

"But?"

"He's … I don't know how to say this without sounding disloyal. You have to understand he saved my life, literally from a burning building, and I don't want you to misunderstand. I love him. But, he's changed….. At the start of all this, he had this vision, we'd get a group together of like-minded people, and we'd build a proper community where we shared a common goal and values. But I've noticed that things have changed……"

"In what way?" Ronnie asked. He could see Angela was struggling to find the right words.

"I think Devlin is ill, he's become paranoid. He thinks that others in the community can't be trusted, and he's begun to impose a whole lot of rules. His men, the guard, he has them watching people. He encourages them to report any inappropriate behaviour or infringements of the rules. I don't see how this can last; there's no long term safety here for Eve."

"So why don't you just leave, with Eve? You can come

with us. We'll help you."

"No, I couldn't possibly come with you. There's no way Nairne wants me coming back to Scotland. There's no way she would want that. And besides, I do love Devlin, I just....... I worry about what the future will hold for Eve. I worry about what will happen if Devlin's brave new world doesn't work."

"Are you afraid of him?"

"No, he'd never harm me....... He loves me. He loves Eve. In fact, I think he loves all of us in his own way. We are his creation."

Ronnie was not convinced. Angela looked scared, in fact she looked like someone who had lived with fear for some time.

"Okay, so you want Nairne and me to take your daughter with us. You understand that means you will probably never see her again. Is that what you want?"

"Of course not, I want to have her with me. I want to look after her, to be there for her..... But this is for the best. Nairne's right, motherhood is not my thing. She really would be better going with you. From what you've said your community sounds like a safe place where she would be loved and looked after."

"And what about you?"

"What about me? I stay here with Devlin."

"And if you're right and this place falls apart, what then?"

"I'll be fine, I can look after myself. You know Nairne didn't inherit all her survival instincts from Daniel," Angela laughed, trying to lighten the mood. She placed her arm through Ronnie's. "You know, my daughter has made a good choice with you, Ronnie. She really has."

"Let's say I could persuade Nairne to do this, to take Eve with us, what about Devlin? She is his daughter. I am assuming he would have something to say about this."

"We wouldn't tell him."

Ronnie stepped back, pulling his arm free and turned to

stare at her.

"You want us to steal his child?"

"It's the only way. He would never agree to it. He would see it as a betrayal that I don't believe in his vision. He wouldn't understand. But if you and Nairne just took her, without my knowledge or his.... . He would be angry, of course he would, but he would have no idea how to find you, so what would he be able to do?"

"He could come after us."

"No, no he loves Eve, don't get me wrong.... But he believes that the children belong to the community, he doesn't love her any more than he does any of the other children in the nursery. He'd get over it." She looked into his eyes and saw the horror at what she was saying. "Honestly, his life is so busy with all of us to look after....."

"And what about you? Could you really let her go, never see her again?" Ronnie was puzzled. Angela obviously loved her daughter. He could not believe she would choose to stay here with Devlin rather than leave with them.

"Oh Ronnie, Nairne and Zane are proof that I can just walk away and not look back. I've done it before, I can do it again," she retorted. "If you have any doubts about my ability to do that, just ask Nairne."

"I have to say I don't like this, not one bit. I think if you are so worried about Devlin's mental state you and the others here need to challenge that, sort this out properly."

"Perhaps you're right, but it doesn't change anything. I still want you to take Eve. What we've built here, it won't last. We should have left the city. We should have tried to find somewhere remote, with more land, with clean water, but Devlin believes that there is so much to be gained from within the city. I know this isn't going to work in the long run and when it falls apart it's not going to be pleasant. So Ronnie, will you do it, will you speak to Nairne, please? Can you at least persuade her to go and meet Eve, I know if she does that she'll just adore her."

"I'll give it a try."

Nairne was enjoying the work outside in the garden, although she was not convinced she would wish to spend much time in Susan's company. The girl had been polite, if somewhat reserved, but there was an uncomfortable undertone of jealousy. Nairne couldn't decide exactly what she was jealous of. It appeared she had some animosity towards Angela, and towards Alex. She was curious about Ronnie, asking lots of questions about their relationship and about him. Nairne got the distinct impression that Susan preferred the company of men to that of women. She also spoke very highly of Devlin, in fact he sounded like some sort of God-like creature, an infatuation perhaps. Nairne could not understand it, as she had found him to be exceptionally arrogant and annoying. To hear Susan speak it was as if they were all bearing witness to the second coming.

"Once you get to know him, you'll see just what a great man he is. Honestly, we would not have stood a chance without him. It takes a special kind of person to be able to lead people the way he leads us," Susan commented.

"But what about other people's points of view, is there not some sort of democratic process?"

"Oh no, you can't just trust everyone to make the right decisions, that's what we did before and look where that got us. It is much better if appropriate people are in charge and they can take the responsibility for the rest of us. Really, you should speak with Devlin. He will explain it."

"I bet he would," Nairne replied, trying to hide her contempt for the very idea that it was better to have one person in control of everyone.

"Devlin says democracy is a luxury we can no longer afford. He says that if we had not had such liberal attitudes, then the world would never have got into such a state."

"What, so climate change is a consequence of the liberal minded west? That's an interesting way of looking at it."

"See I told you, but really you need to speak with him and get it directly from him. He is so much better at explaining it all."

Nairne let the topic drop as there was something else she was very curious about and she thought Susan might be in a relaxed enough mood to tell her something about it.

"Susan, I was wondering about the room we are in, it obviously belonged to someone. The wardrobe is still full of clothes. Who used to stay there?"

"Oh, that was Ralph's room, but he's gone now."

"Ralph?"

"Yes, I didn't know him very well. He was just a boy, late teens, a bit of a, you know…..a bit of a soft character. He worked with Alex in the store room and did some other tasks like looking after the animals. And he was responsible for managing all the equipment for the garden but he was a bit lazy. He was a fat boy, you know the sort. He really didn't fit in here. I'm not sure how he came to be here, but he's gone now."

"So where did he go?"

"Oh, I've no idea, he's just gone."

"What, like disappeared?"

"No, no nothing like that. He was caught stealing so now he's gone."

"Stealing what?"

"Food! Like I said, he was a fat, greedy boy, and he was caught, so he had to go. He got off lightly, I can tell you. I don't think anyone would have complained if Devlin had carried out the proper punishment, but that's what I mean, Devlin is such a good man, so kind and generous. He was willing to let Ralph go and leave the community rather than extract the full punishment from him."

"So what was the full punishment?" Nairne asked, trying to keep her voice steady, her mind racing at what this could involve; a public flogging or extra work duties?

"Chop off his hand, of course. That would have stopped him stealing again." Susan made the statement as if it were the most obvious and natural thing in the world.

"Chop off his hand? Are you serious, for stealing some food? If you had done that he would probably have bled to death, or worse, died of blood poisoning. That is barbaric: it's like something from the middle ages."

"See, that's what I mean, Devlin is such a good man he just expelled him from the community."

"So why didn't he take his stuff from his room? He left family photos and all his clothes."

"He wasn't allowed to take anything with him. That was part of the punishment. He was stripped of all his clothes and taken across on one of the boats to the mainland and dropped off."

"What with no clothes, no weapons, nothing at all?"

"Yes, of course. If you break the rules you must expect to be punished otherwise there would be anarchy." These appeared to be Susan's final words on the subject. She stopped digging and stood up and stretched her back. "I think we are just about finished for today. Thank you for your help it was good of you."

"I enjoyed it," Nairne replied. "I'll help you take these things back to the house. I take it the tools go in the store room over there?" She pointed to the cricket pavilion.

"Yes, if you don't mind returning the tools I'll take the barrow back to the kitchen so Alex can get this stuff weighed and recorded."

"Great, maybe I'll see you later at dinner," said Nairne, picking up both forks, the shears and the plastic buckets they had been using. They had unearthed a reasonable volume of potatoes, but the tubers were small and there were signs of disease on some of them which meant they would not store. Susan had the potatoes piled up in trays on top of the wheelbarrow. She set off towards the main building.

The tool store was unlocked. The tools were all lined up neatly, cleaned, oiled, sharpened and generally very well looked after. Nairne found a rag and wiped down the tools they had been using, before hanging them up in their allotted spaces. Whoever had looked after this place certainly hadn't been lazy, she thought. It was spotlessly clean and extremely well organised.

She headed back to the main building and straight up the stairs towards her room. She was in need of a wash before dinner. There was dirt ingrained in her hands, under her nails and the bottom of her trousers were muddy. She carried her boots, which were caked in soil. They would need a good clean before she could wear them indoors. She was almost at the door to their room when she heard someone call her name.

Devlin was standing at the far end of the corridor, leaning against the wall, looking relaxed, friendly even.

"Nairne, how are you? I see you have been out helping Susan with some work. That was kind of you but not necessary: you are our guest. After all, I wouldn't want you to think you have to earn your keep." His voice was like oil and it oozed towards her, lubricating everything in its path.

"I was happy to help out. I enjoy working outdoors and since Angela wasn't up to it today I thought it would be useful if I filled in for her. Ronnie and I are used to hard work, and if we're eating your food it is only fair we should do some work in return," she replied.

"Don't run off, I was hoping to have a chat with you. Please, why don't you come along and join me in my office. We can have a drink, there's still plenty of time before dinner is served."

"I was going to get cleaned up." She held up her muddy boots.

"Don't worry about that, come on, you can get cleaned up afterwards."

Reluctantly, Nairne walked back along the corridor and into Devlin's office. She put her boots down just inside the door and took a seat on one of the straight backed chairs. Devlin went over and fetched two glasses and poured them both a drink.

"Whisky? Is that okay for you?"

"Fine," said Nairne, taking the glass.

"Please Nairne, come and join me on the sofa, you look very uncomfortable perched on there." Nairne rose and went over and sat at the opposite ends of the black, leather, three seat sofa.

"So, what do you think of the place now you have had a chance to look around? Pretty impressive isn't it?"

"Yes very," said Nairne. "There was one thing I was wondering about?"

"Oh yes, what's that then?"

"I suppose it's two things really. Firstly, how do you manage for fresh water? There doesn't seem to be a supply anywhere on the site, and secondly, how much do you have to supplement the food you require from trips to the mainland?"

"Good questions, these show a good, sharp mind. I like that. The water, you're quite right, we don't have a fresh supply; however we do have a swimming pool and we've rigged up a system of water butts, downpipes and filters which collect all the rain-water which falls on the buildings and paved areas and we store that and use it. Obviously it needs to be treated to stop infection and we boil it before use. You'll have seen we've converted to dry toilets and we have a composting system for that waste."

"So what happens if you have a drought? A couple of years ago we had two really dry years one after another. With the numbers you've got here you must need quite a lot of water."

"Well, you can see we're managing fine, so far," Devlin replied, not altogether as happily as before. "And we do still bring in goods from the mainland, but I think we could get by. It's still good to be able to trade for some luxury items." He indicated to the drink in his hand.

"So what do you trade with? I can't imagine you have lots of spare food, so what is it that you take over to the mainland?"

"Oh this and that. Anyway, nothing for you to worry about. The community is on a firm footing, so if you're worried about your mum, you shouldn't be. I'll look after her."

"No, I'm not," said Nairne. "I was just curious."

"Talking of curiosity, I would really like to hear all about how you found us."

"As you can imagine, it took us a bit of time," Nairne replied. "But there's nothing much to tell. We met a girl who used to be part of your group when you lived in, where was it now," she racked her brains for the information Angela had given her earlier. "Yes Brixton, I think her name was Liz or Lizzie. We met her further North, and when she heard my name she said she knew a woman called Angela Grear who was Scottish. To be honest, I was pretty sceptical, you know the police had told us Angela was dead...... it was a bit of a shock to find out that she was still alive. This was months ago, but since Ronnie and I were doing a bit of travelling anyway, we thought why not....." Devlin nodded.

"Lizzie, interesting, yes I remember her. That was a long time ago. Lucky for you - a chance meeting like that."

Nairne could feel the colour rise in her cheeks, she sensed he didn't believe her, but he was not going to challenge her outright.

"Thanks for the drink, but I'd better get cleaned up and changed before dinner. Ronnie will be wondering where I have got to." She stood up and placed the glass on the table. Devlin stood up.

"Well, it was good to catch up, I'll see you at dinner."

Devlin opened the door for her and she could feel his eyes following her down the corridor.

TWENTY FOUR

"So how did you get on with Angela?" Nairne asked.

Ronnie was lounging on the bed.

"It was interesting. She *is* afraid of him. She won't admit it, but she is definitely afraid of him. She said he was delusional. And she still wants us to take Eve with us but without him knowing anything about it."

"She wants us to kidnap Devlin's daughter and sneak out of here? She is the one who is delusional."

"Nairne, I think we should consider it. I know it seems like a crazy thing to do, but if your mum is right then this place will eventually implode. If Devlin gets worse…"

"And what about us? Does she think that he'll just let us go, without any fuss? He'll come after us. You know he will."

"Angela reckons he'll be annoyed, but she thinks he'll let us go. She says he doesn't show much interest in Eve and the community has quite a few children. She could be right. Anyway, he would have trouble finding us."

"Did she tell you how they deal with people who break the rules? Did she tell you about Ralph, the boy whose bed you are lying on?" Nairne asked.

"No, what happened to Ralph?"

"He was expelled for stealing."

"It seems a bit harsh, but you know as well as I do a community like this can only work if people trust one another."

"Ronnie, they stripped him naked and dumped him on the mainland; that was after Devlin graciously showed mercy and decided not to chop off his hand."

Ronnie looked at her in disbelief.

"I'm not making this up," Nairne continued. "Susan told me all about it. She thought it showed what a kind and generous man Devlin was."

"But don't you see, if this is true then Angela has plenty of reasons to believe Eve is in danger. Who knows what Devlin might do next?"

"Yeah, to us!"

"Nairne, you risked your life for Subhash and Sahasra without giving it a second thought and Eve is your sister."

"Yes, but we weren't kidnapping them from their parents. We were trying to save them from a bunch of psychopaths."

"Exactly, what do you think Devlin is if he would consider chopping off a boy's hand because he stole something?"

"Okay, I know what you're saying, but what about Angela? Why doesn't she just leave and take Eve with her? She could come with us. We could help her to find somewhere safe."

"She knew you wouldn't want her to come back with us, so she is willing to stay here and let us take Eve."

"That's big of her. She'd like us to risk our lives for her new kid, but she'll just stay here and that's because I don't want her to come and live with us. She is so good at making herself seem like the martyr."

"Nairne. I know you don't like her, I can even see why. She let you down, but you are better than that. If your sister needs you then I know you'll do the right thing. I think at least you should go and meet your little sister. If we are going to do this, then she needs to have a chance to get used to us, to trust us. Taking an uncooperative toddler away without getting caught could be very difficult."

"What now? You want to go and do that just now?"

"No time like the present, come on. We still have a bit of time before dinner. We'll stop off and get your mum and then go along to the nursery."

Reluctantly, Nairne followed Ronnie down the hallway towards her mother's room. Angela was sitting on the edge of the bed when they entered. She immediately put on a bright smile.

"Nairne, Ronnie, how lovely to see you both. Nairne, I hope you didn't work too hard this afternoon."

"No, it was fine, Susan was very.....welcoming."

"Yes, Susan can be a bit of an acquired taste, I think," Angela replied.

"We thought it would be useful if we could meet Eve properly," Ronnie said.

"What? So have you agreed, will you take her?" Angela was gushing and they could see the excitement in her eyes.

"Hold on, we haven't agreed to anything yet, we just thought if we are to consider this then we need to get to know her. I mean, it would be totally unfair and impractical to take her if we are complete strangers to her. But I'm not saying we'll do this," Nairne replied.

"Oh just wait, you will love her. Honestly, she is such a sweetie, and she's no bother, really, she's a very easy child."

Nairne looked to the heavens, when her mother was this hyper there was no point in arguing with her.

The nursery was quiet. The children were due to have their dinner and when Nairne, Ronnie and Angela entered the room one of the women was making sure everyone had washed their hands. Eve turned when the door opened and squealed in excitement. She charged across the room towards Angela, arms outstretched, giggling. However when she saw Nairne and Ronnie she faltered for a moment, unsure of whether to keep going or to head back to the others.

"Eve, darling." Angela bent down, reaching out and Eve let herself be swung up into the air, before Angela settled her on one hip. She brushed Eve's unruly curls from her forehead.

"I've brought you some visitors. This is Ronnie and Nairne. Can you say hello?"

Eve giggled in response and hid her face against Angela's shoulder.

"She is quite shy," said Angela. "Although once she gets

going there is no stopping her."

Angela introduced Nairne and Ronnie to the two women who ran the nursery. They both smiled and nodded in acknowledgement. Janette, the older of the two, was in her late twenties and mother to one of the older children. Carron, the younger, was barely older than Nairne. She was slim with long, light brown hair, which hung loosely over her shoulders, and she wore glasses.

"So, Eve is your little sister then?" Carron asked.

"Yes, I guess she is," Nairne replied. "So I wondered if it would be all right if I came and spent the day with you tomorrow. We're not going to be here for long and who knows when I might see her again. If you don't mind, I'd be happy to help out."

This statement brought looks of amazement from Angela and Ronnie. Carron looked to the older woman before replying.

"That would be fine with us. As long as it is okay with Devlin." She glanced nervously at Angela as she spoke. They were both aware that Devlin was keen that parents relinquished individual control over the children and limited their contact time. The children were the responsibility of the community, not of individuals.

"I'm sure it will be fine with Devlin, under the circumstances," Angela replied. "I'll speak with him this evening."

They left Eve in the nursery, sitting at the table eating her dinner.

"That was a great idea volunteering to help out," Angela said, as they walked down the corridor. "I am so grateful to you, you have no idea what this means to me." She squeezed Nairne's arm affectionately

"Hold on, I haven't said we'll take her yet. I just think if it is a possibility then she needs to be able to trust us. But I'm still not convinced about this. If you think this is the right thing to do then come with us."

Angela stopped in her tracks. Her face was a mixture of

surprise and confusion at Nairne's offer.

"No, I can't. It's not that I don't want to, but I can't."

"Because of Devlin? He doesn't own you. If you don't want to stay with him then we'll just tell him and you can come with us," Nairne replied. She just couldn't understand this loyalty to Devlin. Angela had never shown loyalty to anyone.

"Nairne, you don't know what it means to me that you would consider taking me back with you. After everything...... but really it is for the best if I stay here. I know Devlin doesn't own me, but I do love him. I just know that your sister would be safer with you."

"I don't understand how you can say you love him if you are frightened of him. That's not what love should be about. For God's sake, why won't you just come with us?" Nairne could feel her temper rising, she wanted to shake Angela, make her see how stupid she was being. Ronnie intervened.

"Nairne, it has to be your mum's choice. We can't make her come with us but the offer is there. At least think about it."

"Okay, I'll think about it, but please, you will take Eve won't you? Regardless of my decision." Her expression mirrored the desperation in her voice.

"Yes, we'll take her," Nairne replied, her tone flat and defeated. She knew Angela would not come with them.

"Thank you Nairne, I don't deserve to have such a wonderful daughter. I really don't." She hugged Nairne, holding her tight. She could feel Nairne remain stiff and unyielding. Angela let go, wiping tears from her eyes. "Oh, God, what am I like?" she laughed nervously. "We'd better get downstairs for dinner. Devlin hates it when people are late."

When they entered the dining room Angela could see that seats had been left for them at the top table, one for her on the right side of Devlin and two for Nairne and Ronnie on the left. Alex was sitting at one of the other tables with Susan, who looked displeased at the new seating arrangements. They were just in time as Devlin rose to his feet and called everyone to order. Within seconds silence fell. He let the silence last, waiting until he had everyone's full attention and then he smiled. Nairne thought she could feel the relief in the room, as the smile indicated Devlin was in a good mood.

"Good evening to all of you, as always it is good to see so many community members gathered together after a productive day's work. And as you will see, and most of you will already know, we have visitors staying with us." He turned towards Nairne and Ronnie who could feel every pair of eyes in the room focusing on them.

"This is Nairne, Angela's daughter and her friend, Ronnie. They will be staying with us for a few days and I know I can rely on all of you to make them feel welcome. As you can imagine they are keen to find out all about our successful thriving community, and to be able to take back some of the good ideas we have implemented to make our community safe and productive for all of us. Not everyone is as lucky as we are here, and if we can share some of our good practices to help Nairne and Ronnie's community back home get on their feet, then we will gladly do it. Now, please, everyone enjoy your meal and may we thank the Lord for this food."

He sat down and turned to face Nairne. She could feel the colour rise in her cheeks. The idea that they had come down here to find out how to run a community from this man was laughable. They'd seen enough to know there was no way this site was producing enough food for all these people. Devlin and his guard were getting supplies of food and other materials from the city, but it was unclear what they were using to trade with. She bit her lip. They just had to manage a few more days and then they were leaving.

"I wondered if I could spend the day in the nursery tomorrow. I'm really interested in the communal way you are raising the children. We can see how much more efficient that is than parents just looking after their own. In our own community, we have a few young children and I think we can learn something from your methods. I met Carron and Janette earlier today but I wanted to check with you that you are happy for them to share their experience with me," Nairne could hear her voice speak the words, even though she couldn't quite believe she was managing it.

"Nairne, that would be fine. I didn't think you would be the type who wanted to get involved in childcare, but I suppose that natural maternal instinct is difficult to overcome. Of course, we'd be delighted for you to spend some time with our children, and I am sure while you are doing that we can find a useful task for Ronnie," Devlin beamed at her.

"I was hoping to spend some time with Alex, if you don't mind. I'm really keen to see how you manage to keep control of all the food stock, and the systems you have in place to ensure you have sufficient supplies."

"Ronnie, I am sure we can find something more interesting than that to keep you busy. Why don't you come with us on our trip tomorrow, and you can see at the sharp end just how we keep our little community afloat. I can always use another dependable man in the squad." The offer felt like a threat, but Ronnie could see this was a challenge that Devlin wanted to set for him.

"I'd be happy to go with you, if that would be useful," Ronnie replied. Nairne glanced at him and he could see she was far from comfortable with the idea.

"Devlin, are you sure?" Angela cut in. "I mean you and your men are used to going to the mainland and dealing with any situation. Ronnie is our guest. It can be dangerous over there."

"Oh Angela, don't be such a worrier. The boy will be fine, and surely you want to be sure your daughter has chosen a young man who can take care of himself and her.

It will be good for the lad."

"Angela, it's fine. I'd be happy to go, honestly," Ronnie replied, putting on his most convincing smile.

TWENTY FIVE

Nairne arrived in the nursery at eight thirty, just in time to help clear away the breakfast dishes. There were eight children, three of whom were old enough for school lessons and who spent the day in the adjacent room with the community's designated teacher, Rosemary. Nairne was left with Carron, Janette and the five younger children. The two women were welcoming and seemed pleased to have the extra help. The children were shy to begin with, but by ten o'clock Nairne was an accepted part of the furniture.

She was not a natural with young children. She lacked any real experience, however she knew she had a limited amount of time to get Eve to a point where she would trust her, so she entered into the spirit of the day wholeheartedly. By mid-morning she was on the floor with Eve, Adam, and Jacob, a boisterous four year old. They had a large pile of wooden blocks and all three children were trying to build taller towers which were then recklessly knocked to the ground. Nairne looked up to see Angela standing outside the main doors looking in. Nairne waved, but Angela just waved back. A few minutes later she was gone.

"Eve, would you like to sit next to Nairne for your lunch?" Carron asked as she arranged the children's plates on the table.

"Yes!" Eve exclaimed, grabbing Nairne by the hand and pulling her towards the table. Nairne sat on the floor next to her sister, who was perched on a tiny wooden chair. Lunch was a messy business but the children were all in good humour and the two women were very relaxed with them. Nairne was tired; she was not used to looking after children, and they were quite demanding. Adam sat opposite her, his dark curly hair framed a lovely face with dark eyes, just like Eve's. Nairne watched him carefully. He was a very reserved little boy. It crossed her mind that he and Eve could be brother and sister. The thought almost floated away, but suddenly Nairne was aware of a feeling of anxiety. They did look like each other, but surely lots of small children looked alike.

"So how are you holding up?" Carron asked, sitting down to join them. Janette was taking the opportunity of an extra pair of hands to do some spring cleaning of the toy store.

"They certainly keep you on your toes," Nairne replied. "I don't have much experience with children. I don't think I'm a natural, but I'm enjoying it."

"You are doing fine. It can be quite hard work, especially the noise levels when they are excited, but you soon get used to it."

"Not all of them are noisy," Nairne replied, "Adam here is a very quiet little boy, aren't you?" He stared up at her with large saucer like eyes. Carron ruffled his hair and put her arm round him. "Adam is a little treasure. My very own treasure."

"He is a lovely looking boy, who does he belong to?" Nairne asked, trying to sound as casual as possible.

"Oh, like all the children, Adam belongs to all of us," Carron replied defensively. She looked sad as she spoke and Nairne sensed that this was not a topic worth pursuing. "Are you able to stay with us for the rest of the day?"

"Yes, if you don't mind."

"Yes, yes, yes!" squealed Eve, happy to have such a dedicated playmate for the whole day.

"I guess that is your answer," said Carron laughing.

"Could we take them outside to play?" Nairne asked. "Maybe a walk in the garden or into the woods?"

"Oh, I think that would be a great idea. I'll just let Janette know, then she can do some tidying in here while we are out from under her feet. I'll get their coats and shoes, if you can help me get everyone ready."

Nairne helped each of the children into their shoes and jackets.

"So where is Ronnie today?" Carron asked, as she pulled on her own boots and zipped up her coat.

"He went out with Devlin and his men on a trip to the mainland for supplies."

Carron looked surprised.

"Is that unusual?" Nairne asked. "For a newcomer or a visitor to be taken on a trip?"

She had felt extremely uneasy about the whole thing ever since Devlin had suggested it, but she knew Ronnie had little choice without appearing to doubt Devlin's judgement.

"Devlin and his guard are a very tight-knit group. They have known each other a long time, some of them from before all of this. They served together, and he likes to keep them apart from the rest, you know the way men do that, their own private club. Devlin trusts all of those men with his life. I'm surprised that he would take someone he doesn't know. It can be dangerous out there."

"Ronnie can look after himself. We have had quite a lot of experience of 'out there' and so far we've managed to stay alive."

"Yes, I guess he managed to get you here safely, so you must trust and rely on him for so much. I can't imagine trying to go on such a treacherous journey with only one man to protect me," Carron replied, without any hint of sarcasm.

Nairne let the comment pass. She felt as if she had been plunged back into a different world where women were simpering chattels, to be protected and provided for. She wondered if such a time had ever really existed, but Devlin was doing a good job of creating such a place.

The boat trip across took less time than the journey with Nairne a couple of days earlier. The river was quieter, and they docked at a remote spot to the east of the island. Devlin had introduced him to the three men who accompanied him on his trip. Don, Ed and Liam, nodded in turn as they were introduced. Ronnie had met Don previously and he recognised Liam as one of the guards on duty the day he and Nairne had arrived.

They were a quiet bunch and there was little idle chatter on the crossing.

"What are we looking for?" Ronnie asked. He had noticed they had not taken much with them to trade with, and he assumed that the group had a clear idea of what they needed and where to find it. He had also noticed they were well armed and they all looked as though they knew how to handle themselves.

"We'll see what there is to trade," said Devlin. "Sometimes, like today, we come over for very specific resources, but usually we just have a look and see what there is."

"Nairne and I passed a big market at Hampstead Heath, on the way through the city. We didn't have time to stop and go in but it looked like they had a wide range of goods being traded. Is that where we're heading?"

"No we tend not to go that far. Don't worry, just stick with us. Do as we say and enjoy the ride," Devlin laughed and the others grinned in a conspiratorial manner.

Ronnie's sense of unease began to increase, but there was little he could do but go along with whatever the others did.

They tied the boat up and the five of them stepped onto dry land once more and set off down the narrow alleyway in single file, with Devlin in the lead and Don at the rear. Ronnie was sandwiched in the middle, the only one of the group who was not armed. They were carrying three rucksacks, he assumed full of items to trade, but no one had said what they contained. From their size and weight he doubted it could be food, as there was insufficient bulk to make them worth much. Perhaps it was alcohol, or cigarettes, or some other precious commodity. The alley appeared to be a dead end, however to the left there was a doorway. Devlin paused and removed a set of keys from his pocket before unlocking the large padlock and removing the heavy chain which held the workshop doors together. Inside was pitch black, and as they entered Devlin switched on a small hand torch, shining it behind them. Don, who was last to enter, looped the chain through the handles on the inside and inserted the padlock, clicking it shut.

"So the only way back to the boat is through those doors. That means we know the boat will still be there when we get back," Devlin said. "Right guys, are we ready?" They all nodded in agreement. The space they were in had been a car repair workshop. There was an inspection pit in the floor, now full of foul smelling water, and a stack of abandoned tyres lay piled against the far wall. There was a roller door, for vehicular access and a pedestrian door on the opposite side with the window boarded up. The doors were both padlocked shut. Once again Devlin produced the key and unlocked the pedestrian door. They emerged into a wide street, where almost all the buildings were boarded up and there were no signs of habitation.

"We're too close to the water here for people to feel safe in these properties," Devlin remarked. "When we get a high tide, some of these places will be flooded up to the first floor. You'll see as we head further in where the occupation really starts." With this he strode off down the road. Ronnie followed with the others. He could sense a change in the group. They were focused, moving as a single unit. Rifles were held in a ready position, eyes and heads were mobile, watching out for any unexpected danger or threat. Devlin appeared to know this route well. He did not pause or hesitate at any of the junctions. Within a few blocks they began to see signs of life. There was a smell of smoke from cooking fires and in one or two buildings they passed they could hear voices from within. Outside one property was a large Alsatian dog tied with a sturdy rope to the railings. It barked and strained to get at them as they passed. Ronnie could see it was thin and under-fed, its coat patchy and bare in places. He guessed meat was probably pretty difficult to find now. The men paid it little attention. They proceeded down a number of streets and alleyways, turning in this direction and that, and Ronnie became aware that at all costs, he could not let them out of his sight. If he did he would never find his way back to the boat. For a moment he wondered if this was the plan, to lose him and return to the island without him, giving Nairne some story. Paranoia was a terrible affliction, he pushed the thought from his mind. After thirty minutes or so they entered what had been a sleek middle class terrace. Each house had its own garden. Cars, long since abandoned due to lack of fuel, lined the street: Range Rovers, Audis and Daimlers. Some of the properties were obviously still occupied. The gardens had been given over to growing vegetables, security grilles were fitted to the doors while the windows were protected with bars or mesh screens. It seemed to Ronnie that some residents had obviously had the foresight to plan ahead. Other less well protected properties stood open, windows broken, doors kicked in. A couple of houses had been burnt out. A wide crossroads lay at the end of the street and the group turned left. Up ahead, Ronnie could see a number of large houses, each set in their own grounds. High walls, hedges and sturdy security gates surrounded each property.

"It's the third one on the right," Don said. "The one with the turrets."

Ronnie looked at the house as they reached the security gates. It was a modern three-storey building with fake ornamental turrets and a grand driveway, which was out of all proportion to the house. It was the kind of place he imagined a crime lord would build: flashy and overstated.

Devlin went up to the gates and pressed the intercom. A

security camera mounted on a pole inside the gates moved round to get them all in view.

"Yes," a male voice responded.

"We're here for the trade. We have the items you requested." Devlin slipped the rucksack off his back and held it up in view of the camera.

"Leave the weapons outside the gate. Two of your men can stay out there with them. The rest of you can come up to the house."

Each man made a show of unstrapping their rifles and placing them on the ground. The gates swung open. Devlin, Don and Ronnie walked through as the gates closed behind them. The front door opened as they approached and two burly men emerged, each accompanied by a large dog. Doberman Pinchers had always been a popular choice for guard dogs and seeing the crazed look in their eyes, Ronnie could see why. Their sleek coats told him these animals were well looked after. They looked fit and dangerous. The larger of the two men handed his dog's lead over to his colleague and then proceeded to pat each of them down, checking for any other weapons. Ronnie stood with his arms outstretched, while the burly figure searched him.

"Right, you two can wait in the hall. You," he indicated to Devlin. "Come with me."

They entered the building and he stood and waited with Don, their minder and the two dogs while Devlin was taken through into the heart of house carrying two of the rucksacks. Ronnie looked around. The interior was just as anticipated: decorated in heavy flock wallpaper, with a grand staircase sweeping upwards to a feature window. Above their heads hung an ornate chandelier, each miniature crystal shape cast patterns of light across the space. Ronnie could not imagine what had been in the rucksacks. They did not appear to be heavy and this was obviously a deal that had been planned well in advance. Devlin emerged from the living room a few minutes later.

"That's us, then," Devlin stated. "If we can just pick up our supplies we'll be on our way."

The security guard nodded in response.

"Follow me. Your stuff is through here." He showed them down the hallway to the rear of the property into a large spacious kitchen. On the counter top were various boxes and bags full of cigarettes, alcohol and what could only be described as luxury food items: tinned fish and tinned meat. Don took the rucksack from his back and pulled out a couple of larger holdalls. He began loading the goods into the bags. Within five minutes each of them was carrying a bag full of goods.

The bodyguard showed them back out to the front door.

"Pleasure doing business with you," said Devlin.

Liam and Ed were still waiting at the front gates and once the gates closed behind them they each retrieved their weapons.

"Come on let's get this stuff back to the boat," Devlin instructed. "And guys, keep your eyes open." The others nodded in response and they set off back towards the boat. Ronnie was pretty sure they went back a different route. He guessed Devlin would be wary of following the same route twice, in case they had been noticed by anyone on the way. Their return journey was uneventful and once inside the lock-up Don took the bags and put them against one wall before covering them with a tarpaulin.

"Right lads, are we set?" Don asked. Each nodded in turn. They all looked excited. Ronnie could sense the change almost like an adrenalin rush that had swept through the group.

"Where to now?" he asked.

"Wait and see, just wait and see," said Devlin laughing. The others joined in.

"Is this not the same street as before?" Ronnie asked. They had travelled a different route but the row of houses ahead looked familiar.

"That's right," said Devlin. "You've got a good sense of direction, Ronnie. That's a useful skill. Ever spent any time in the services?

"No."

"I guess you're too young. It had all turned to shit by the time you would have been old enough," Devlin replied.

"I don't think it would really have been my scene," said Ronnie. "I've never been much of a joiner."

"It would be the making of you," Devlin replied. "There is nothing like the bonds you make in the forces. Nothing like them, not wife, not kids. These guys here are my brothers. Right lads?" The others nodded their approval.

"So why have we come back? Is there more stuff to pick up?"

"You could say that," Don interjected. "Just watch and learn."

They approached the property from the opposite end of the street this time. Don, Liam and Ed stayed back. Ronnie and Devlin stopped at the gate.

Devlin pushed the buzzer. The camera swung round to face them. Devlin looked up at it, smiling. He took his rucksack off holding it up to the camera.

"Yes, is there a problem?" The security guard's voice came through on the intercom.

"No problem. I realised we missed a few bottles. They'd slipped down inside the rucksack. I thought I would come back and drop them off. Do you want me to leave them here or come up to the house?"

"Hold on. I'll come down and get them," the voice clicked off.

The front door opened and the security guard walked down the gravel drive with a dog lead in one hand and an over excited dog bouncing and pulling on the end of it. Devlin undid his rucksack and pulled out a number of small bottles of medication in a clear plastic bag. He held his hand through the gate.

"Sorry about this, but I didn't want your boss to think we were trying to rip him off. I like my customers to be satisfied with the service."

The security man nodded and held out his hand to take the bag. As he leaned forward. Devlin dropped the bag and grabbed his hand yanking his arm and shoulder through the gate. He flailed uselessly, letting go of the dog's lead and trying to use his free hand to push back from the gate, but Devlin twisted him around and pulling a knife from the sheath on his waistband, he plunged the blade into the guard's neck while pulling his body backwards. The frantic dog jumped and snapped, but Devlin was protected by the body of his unfortunate victim. Ronnie stepped back in shock as blood sprayed from the wound covering his jacket and face. This was not what he had been expecting. He glanced up and down the street. There was no sign of Don or the other two. Then he saw movement. They had scaled the walls and were now on the other side. The dog heard them and set off bounding in Don's direction. There was one shot and the barking stopped. Ronnie saw the three figures hurrying up towards the front door of the house, which lay open. Don went in the front, while the other two circled the property.

Devlin had let go of the guard, whose lifeless body slumped to the ground. Moments later the gate began to open. Devlin stepped through the widening gap and gestured to Ronnie to follow him. Ronnie wanted to turn and run, get as far away from these men as he could, but he knew that was not an option. Once through the gate Devlin took hold of the guard by the leg and told Ronnie to take hold of his other leg and they dragged his lifeless, bloody corpse out of sight to one side of the gate.

When they entered the house the other guard was already in the hall, his hands up in the air and a gun pointed at his head. He looked stunned at this unexpected turn of events.

"You have no idea who you're messing with," he said to Devlin as they entered the hall. "You'll pay for this."

Devlin put his hand up to his mouth and indicated that he should be quiet. The doors to the living room were shut.

"Right, tell her to come out here, say that you need to see her," Devlin instructed.

The guard remained silent. Devlin took out his knife which still bore the evidence of the killing outside and placed the tip of the blade under the guard's eye.

"Call her now!" Devlin's tone made it clear this was not a negotiation.

"Mrs Hemsworth, Mrs Hemsworth. Can you come out here please?"

They all waited and heard approaching footsteps. A key turned in the lock.

"David, was that a gunshot I heard, is everything all right?" She was already at the end of the sentence by the time the door swung open. Her face took on a look of absolute terror as she saw her guard with a gun pressed against his temple. Mrs Hemsworth stepped back pushing the door closed, but Devlin shoved it open and barged into the room. Ronnie and the others followed him.

It was a grand living room, with plush, cream coloured carpets, another large chandelier hung from the centre of the ceiling and two long white leather sofas sat against each wall. A spacious bay window looked out over the grounds. There were metal grilles on the windows. The room was dominated by the large, unwieldy hospital bed which took centre stage. A man was lying in the bed connected to a drip. He was pale, his grey hair was thinning on top. His breathing was steady and he was heavily sedated. He looked as though he had been a large, well-built man, but his body was now ravaged by illness. Mrs Hemsworth backed away until she was at the side of the bed.

"Get out of here!" she screamed at Devlin. She was in

her forties, and was impeccably dressed. In fact it looked as though she had been totally unaffected by what had been going on in the world. Her hair was styled, her clothes were beautiful but impractical. On each hand her fingers were adorned with rings and around her neck hung a set of pure white pearls. She was sobbing, but even in this distressed state she was an unusually beautiful woman.

Devlin ignored her outburst and walked around to the other side of the bed, where a tray of small medicine bottles sat on the bedside table. They were identical to the ones Ronnie had seen him offer to the guard. Devlin opened his rucksack and placed the bottles inside, then he rummaged through the drawers of the cabinet and removed other medicine bottles.

"What are you doing? He needs those. Please! My patient can't manage without those medicines. What are you doing?" the words were spoken by the only other person in the room, a man of about thirty. He was unassuming, below average height with short neat brown hair and a pleasant face.

"So what will happen to him without these?" Devlin asked, holding up the rucksack full of medicine.

"Without those I can't treat him and it is likely that he will die," the man responded.

"So you are the doctor then, a real doctor?"

"Yes…" the man hesitated. "I am a fully qualified doctor."

"Right Don, take him outside."

Don walked over and grabbed the man by the arm and began to frog march him towards the door.

"But, I can't!" He tried to pull away. "My patient, Mr Hemsworth needs care, I can't leave him…" Don continued to drag the man out of the room and down the stairs into the front garden.

"What about my husband?" the woman protested. "You heard what the doctor said, he needs care and medication."

Without a moment's hesitation, Devlin pulled out a

hand gun from the holster on his belt and shot the sleeping man twice in the chest.

The woman screamed, a shriek of absolute terror, and flung herself onto her husband's body, clutching him as the blood soaked into the front of her blouse. Devlin pulled her off and turned her round. He could see the fear in her eyes and Ronnie began to feel his pulse race. Devlin looked her up and down then he reached out his hand towards her chest. Ronnie could see her shrink back. Devlin took hold of the string of pearls and rubbed the precious beads between his fingers.

"Take them off," he ordered.

She fumbled with the catch and let him take the necklace from her. She was shaking, small sobs escaping from her. Devlin reached up and wiped a tear from her face, before walking from the room. Ronnie just stood there looking at her as the others followed Devlin out of the door.

"I'm sorry," Ronnie whispered, as he turned away. He glanced back as he reached the door, but she was just standing there, frozen to the spot.

TWENTY SIX

It was dusk by the time they rowed back across the water. The weather had taken a turn for the worse, and heavy rain fell soaking them and their cargo. The doctor sat with his hands tied securely and head bowed. Water ran down his face and dripped from his hair. He had barely spoken since he had been dragged from the house, other than to ask where he was going.

Ronnie sat in the middle of the craft, helping Don row. He too had been almost silent. His mind was still reeling from the events of the day and the violence he had witnessed. He just wanted to get back to the island, get Nairne and get the hell out of there. Angela was wrong about Devlin; he was already past the point of no return. As they reached the dock Devlin climbed out of the boat and moored it, tying the rope securely. Everyone climbed out after him. The doctor was man-handled roughly onto dry land.

"Please, what do you want from me?" He was frightened.

"Do you have a name?" Don asked.

"Harry. My name is Harry Dunn."

"Then welcome to your new home Doctor Dunn," said Devlin. "Don't worry you will like it here, plenty to eat and drink, good company, safety and security. What more could you ask for?"

"So how long do you intend to keep me here?"

"For as long as we need us. We have a whole community of people here who can benefit from your experience and skills. How much more rewarding will that be than treating one person?"

"But, what about my family……. I have a wife and a son. They'll be expecting me home, what will happen to them? Please, you need to let me go back." He looked panic stricken.

"Doctor Dunn, Harry, calm down. Don't worry, we're not barbarians. If you tell us where to find them I'll have a couple of the boys go over there tomorrow to pick them up and bring them here. Honestly, you will not get a better offer than this. We are safe over here, secure, and we can easily accommodate your family."

"But we have a home......" Doctor Dunn's words trailed off. He could see from the expression on Devlin's face that this was not a negotiation. Devlin untied the ropes from the man's wrists and put a friendly arm around his shoulder.

"Come on, have a look around and you will see this is the best thing that could have happened to you and your family."

Ronnie walked behind them as they approached the main building.

As they entered the building, Don took charge of their new guest and took the man upstairs to get him settled into his new accommodation. Devlin turned his attention to Ronnie.

"Not a bad day's work, what do you say?" Devlin beamed.

"Yes, I can see that a doctor is a valuable asset to the community," Ronnie replied, trying to keep his tone even and his views to himself.

"Now you can see just how good our set up here is. I knew we needed a medical expert, with a group this size we need to have someone on hand if there is an illness or an accident, so when I heard about Hemsworth I knew that was our chance. Best bit is it didn't cost us a thing. Look, I guess you'll want to get cleaned up before dinner. Thanks for your help today Ronnie."

The words felt like an accusation, as though Ronnie had been complicit in the crime, a knowing participant.

Nairne was sitting on the chair at the small desk leafing

through a book when Ronnie entered their room. She glanced up.

"Are you all right? What happened?"

Ronnie was pale. He looked shattered. His jacket was stained and Nairne could see blood on the back of his hands and smeared across his cheek. She got up and went over to him. He pushed the door shut and slid down onto the floor, his head in his hands.

"Ronnie, what happened?"

"Devlin is what happened. Your mum's wrong about him. He is completely crazy. We need to get your sister and your mum, and we need to get out of here as soon as possible."

There was a murmur of approval as Devlin introduced Doctor Dunn after the evening meal. Their own doctor. Everyone could see what a great achievement this was for the community and Devlin revelled in the praise. Doctor Dunn, stood silently with Don next to him.

"So, as of tomorrow, we will have our very own medical practice. We're setting up a room as I speak. I have asked Doctor Dunn to see each of you for a general check-up over the next few days. Obviously, we are unlikely to keep the good doctor fully occupied, so he will also accompany us back to the mainland, where he can use his skills to help others in exchange for supplies for the community. So, he will more than earn his keep. We will also be looking for a volunteer to work with the doctor to learn from him. Let's raise our glasses and welcome Doctor Harry Dunn!"

Everyone stood and raised their glasses in a toast. The doctor looked overwhelmed but Nairne and Ronnie guessed it was with fear. The man was now a slave working for the community here and on the mainland. Ronnie could see why Devlin was so keen to locate his family and to bring them over to the island, as that would secure the doctor's co-operation.

As the meal ended, Devlin left with his men to plan the

following day's activities so Nairne took the opportunity to invite Angela out for a walk with them both.

It was an overcast and wet evening so they put on their coats and boots and set off up the drive. The light was fading fast and Angela had been aware that they had attracted some surprised glances when they had left the warmth of the main hall.

"You two are being very mysterious, could we not have had a chat indoors?" Angela asked.

"No," Ronnie replied. "We needed to be sure we would not be overheard."

"We've got something to tell you. You need to come with us and we need to leave as soon as possible," Nairne said.

"But Nairne I've already explained, I'll be fine here with Devlin and I know you don't want me coming to live with you. I understand, but really I'll be fine if you can just take Eve. I saw you together today she looked so comfortable with you."

"Ronnie tell her what happened."

Angela glanced at Ronnie inquisitively. Ronnie took a deep breath and gave a short graphic version of the day's events. Angela listened intently and her expression became more and more grave.

"It isn't just that he murdered a man who posed no threat to him, it was the way he did it. The way he seemed to feel nothing at all, no guilt, no compassion, nothing. And there's something else. He took a string of pearls from the woman. I thought…. when he went to touch her…. But he just took the pearls from her and…."

Angela put her hand up to her neck, her fingers closing around the string of pearls, Devlin had presented her with not two hours earlier. She felt the smooth perfect surface of each individual pearl.

"I'm not defending what he did, but if that man was dying and Doctor Dunn had decided to come back here, maybe he thought he was doing the kindest thing…."

"Angela, mum, you're not listening. He shot the man twice in the chest like it was a perfectly normal thing to do. The doctor didn't choose to come back here, he was forced at gun point. And the pearls that you're wearing, he took them from the murdered man's widow." Nairne's voice was urgent and panicked.

"Mum, please, you need to believe us. It is not safe here, just come with us."

TWENTY SEVEN

Doctor Harry Dunn sat in his new surgery. He glanced around the room. It was quite impressive. The community had managed to gather a remarkable amount of medical equipment, some basic instruments for dentistry, surgery and a good collection of drugs. They had pain killers, insulin, tranquilisers and anaesthetic. It was as if someone had done a smash and grab raid on a hospital. He guessed some of the medication would be past its official use by dates, but in comparison to what he had been working with over the last year it was remarkable. A couple of community members were sorting through the supplies for him and compiling a proper inventory. They had even left him a supply of notepaper and folders, one for each community member so he could make up basic medical records. He sighed deeply. That morning he had given Don directions to where his family lived. He had written a note to his wife to tell her to come with Don and that it was all going to be fine. A wave of nausea came over him as he thought about what he had done; bringing his wife here with these people. He knew that Devlin was out of control and he'd seen first-hand how callous they were, but what choice did he have. Leaving his family alone in the city was potentially an even more dangerous scenario.
So far, Doctor Dunn had seen six patients and checked them over. They were all in remarkably good health and he guessed that food supplies had been reasonably constant for this group. He finished his cup of tea and opened the door of the surgery and called in the next patient.

His morning surgery ended with his eighth patient of the day. He recognised her as soon as she entered the room. She had been sitting next to Devlin the previous night at dinner. Angela introduced herself and sat down in the chair. She was older than any of the other women in the community that he had seen so far. She seemed nervous, and he noticed that as she sat she held herself carefully.

"So Angela, I'll just run through some basic checks. I'll weigh you, check your blood pressure and listen to your heart. Nothing to worry about. Then if there is anything in particular you wish to raise then please do."

Angela nodded and moved forward in the chair to slip her shoes off before standing on the scales. He could see her wince.

"Are you in pain?"

"Just my back," she replied. "It has been sore for quite a while……. but I doubt there is anything you can do for me, Doctor."

"I can have a look at it. If it's a disc problem or muscular we can sort out some exercises which may help."

"Perhaps, but I don't think it is……"

"So what then, do you have some reason to think it is something else?"

Angela nodded and he could see the fear in her eyes.

"Doctor, I found something. It was a long time ago, well over a year…… a lump. I know what that means and I know there is nothing anyone can do for me……. So I think my back is just the next stage…….. But it would be good if you could tell me how long I might have. And if you will be able to help me when the time comes."

"Let me take a look first. I want you to tell me about any other symptoms you have had. There could be a variety of causes and I don't think you should be jumping to conclusions just yet." He sounded reassuring and calm. "Have you discussed this with anyone else?" He knew she was Devlin's partner, and he now began to wonder if this was the reason he had been brought here, but if she was right and this was some sort of cancer then there would be little he could do, except help manage the pain.

"Oh no, and you mustn't tell anyone, please."

"But Devlin said he wanted to know if I found any

significant health issues within the community. I'm not saying this is, but if it is.....""

"Please don't tell him. If it turns out to be serious then I just need a week or two more then it won't matter if he knows. I know it's a lot to ask but please."

"Okay, I'm not happy about discussing my patients with anyone, but you do understand my position here. My wife and son will be arriving later today, and I need to make sure that I don't do anything to jeopardise their safety." He could see the terror in Angela's eyes, no longer about her health, but about Devlin finding out something serious was wrong. "Angela, I want to be able to act as your doctor, and I want you to trust me. Let's have a proper look and see if I can at least identify what this is before we both start getting into a panic about Devlin. Agreed?"

She nodded in response. She could see she was placing him in an awkward position but she just needed a little bit of time.

An entire day of heavy rain, which showed no sign of letting up, had prevented anyone from undertaking any work outside. The only people to venture outdoors were Don, Devlin and two of the guards. They set off mid-morning to the mainland to fetch Doctor Dunn's family. Ronnie and Nairne volunteered to give Alex a hand sorting through the various boxes of medical supplies the community had gathered over the last few months. Although Alex had kept all the supplies together, there was no detailed inventory. Some of the drugs would be past their best, but he had agreed with the doctor to check each one and separate those which were still within date. He was also starting on a proper list of all the supplies including bandages and instruments. Nairne had started making a list of the various herbs the community had grown within the grounds, and Ronnie was searching through the library for any books on herbal medicine, which the doctor might be able to use.

The three of them sat in the library. It was a beautiful room with oak shelves lined with hundreds of books. Most had been there when the community took over the place but they had also gathered some on their trading missions. Ronnie and Alex had moved the ten boxes of medical supplies into the library and Alex was carefully unpacking them. They chatted while they worked. Nairne could see why Angela was fond of Alex. He was a kind and considerate young man who just didn't seem to fit in here.

"Do you have any idea when you are going back home?" Alex asked.

"What, trying to get rid of us?" Ronnie replied, laughing.

"Of course not, Angela is so happy to have you both here, but I assumed you would want to get back before the autumn weather settles in."

"Yes, you're right, but looking out there today maybe we're too late already," Nairne replied gazing out of the large leaded library window which was smeared with rain. "We must have had a few centimetres of rain today. And, interestingly the ground is too hard to soak it up."

"And what about you?" Ronnie asked.

"What do you mean?" Alex replied.

"Are you happy here? Do you want to stay here long term?"

"I don't have anywhere else to go and at least here we're relatively safe. As I am sure you can both imagine, survival skills, fighting and what not, aren't really my strong points. I guess I'll stay here. I have one or two good friends here and so yes, this is it for me."

"What about Ralph?" Nairne asked. Alex looked shocked.

"What do you know about Ralph?"

"Susan told me all about his expulsion from the group. Is that the kind of community you want to live in?"

"Not one of Devlin's finer moments, I know, and I'm not going to try and excuse his behaviour, but I couldn't leave your mum here. She's been like an older sister to me. She is the closest thing I have to family. Anyway, where would I go? If I keep my head down, work hard and stay out of trouble then everything will be fine."

"And Susan?" Nairne asked. "My mum seems to think you're keen."

"Oh my God, no!" Alex exclaimed. "Absolutely not! Whatever gave Angela that idea? I was just being friendly. Susan is quite new here and she seemed a little bit….. lost. I suppose I just wanted to make her feel part of the group, and since I spend time with your mum and she works with Susan. I was just trying to help her settle in…." he began laughing. "Me and Susan!"

"It's not that mad an idea is it? Or has Susan already got someone else?" Nairne asked. She hadn't taken to Susan, but she was a very pretty girl. Alex's cheeks began to colour.

"Sorry Alex, it's none of our business. Anyway there was something we wanted to talk to you about. We have a favour to ask of you."

"Of course, anything," he replied.

"Angela has asked us to take Eve back with us to Scotland, to safety and I want her to come with us. Her and Eve."

"What, leave here, leave Devlin? He'd never allow it." Alex looked frightened.

"We aren't planning on telling him. We're just going to sneak out of here at night and take one of the boats. Will you help us?"

"I don't know….. I don't want to get into bother. If Devlin found out I'd helped…… I don't think he likes me much. Part of the reason I've been safe up until now is because of your mum. I know she always supports my position in the group."

"Okay, we understand," said Ronnie.

Silence fell and Alex continued to sort through the boxes. After a while he put down the pen he was holding.

"What do you want me to do?"

"Look, we don't want to put you under any pressure here," said Nairne.

"No, I understand it's my risk and my choice, just tell me how I can help."

"We need to persuade my mum to come with us. She is still trying to convince herself that we should just take Eve and leave her here with Devlin. And secondly, we need help on the night to get out of here. The doors are locked and we need some way of getting our hands on the keys. Can you help?"

"Yes, I think I can do that…… but I have something to ask."

"Yes, what is it?" Ronnie asked.

"Can I come with you? I don't mean all the way to Scotland, but away from here, I can hopefully find somewhere else. I know I have been kidding myself. There's no security for people like me. I know it's only a matter of time….."

"People like you? We can make it look like you didn't help us if that's what's worrying you," Nairne replied.

"No, it's not that, at least not just that….. Look, it doesn't matter, but if Angela is going with you then I think I'd like to go too."

Ronnie and Nairne looked at each other. They had two motor bikes, that would allow them to take Angela and Eve but an extra person would make travelling a much more difficult prospect. However, Alex was willing to take a big risk to help them and he was right, if Devlin or his men suspected Alex was involved he could be in danger.

"Okay, we can help you get to the mainland and to the other side of London. But we don't have sufficient transport for all of us. You'd be on your own once we get out of the city unless we can come up with another form of transport, but it would be better than nothing. We also met some good people on the way down here, they were headed to York to settle down, we can give you details of where they went and maybe you can make your way north and join them. They were in need of some younger people if they were going to make their group tenable. Now we just need to persuade my mother to see sense."

The door of the library opened and Angela entered.

"Alex, you're needed I'm afraid. Doctor Dunn's family has arrived and Don asked if you could get them some supplies from the store."

Angela had seen them standing in the hallway. They looked frightened.

"Great, I'll see you all later, after dinner. We can discuss what we're going to do in more detail," he said as he left the library. Ronnie and Nairne both nodded in agreement.

"What was that about?" Angela asked.

"We asked Alex if he would help us to get out of here. We're going to need access to the keys for the doors and also keys to the padlocks for the boats," said Nairne.

"That's a big risk for him to take, if he gets caught."

"He's coming with us," Ronnie replied. "If you will come too."

"So what about it? Will you come with us?" Nairne asked.

"Nairne, there's something I need to tell you….. I won't be coming with you and I've decided that Eve should stay with me."

Ronnie and Nairne looked at each other.

"So, you don't want us to take her? I don't understand. What's changed your mind?" Nairne asked, her tone unmistakably annoyed.

"There something I should have told you when you first arrived, but with your father and brother…... I just couldn't bring myself to tell you and it was the reason I wanted Eve to go back with you," Angela sighed. Tears welled up in her eyes. "It is such a relief, you've no idea…. I thought, I thought I was unwell, seriously unwell…. I thought I would be dead in a year, maybe two, and that Eve would be left all alone here and that was why I wasn't going to come with you. Devlin is a good man, but I knew he wouldn't cope without me, certainly not with a child. I thought it would be too hard for me, the journey, and what would be the point? I'd be leaving her anyway, but I saw the Doctor today and he said it's all fine. So now I don't need you to take her away. We'll be fine here with Devlin. It's my second chance, with Eve and with you, to be a proper mother. You and Ronnie could stay here, for a while longer. Who knows, maybe you'd like to stay for good. I know Devlin would be fine with that."

"Why didn't you tell us?" Nairne asked her voice raised. "Why can't you just be straight with me just once?"

"I couldn't tell you, when you got here and I found out about your dad and Zane, I just couldn't tell you that I'd be dead soon as well and I didn't want you to feel a pressure to stay or to take me back with you and look after me...... it wouldn't have been fair to you. But now," she wiped away tears which were still running down her face. "Now there's no reason for any of us to leave. I can look forward to seeing both my girls grow older."

"We are not going to stay," Nairne replied. "We will be leaving as soon as possible and we think you should come with us. You, Eve and Alex. But we can't make you."

TWENTY EIGHT

The evening meal was all but over when Devlin took to his feet and called for silence. His expectant audience waited. Nairne glanced along the table at her mother. She looked so relaxed, so happy it was palpable. As Nairne turned her head she caught Susan's eye. She was sitting next to Alex, her expression thunderous. The look was directed at Devlin. The girl's neck was red, her face was flushed, and she could barely remain seated. Her eyes were red raw from crying. Alex was looking down at the table as if his plate of food was the most interesting thing he had ever seen.

"I have an announcement to make, one which I know you will all join me in celebrating. Our good doctor has already proved his worth. Devlin raised his glass in the direction of Doctor Dunn. The doctor was joined at a nearby table by his wife and son. His wife was in her early thirties with a strong face framed by beautiful long dark hair. The boy looked to be about eight years old.

"Yes, our good doctor has already seen many of you and we have some exciting news….. Firstly, though let me ask Susan and Alex to stand up please." They both rose. Alex continued to look down as if hoping a hole might appear into which he could jump. Susan, her jaw jutting out in anger, stared straight back at Devlin.

"Please raise your glasses to Susan and Alex, who earlier today have announced that they would like to get married. To Susan and Alex!" Everyone in the hall raised their glasses and joined in the toast. Nairne glanced at Ronnie who in turn looked to Angela, she smiled but her eyes looked confused. After the toast Alex went to sit down, but Devlin was not finished with them yet.

"So, what I hear you ask has our good doctor to do with this? Well, let me share all the news. Susan is expecting a baby, yes can't you see how she is positively glowing." All eyes turned to stare at the girl. She did not look glowing to Nairne. She looked angry. "Now you all know the rules about pregnancy outwith marriage and I can tell all of you that Susan and Alex are sorry for their behaviour. But I understand, they are young and in love and these things can sometimes happen. So there will of course be a punishment. But we are not barbarians and with Susan in her current condition the punishment must not in any way affect the child she is carrying. So this is what we will do. Alex will be punished tomorrow, and that will be in the form of twenty lashes. Susan's punishment is that she is not to be spoken to by any of you until the child is born. No gossiping, no chatting, no flirting, no conversation unless it is to give her a direct instruction about her duties. And for this period she will be known by all of you as Jezebel. Hopefully, this will give her time to reflect on her behaviour."

Everyone stared at them. Their faces turning from an expression of congratulations to horror. Nairne could not decide if the rest of the community were as morally outraged as Devlin was acting, or if the looks were in response to the punishments being meted out. Devlin put his glass down on the table and sat back down to finish his meal. Susan and Alex just stood there, all eyes upon them. After a few seconds Susan fled from the room, tears running down her face. There was a murmuring from the crowd and nervous glances. Alex just sat back down at his seat, his eyes never leaving the table. He looked utterly defeated. Devlin's guard stayed in place watching for any reactions they did not approve of. Angela got up to follow the girl. Don placed his hand on her arm and whispered in her ear. She sat back down.

When the meal was over Ronnie and Nairne went up to their room, Angela followed them. She came in and shut the door behind her.

"What the hell is going on?" she asked. "You said that

Alex wanted to leave."

"He does," Nairne replied.

"But what about Susan? He can't just walk out on his responsibilities. What will she do if he leaves her in this condition? This is just wrong….." Angela replied. "We need to talk to him and get him to change his mind."

"Who?" Ronnie asked. "Alex or Devlin? We can't possibly stand by and watch Alex being flogged. So what if he got Susan pregnant? Who is Devlin to decide what punishment should be handed out to two adults who had consensual sex? It is ridiculous."

"This is a community. We have rules and everyone knows that. Without the rules where would we be? Alex can't just leave her….." Angela persisted.

"I'll go and find out what is going on with Alex," said Nairne.

Nairne found Alex in the library, finishing off his list for the doctor. He looked up as she entered and indicated for her to stay quiet and to close the door.

"What the hell is going on?" she asked. "I thought you weren't interested in Susan?"

"I'm not," he hissed the words. "In fact, I can't stand her, but Devlin has decided that I am the father of the child, so what am I supposed to do?"

"Deny it. Tell him she is seeing someone else, let whoever got her pregnant take the blame."

"Yeah, except it's Devlin's."

"What?" Nairne gasped. "How do you know?"

"I've seen them together. She is totally besotted with him and it's not the first time. Adam, one of the other children in the nursery."

"Yes, what about him?"

"You didn't notice the similarity to Eve, they are like peas in a pod…. Adam's mum was married to one of Devlin's men, but he is fair haired as was she. There is no way he is the father of the child."

"So where is she now?"

"No-one knows, one day she had just gone, supposedly she ran off but I'm not sure I believe that."

"What, so Devlin makes a habit of sleeping with the other women?"

"Yes…. that's the truth."

"What happens then if you come with us and leave Susan here, with no one to marry?"

"I don't know, but she is not my problem… honestly, I have never ever had anything to do with Susan, not like that…. I was just summoned in to see Devlin and told that Susan and I would be getting married. She just sat there and she confirmed in front of witnesses that it was my child. It is so stupid, I don't even like women…and now….."

"That's what you meant earlier on about people like you."

"Yes, that's what I meant. I think Ralph was also gay, not that he ever said anything to me, too frightened to, but I kind of suspected. The whole theft thing was just an excuse to get him off the island and out of the community……"

"Right, so here's what we need to do, we need to leave tonight."

"But we haven't made any proper plans," Alex replied.

"No, but if we wait you are not going to be in any condition to travel. Not after a flogging.

I'll go and let Ronnie know and get our stuff together. We'll meet you downstairs in the main hall at two o'clock, everyone should be asleep by then."

"What about Angela, is she going to come with us?"

"No, and she wants to keep Eve. She's decided they should both stay here with Devlin. She even asked us to stay, but there is no way we are going to stay here one more day. The guy is out of control."

When Nairne returned to her room Ronnie was trying and

failing to persuade Angela to change her mind.

"At least let us take Eve, she'll be safe with us. I promise you. And our community is thriving, we can provide for her long term."

"But so can I, and with Devlin. You've seen this place, we're doing really well here…..I was mad to even think of sending her away. You have to understand when I wrote that letter to Daniel, I thought I was going to die…… I wasn't thinking straight."

"Angela, there is no way this community is growing enough food to feed itself. You are only getting by because every week the men go over to the mainland and take stuff from other people by force. There's no long term future in that. And Nairne and I have seen the diseases spreading in other cities. How long before you get someone sick here. Please think about it……"

"Oh Ronnie, I know you mean well, but you and Nairne are barely more than children yourself. Honestly, we'll be fine here. Maybe you can persuade Nairne to stay a bit longer."

"No," Nairne interrupted. "We're leaving tonight. I've spoken to Alex and he's coming with us so we need to go tonight before his punishment."

"And what about Susan?" Angela demanded. "He's just abandoning her?"

"It's not his child."

"Well he would say that, wouldn't he?"

"Yes, because it's true. Mum, Alex is gay. He has no interest in Susan or any other women in this community."

"Then I'll go and tell Devlin there has been a mistake, and we'll get to the bottom of this. Make the real father take some responsibility."

"Devlin knows who the real father is, that is not the issue. He has instructed Alex to take responsibility, and Susan is colluding with him telling everyone it is Alex's child."

"But why would Devlin do that?" Angela stood up.

"I'm going to see him right now."

"Because the child is his." Nairne said the words and watched as her mother crumpled in front of her, her face aging almost instantaneously.

"Nairne, that's a cruel and nasty thing to say to me. You have no right…. no right to say such things!"

"Mum, it's true, "

"Oh, I guess Alex told you that. I'm so disappointed in him. I thought he was my friend. To say such a cruel thing, to try and shift the blame onto Devlin…..I'll never forgive him."

"He's not lying, mum, he's seen them together. And she's not the first. Adam's mum….."

"What about her?"

"Mum, Adam and Eve are so alike. They are obviously brother and sister. Everyone else can see it. Please, just wake up and come with us, please," Nairne begged. She took hold of Angela's hands and the two of them stood staring at each other.

Angela pulled away and pushed past.

"Nairne, I can't believe you would say that. To try and destroy everything I have. There is no way that Devlin would do that to me." Angela spat the words. "I know you don't approve of him, but he loves me, he always has."

She stormed out of their room slamming the door behind her.

"That went well," said Ronnie.

Nairne sat down heavily on the edge of the bed.

"Why won't she believe me? Why can't she see it?"

"I don't know, maybe it's just too hard to think she's spent all this time with someone and has been so wrong about them. Whatever her reasons are we need to leave, with Alex and if possible with Eve. I know this is going to be hard but we need to go. Unless you are willing to stand by and watch someone be flogged."

"No, you're right. Let's get our stuff together," Nairne replied.

"And Eve? We can't take her against Angela's wishes," Ronnie said.

"I know, I know but leaving her here….. What do you think her chances are?"

"Who knows? She could make it. There is no way this group is going to hold together long term, but that doesn't mean your mum and sister won't make it."

TWENTY NINE

Angela sat on the edge of her bed. She had been down to Devlin's office. There was no sign of him. She could feel a tightness across her chest. A day, which had been so wonderful, she had got her life back and now...... for Nairne to make up those hurtful stories. She just couldn't believe it. She was tense, her neck ached and she could not settle. Glancing at her watch she stood up and strode towards the door; she would speak to Susan and get to the bottom of this whole mess.

She reached Susan's room. Her hands were sweating and she could feel herself tremble as she knocked firmly on the door. She waited. There was no answer. She knocked again.

"Susan, it's Angela. I need to speak with you." Her voice sounded loud and strained. She grasped the door handle and turned it. The door was locked. She hammered on it, her temper rising.

"Susan, open this door. Open it now. I need to speak to you!" She rattled the door backwards and forwards. A door opened further down the corridor and Carron poked her head out.

"Angela, is everything all right?"

"Yes, it's fine. I'm looking for Susan...... it's important."

"I haven't seen her, not since dinner. She was very upset about Devlin making that announcement and everything. Alex was here a while ago..... But as I said to him, she hasn't been back to her room," Carron replied.

Angela stormed off down the corridor without another word. She would find Alex. He could look her in the eye and tell her it was not his child.

Alex's room was on the opposite side of the main building

where the other single men lived. It was a floor below the room currently occupied by Nairne and Ronnie. Angela went down the stairs, her heart was thumping, and she could feel her temper rise. She could see a narrow band of light beneath his door. She knocked on the door, opened it and walked in. Alex spun around. He was standing next to the bed stuffing items into a small rucksack. He jumped, startled by this sudden intrusion.

"Angela, you gave me such a fright…. I should have locked the door." He put his hand to his chest as he spoke. "I'm glad you've come, I wanted to see you before I left…..you know I'll miss you so much. You've been such a good friend to me… Angela, is everything all right?"

"What do you think? How can you just walk out on your responsibilities? I thought better of you Alex. I know Susan can be difficult, but she's young…… you can't just run away like this. I know you may think that Devlin is wrong to punish you, but you must realise that for a community like this to work, there have to be rules. It's what we all agreed to, remember?"

Alex looked shocked.

"We never agreed to Devlin handing out punishments, not like this. I'm going to be flogged and for something that has nothing to do with me. It's not my baby. As I said to Nairne….."

"Yes, she told me what you had said. I just can't believe you would make up something so hurtful."

"But I'm not making it up, honestly!"

"You expect me to believe you, and all this nonsense about being gay…. If that's true why did you never say anything to me?"

"Because I was afraid to tell anyone. I could see how intolerant they are; Devlin and his guard. I knew what would happen if they found out."

"I don't believe you Alex, not for one minute, not any of it! And you should think carefully about trying to leave. You should be man enough to take your punishment, ask for forgiveness and take care of your responsibilities."

With this Angela stormed back out of the room slamming the door behind her. Alex slumped down on the chair next to his bed. His legs were shaking. Angela had been his one true friend, and even she did not believe him. He looked at his watch; there were six more hours before he was meeting Ronnie and Nairne. He just had to hope Angela wouldn't say anything.

Ronnie and Nairne lay together on top of the narrow bed. They were meeting Alex downstairs at two o'clock, once everyone in the building was asleep. Already packed and ready to go, grabbing a couple of hours sleep before leaving had seemed like a good idea. Ronnie's breathing was deep and regular, while Nairne lay there, her mind racing. She didn't want to leave like this, sneaking away in the middle of the night, the angry words hanging between her and Angela, but she also knew they could not stand by and watch someone being flogged. She felt bad about leaving Eve, but Ronnie was right. It was Angela's choice and responsibility. Maybe she would see sense and come with them. Nairne looked at her watch; it was just after ten thirty. Gently, she lifted Ronnie's arm, which was draped over her waist, and moved it back. Then, with as little sound as possible, she stood up and sneaked out of their room. She would go and speak to Angela, try one last time to persuade her to come with them. She cut down the back staircase to the floor below. The building was quiet and most people had turned in for the night. Walking down the corridor to Alex's room Nairne knocked gently at the door and opened it, mindful that she did not want to be caught sneaking around in the men's quarters at this time of night. Alex looked up as the door opened, hoping it might be Angela, now she had time to calm down. Nairne stood in the doorway.

"Can I come in?" she whispered.

"Yes, of course, please."

"I just wanted to check you were ready for later…." She could see the rucksack neatly packed. He even had his boots on ready to leave. "You might want to get a couple of hours sleep before we go. Ronnie is out like a light, but I couldn't settle. I'm going to have one last go at talking to my mum... I know it's unlikely, but I thought I'd give it a try," said Nairne.

"Yes, you should do that," he replied. "She came to see me earlier. She was so angry. I never wanted to hurt her, Nairne, I'd never do that. But she was so upset. I feel terrible leaving like this."

"Why don't you come with me? Let's see if we can persuade her."

"I'm not sure. I don't want to make things worse," he replied.

"We've nothing to lose. All she can say is no and if we give it one more go then at least we will both know we have done everything we could."

Nairne held out her hand and Alex stood taking it in his and followed her back out into the corridor.

"I told you already I don't know how she tracked me down. And anyway you are just trying to change the subject. I want you to tell me about Susan. I want you to tell me that she is not carrying your child!"

"You want me to tell you the truth, then tell me why you sent for that daughter of yours. Tell me why Angela. Do you want to leave? Is that it?"

"I didn't send for her. She told you she met Lizzie, she told her where we were and Nairne tracked us down...... you can hardly hold me responsible for that."

"But I know that is a lie Angela. I know it for a fact. Do you want me to get Nairne down here and ask her why she lied to me? Do you want me to get the guard to question her? Do you?" Devlin roared at her, his voice full of threat.

Angela was so angry she could barely think clearly. It was a bluff. She was sure of it. How could he know Nairne was lying? How could he be so sure?

"Why would she lie? Why would she do that?"

"Like mother, like daughter," said Devlin. "Like all

women. You were made to tempt us, to torment us, to manipulate us………Take Lizzie for example. Oh yes, Lizzie, you probably thought she was your friend……" Devlin laughed. "So it may surprise you to know that shortly after Eve was born I was forced to deal with Lizzie…. she was trying to split up the group, drive a wedge between me and the guard, threatening to tell Don that I had made advances towards her…. and I told her straight, no woman was going to come between me and my men. No woman was going to dictate to me. So, I know that Lizzie didn't meet your precious, lying daughter. I know it because Lizzie is not in a position to meet anyone or speak to anyone."

"What did you do? Devlin, tell me, what did you do?" Angela's voice was barely a whisper. She could feel sweat running down her back, her flesh felt prickly and hot and cold. Devlin was on the other side of the room, his back to her. The flames from the fire cast mad, dancing shadows across the room. Angela remembered Lizzie, she was a quiet unassuming girl, always very nervous. The others had teased her. She had not been very bright or particularly pretty, in fact she just didn't leave that much of an impression, and she had simply vanished one day. No one had given it much thought. They had just assumed she had moved on.

Angela tried to keep her breathing under control. She needed to get to the doorway and get out of this room. Devlin turned slowly, facing her. His face looked incredibly calm, as if a great weight had been lifted from his shoulders.

"You want to know what I did. I'll tell you what I did Angela, when you admit to me that you sent for your daughter."

"Fine, you're right……I did send for her…. . I was feeling depressed. And guilty about having left my children behind. I just wanted to make sure they were safe, that was all. I'm sorry we lied. I didn't want you to think I was unhappy here. I didn't want to hurt you, Devlin. You know that I love you. I always have ever since we first met. You saved me......I'll always be grateful for that ....."

Devlin crossed the room, moving towards her. Angela stepped back, every fibre in her body telling her to run. She tried to remain as calm and placid as possible inching backwards, past the bottom of the bed. He was between her and the door. She could not escape the room, so she knew she had to talk her way out of it.

"I should have left you to burn. You don't even know when we met.... . You think I was just passing and decided to risk my life to save you. I worked in that building for almost two years. I served my country, I risked my life for this country, and I came back to some shitty job in some shitty building, pandering to the needs of rich, lazy whores like you. Cleaning your staircases and fixing your leaking taps and dealing with your rubbish. You never looked the road I was on ...... you never knew I existed. I was no more important to you than the shit on your shoe. But I showed all of you, spreading filthy disease. I showed you all. I made sure that pestilence didn't spread. But I should have left you to burn." He stepped forward and took her head between his hands. His voice raised, speckles of saliva hit her face as he spoke. Angela backed away, her hands against his chest as she tried to push back from him. His hands felt warm against her skin, gentle, his fingers caressed her hair. "My beautiful angel. I should have left you to burn......." He slammed her back and her head crashed against the wall. Pain seared through Angela's brain and she screamed, pushing and fighting against him. He pulled her forward and slammed her head back again, roaring as he did so, a sound of pure anger.

They heard the raised voices and the crashing and banging noises as soon as they opened the fire door into the corridor. Angela and Devlin were the only people who slept in this area of the house. Devlin liked his privacy. Their apartment was on the left hand side of the corridor. The voices were raised, but Nairne and Alex could not make out the words. It was definitely an argument. Alex hesitated.

"Nairne, we should go back. We don't want Devlin to find us wandering about out here......" He pulled at her arm, back towards the stairway

"No, I want to make sure mum's okay. This sounds like a real slanging match..." She walked towards the source of the noise. A scream broke through, her mother, then a thud which they could both feel as well as hear like a weight slamming into something. A second silence then another thud and another. Nairne ran towards the sound. She reached the door of the bedroom and turned the handle. It was locked. She rattled on the door. She could hear Devlin now, his voice raised shouting.

"I told you, I told you not to do that! Not to question me! I told you! I told you!" He sounded almost hysterical. Nairne looked at Alex, she thumped at the door.

"Mum, it's Nairne let me in! Mum, what's going on? Open the door!"

Devlin continued to rant.

Nairne pounded on the door.

"Here, we'll break it down," said Alex, who had grabbed a fire extinguisher from the hall. He held it at waist height and slammed it into the door to the left of the handle. The wood began to splinter. The door jamb began to give. He hit it again and again and on the fourth attempt the door flew open. The room was in semi-darkness and in silence. Nairne rushed in. The only light was cast from the open fire on the opposite wall. Devlin was standing to the side of the bed. He ran his hand through his hair. Nairne could hear his breathing, it was ragged and forced as if he had just exerted himself. He was looking down at the floor between the bed and the corner of the room. Nairne walked towards him and followed his gaze. Angela was sitting on the floor, her legs stretched out in front of her. Devlin pushed past Nairne and paced across the room

"Mum?" Nairne whispered.

Alex located the light switch and the room was suddenly

bathed in light. Nairne walked towards Angela whose face was very still as if she was sleeping. Nairne's eyes travelled from her mum's face upwards, following the crimson streak which decorated the wall. She stopped in her tracks, gasping for breath. Alex was behind her now.

"Oh my God….." She heard him whisper and felt his hand on her arm holding her back, pulling her back towards the door. She pulled forward towards Angela.

"Nairne, we need to get out of here!"

Nairne knelt down and touched her mother's face. Angela's head lolled forward to one side and lay there unmoving.

Devlin was ranting now. He was over at the other side of the room rooting around in her mother's possessions, casting clothes to the floor, searching for something.

"I told her, if I told her once I told her a hundred times not to question me. But no, no, no she went on and on and on." He held his hands up to his head. "But I showed her. I showed her who is boss. She's learned her lesson…… and you two. Yes, you." He turned to stare at them both. Nairne and Alex edged slowly round trying to get to the door. "I know the two of you have been filling her head with all this nonsense but no more. I know what you are Alex. I know what you are, an abomination and you will be dealt with. Do you hear me? You will be dealt with. Angela, tell them what you told me, tell them…. I want Alex to hear it from you, his accuser. Angela!"

He strode past them and knelt down in front of Angela grasping her by the shoulders and shook her.

"Angela, tell them," he shook her more roughly.

"Angela….. Nairne get the doctor, quickly, get the doctor. Can't you see your mother isn't well? Go now."

Nairne fled from the room with Alex behind her. They could hear Devlin shouting at Angela.

Once in the corridor Nairne breathed in deeply and then vomited onto the carpet. She struggled to breathe, her body retching again and again.

"She's dead, she's dead," Nairne sobbed. Alex grabbed

hold of her and dragged her along the corridor.

"Nairne, he is crazy! We need to go now. Go and get Ronnie. I'll get Eve. Go on. We don't have any time to waste."

"But he killed her, I can't just leave. He killed her!"

"Nairne, if we don't get out of here he'll kill us too. Come on. He pulled her towards the stairway. Shoving her towards the stairs, Alex took off downwards. "I'll get the doctor and then Eve. Move Nairne!"

Nairne pulled herself up the stairs her legs shaking. She staggered along the corridor and through the door into their room.

"Nairne?" Ronnie stirred and sat up. "What's wrong? Is it time, Nairne?" The room was dark but he could hear her breathing, and sobbing.

"Nairne?" He switched on the bedside lamp. She was standing with her back to the door, shaking. Her face was white, sweat beaded across her forehead.

"What the hell? What's happened?" Ronnie stood up and crossed the room.

"He killed her Ronnie. She's dead."

"What are you talking about?"

"My mum, she's dead. I went downstairs to see Angela with Alex. We were going to try and persuade her to come with us and……. he killed her."

"Who killed her? Nairne, who did this?"

"Devlin, it was Devlin, he……beat her head against the wall, again and again and again…." Nairne's voice was shaking. "She's lying down there in her room. There was so much blood, all over the wall. She's dead. Dead. And she had told him about us leaving, about Alex, about everything…."

"Christ, we need to get out of here. Where's Alex?"

He went to get the doctor and Eve. He said he'd meet us downstairs. But she's dead. I know she is….. Devlin is mad, raving mad."

"Right, come on. We are getting out of here. Come on, right now." Ronnie picked up their rucksacks swinging them both over his shoulder and bundled Nairne out of the door. They crept along the corridor and down the back stairway, pausing momentarily at the floor where Angela's room was. There was already a small group of people in the corridor and lights were beginning to be switched on throughout the building. Ronnie pushed open the fire door into the corridor. He could hear Devlin screaming.

"No! No! No!" The sound was pitiful.

"It was Alex, he killed her. Find him!" he was bellowing at the top of his lungs. Ronnie let the door close and pulled Nairne down the last flight of stairs towards the rear door of the building. Up ahead they could see a silhouetted figure. Ronnie stopped and waited.

"Ronnie?" the voice whispered from the darkness.

"Alex? What about Eve?"

"She's still upstairs. I couldn't get along to the nursery without being seen. And they're looking for me."

"I'll go," said Nairne. "You two get the boat ready, I'll be right behind you." With that, she ran back along the corridor to the stairwell. She was on auto pilot. They had to get away and they had to get away right now. Nairne climbed to the second floor and sneaked along past the school room and nursery until she got to the children's dormitory. They were all sound asleep. She opened the door and entered the room, six single beds lined the room. Eve was in the third bed along. She tiptoed across the room and knelt down beside Eve's bed. She could see her chest rising and falling gently. Nairne leaned over and whispered gently in her ear.

"Hello Eve, shhh, it's all right shhh." She bundled the child up in the blankets which covered her and gently lifted her up. Carefully, cradling the sleeping child against her shoulder she tiptoed back out of the door towards the stairs. Eve squirmed and moaned in her sleep. Nairne gently rubbed her hand up and down her back whispering in her ear reassuringly. She walked back towards the door, as quietly as possible and opened it slipping out into the corridor. Carron stood at the end of the passageway.

Nairne froze.

"What are you doing?" Carron whispered, her voice was tense.

"I'm taking her away. I'm taking her back to Scotland."

"But why? What's going on? What's all the commotion? I thought there was a fire or something."

"No, nothing like that," said Nairne, approaching the other girl. "It's my mum, Angela, she's dead. Devlin…….. He killed her……I need to get Eve away from here, please, don't tell them. Please."

She could see the girl was torn, unsure of what to do, unsure of where her loyalties should lie.

"You will take good care of her?" she asked, her voice breaking.

"Yes, I promise. She's my sister. I'll look after her I promise."

The girl nodded and stepped back into her room closing the door behind her. Nairne let out a sigh of relief.

The back staircase was deserted and she rushed down the two flights. At the bottom there was a fire door separating the stairwell from the main corridor which ran from the main hallway to the kitchen. She peered through the small window. There were men, rushing about, lights were being switched on. She could hear raised voices and heavy footsteps descending the main staircase. Opening the door slowly, she stepped into the corridor, clutching Eve to her chest, praying the child would not wake up. She crept towards the kitchen and pushed open one of the swing doors. The room was in complete darkness. Nairne moved carefully, aware that she did not know the layout of the room and any noise could bring them straight to her. Reaching the rear door she turned the handle. It was locked. She looked up, there was a bolt at the top of the door. Stretching up she pulled it down and tried again, the door opened. Outside the darkness was impenetrable and she almost stumbled down the three steps. A light, over at the edge of the trees, just a faint flash, one, two, three, caught her attention. It was Ronnie. She crossed the lawn, aware that if anyone looked out, or shone a light from the house she would be completely exposed. There was a strong wind blowing and rain lashed against her face. It was cold. Eve began to squirm and moan in her arms. Nairne pulled the blanket around the dosing child and whispered to her. She was only a few metres from the trees when the external lights on the building sprung to life. The lawn was suddenly awash with bright floodlights and from the building the sound of an alarm cut through the air. Eve woke properly now, she filled her lungs and let out an almighty cry, struggling and pushing against Nairne. Nairne just kept going and within a few seconds she was in the woods, with Ronnie at her side. The child continued to wail.

"Where's Alex?" Nairne's voice was whipped away by the wind.

"Gone to unlock the boat. Come on!" Ronnie shouted into her ear and began to pull her along deeper into the woods, the torch in his other hand moving backwards and forwards trying to light a path for them through the tangled undergrowth.

The ground was uneven, and they were heading downwards towards the water, towards the dark, unforgiving swollen river. Eve's cries were beginning to reduce and Nairne could feel her shaking inside the now sodden blankets. She was cold, scared and confused. Nairne continued to talk to her gently, as they rushed onward. The atrocious weather could be to their advantage. It made searching for them, or hearing them thrashing around out here more difficult.

Ronnie glanced backwards, Nairne was right behind him, but he could see lights now, a line of them spreading out across the lawn. They were organised and moving towards them. He guessed they would be heavily armed. Their gun was still locked inside the house in the store room but he had the bow and arrows. No one had seen that as a threat more of a curiosity. But although he knew it could be used as a lethal weapon, they would stand no chance against a group of armed men. He could see Nairne tiring. Eve was heavy, especially in those blankets. He stopped and pulled off one of the rucksacks. Dropping it to the ground he held out his arms and took the child from her. Nairne paused for a moment, then picked up the rucksack, and they began running again, picking up speed, Nairne, in the lead now, Ronnie's torch in her hand. She could see the end of the woods up ahead and then there was about fifty metres to the boat house.

Alex was waiting for them. There were five boats. He had unlocked the padlock around the one nearest the entrance to the boat house and he had taken one of the life belts and put it in the boat. The boats all had small outboard motors, but getting fuel for them had proved to be increasingly difficult, so it was of no use. He sat and waited. He was shaking, not just from the cold but from fear. He had heard Devlin shouting the accusation that he had killed Angela. If they were caught he would be executed, he had no doubt in his mind. He saw the flash of torchlight moving swiftly down the driveway. Ronnie came through the door first, a screaming infant in his arms, looking like a bundle of wet blankets. He handed the child to Alex. Eve looked up at him, her cheeks ruddy from the crying, garbled words escaping from her mouth, between breaths. Ronnie climbed into the boat. Nairne, just behind him, slung the rucksack off her shoulder into the boat. She sat next to Ronnie and they pushed off from the side of the boat house and out into the dark, twisting waters. The storm was fierce, strong winds immediately hit the side of the craft sending them spinning. The current was strong, much stronger than it had been during the day.

They took an oar each and attempted to steer the craft, finally managing to turn it in the right direction.

"One, two, three, pull," said Ronnie. "One, two, three, one, two, three." They fell into a rhythm. The pull of the river was extreme and it felt as though they were making little headway in getting across.

"High tide," said Alex. "We're going to get hit with the

high tide any time now. Oh God, they're coming!"

Ronnie and Nairne looked up, they could see the lights from torches as two boats emerged from the boat house. They pulled harder on the oars. She could feel the muscles in her arms screaming from the exertion, but they both knew those boats were being rowed by young, fit men who did this crossing regularly. They were going to catch up. Moments later they heard the first shot. It went wide missing them all, but it was followed by another and another. The two boats were gaining on them. They were not going to be able to outrun them.

"Stop shooting!" Alex shouted, at the top of his voice. He waved the torch back and forwards. "Stop, you'll hit Eve!" he hollered. The closest of the boats was only ten metres away. They could see Devlin sitting at the bow of it while Don and one of the others rowed. It cut through the water, getting ever closer. From here Devlin could see the three of them clearly and he could see the small outline of Eve, held tightly in Alex's arms. Ronnie and Nairne stopped rowing. It was futile. The boat pulled alongside them now. Devlin looked remarkably calm as he stood up.

"You can put the gun down," said Nairne. "We'll come back with you…" Devlin put the rifle to his shoulder and pointed it squarely at Alex. The young man screamed and turned to shield the child in his arms from the inevitable shot. Devlin pulled the trigger.

The tree trunk swirled through the water, bobbing along like a twig, turning this way and that as the current caught at its remaining branches. It surged upstream, the tidal flow hot on its heels, a wall of water pushing upwards into the heart of the city. It hit the side of the boat and Devlin's shot went wide as he slipped and toppled backwards into the water. His body crashed into the swirling darkness, as the boat spun out of control, the oar slipping from Don's hand. He reached over and grabbed wildly for the side of their boat, but the current pulled the boats apart and they continued to spin around getting further away downstream. Nairne looked over the side, as Devlin resurfaced, his expression of fear apparent. He gasped for air and tried to stay afloat. He was several metres away, flailing in the water.

"Quickly, throw him the life belt," said Alex.

Ronnie looked at Nairne.

"Ronnie, throw it to him we can't let him drown!"

Ronnie threw the life belt into the water and Devlin grabbed for it, one arm grasping the float. Ronnie began to pull the rope inwards dragging Devlin towards the boat. Soon he was almost within reach. Ronnie reached over the side of the boat extending his arm as far as he could.

"Grab my hand!" he shouted to Devlin. Devlin was clinging to the life belt. Ronnie reached out further. Devlin uncurled one arm and stretched forward. Their fingers touched as the next surge hit them. The force of the water pulled Devlin under and their grasp was broken. The boat rose with a swell of water. Devlin appeared again, several metres away, gasping for breath, he swung one arm out then the other trying to swim towards the lifebelt.

"Watch out!" Nairne yelled, knowing it was futile, as the wind tore her words away. The pallet which was bobbing up and down on the water careered into Devlin, striking him on the side of the head. The force of the blow lifted his head and shoulders out of the water for an instant and then he went under. Ronnie grabbed the torch from Alex and swung it back and forwards on the water but there was no sign of him. They all looked out into the dark and swirling river, checking each side of the boat.

"It's no use, he's gone," said Nairne. "We need to try and get across to the other side."

Ronnie sat back into his seat, and they each took hold of an oar and began to pull.

THIRTY

"Are you sure you don't want to come with us?" said Nairne.

"No, I think I should stay here. As you have said if this group is going to make it they need some younger people and they've been so kind and generous to all of us. I feel I can really be useful here," Alex replied. "And there's talk of the city opening up again. It's been almost two months since anyone within the city walls has become ill. Anyway, are you sure the three of you don't want to stay here? You know they'd like you to. I don't think they would have managed this winter without you and Ronnie to help."

"I know, and we've really loved being here and helping them to get set up, but I think we need to get back, to get home. I have to think about Eve now, and I know back home that she'll have a good chance. I think you will all be fine here now they're a bit more organised. I'm sure our friends will think we're never coming back. We said we'd be gone for a couple of months, not seven, but there was no way we could have travelled that distance with Eve, in winter. It would have been too risky."

"You have the map Alex?" Ronnie asked.

"Yes, we've put it somewhere safe. And who knows, maybe we will come and visit if that is all right. Ernest and Arnold are already talking about trips to other places to find out how others are coping, so if we ever get organised enough your place will be on our list."

Nairne leant forward and hugged Alex. She could feel tears welling up. She fought them back. Eve stood, arms outstretched.

"Alex, Alex, Alex," she sang at him. Alex leaned down and scooped her up into the air swinging her round.

"Will you be good for Nairne?"

The child nodded, squealing with delight as he swung

her round. She was getting heavy and big. He could see Angela in her when she laughed. He handed her to Ronnie who helped put Eve into the harness on Nairne's back and then they both climbed onto the bikes.

"She is going to miss you," said Nairne. "You've been like a brother to her and to me. I'm glad my mum had a friend like you."

"Thank you Nairne, now you'd better get going before you have us all in tears," he laughed, self-consciously.

Arnold and Ernest and a few of the others stood close by to wave them off. They pulled the visors down on their helmets and started up the engines. Nairne turned to wave at the small group huddled together on the quiet suburban road.

Paul sat at the desk in their living room, a plan of the walled garden in front of him. He laid out the crop rotation plans from the previous three years and then began to mark out the planting plan for this spring, making sure the rotation policy was adhered to. He needed to complete it by Friday for discussion at the committee meeting. The weather was already unseasonably warm so they wanted to take advantage and get things started early. Who knew what the summer months would bring. The door burst open and Subhash rushed in screeching to a halt next to Paul's side.

"Come quickly, come quickly!" The small boy reached up and tugged at Paul's arms. "Come on, they're back, they're back!"

"Subhash?" Paul looked at him questioningly. The boy nodded, his usually solemn brown eyes sparkling with pleasure.

"Dog. Dog, come on!" Dog rose to his feet, stretched, yawned and followed Paul and Subhash from the room. A small group had gathered at the front door, there was an obvious commotion. Paul made his way down the stairs, carefully, a stick in one hand and his other holding tightly to the banister. Dog rushed ahead of him barking madly, tail thrashing from side to side, clearing the bodies out of the way. The group parted and there they were, two figures with helmets on, but visors lifted. Beside them stood a small girl. Dog pushed his way through the throng of people. The girl squealed and hid behind Nairne's legs, arms outstretched wanting to be lifted from danger.

Dog jumped up, his paws on Nairne's chest. She put her arms around him rubbing the fur on his head and ears. The group began to disperse as Paul reached the bottom of the stairs and Arthur shouted out to everyone to give them all some room. Paul and Nairne looked at each other and then he looked down at the child hiding behind her. His eyes questioning.

"This is Eve, everyone, my little sister."

RACHEL MEEHAN lives in rural, southern Scotland and has been writing fiction for a number of years. Earth's Descent is her fourth novel.

She lives with her husband, and their house is situated well above sea level where they grow much of their own food and generate some of their own electricity.

For more information on other titles:
www.Cherryhousepublishing.co.uk

If you enjoyed this book please post a review or get in touch at:
Cherryhsepublish@aol.com

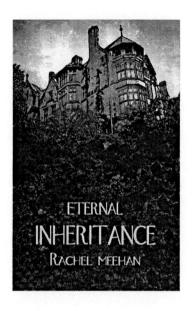

Read an Excerpt from Eternal Inheritance

Twelve year old Sarah is happy living in rural Scotland with her grandparents until her father, Edward Parnell, comes to call. Now Sarah is running for her life.

Against the odds she sets off on a journey full of mystery and danger, finding along the way that there are strangers who will risk everything for you.

Eternal Inheritance is an adventure novel full of twists and turns. There are friendships and bonds, betrayals and lies as Sarah finds herself caught up in a plan for her future that was devised before her birth.

ONE

"Wake up Sarah, wake up!" Her grandmother's voice, although only a whisper, had an edge of urgency that penetrated her sleep. The pounding noise, which had infiltrated her dreams, rang out loudly in the waking world; the walls of her room appeared to shake with the force.

Struggling to open and focus her eyes in the dimly lit bedroom, Sarah watched as her grandmother lit another candle and placed it on the bedside table. Then the slight figure moved quickly and silently round the room opening and closing drawers, removing an assortment of items which she crammed hastily into a small grey canvas rucksack.

"Quickly now darling, there's no time to lose. Get dressed, you need to leave!"

Still trying to grasp the words, Sarah pushed back the covers reluctantly; the cold winter night's air engulfed her body as she reached over for her clothes, which lay folded neatly on the easy chair next to her bed.

"Go where Gran? It's the middle of the night!"

Without pausing, her grandmother crossed the bedroom, reached behind the antique wardrobe and removed a wooden pole with a brass hook at one end. Crossing over to the left corner of the bedroom she reached up and hooked the handle of the loft hatch and pulled. With a click the wooden hatch swung open and an extendible aluminium ladder slid down.

Outside, the rain lashed against the windows of the solitary white cottage. It was only now that Sarah became aware of the lights; instead of the total darkness, which usually encompassed their house, there were car lights outside. Still tucking her tee shirt into her trousers and fastening her belt, Sarah moved over to the window and tentatively pushed back the edge of the curtain. She could see the shadows of two people outside the front door cast by the light of the outside lamp. There were three vehicles parked outside. The black one, which was parked on the grass verge opposite the cottage, was in complete darkness. The other two were police cars, with headlights on, sitting directly outside the gates of the cottage. Three policemen wearing raincoats stood huddled together. The youngest, a tall lanky young man, grasped a leather dog lead in his left hand while the large brown and black Alsatian sat patiently, rain soaking into its thick fur.

"Get back!" Her grandmother's voice sounded panic stricken as she pulled Sarah away from the window, thrusting a waterproof jacket into her hands. Still the pounding at the door continued and now she could hear her grandfather's voice from the hallway.

"Who's there? Hold on I'm coming…."

"It's the Police Mr Miller. Now open the door."

The old man did not open the door, but stood firmly in front of it with an air of anticipation.

"What do you want at this time of night? I'll need to see some identification."

"Mr Miller, don't play games, you know who we are and what we want. Now open the door and make this easy for everyone," the faceless voice called back.

Sarah strained to hear the conversation as her grandmother held her firmly by the shoulders and looked straight into her eyes.

"Sarah, there's no time to explain. You know we were planning on leaving at the beginning of the year, well you need to leave now and we'll be unable to go with you – not right away at least. You have to trust me, it's very important. Your life depends on it. Go to the tree house as quickly as you can, but go the long way round, down to the bridge and along the river. When you get to the river, don't go along the bank, you need to wade through the water. It will stop the dogs following your scent. You can't use the back door as they may have the house surrounded so you'll have to go up to the attic and through the skylight. Do you understand?"

Sarah felt sick. She was frightened. Her grandparents had spoken of leaving the cottage, but together, not like this.

"But Gran, I don't understand, what about you? Why can't you both come with me, and when can I come home?"

"You can't come back Sarah; whatever happens don't come back to the house and be careful. We'll join you by seven o'clock tomorrow morning, if we can. If we're not there by then don't wait for us. There's an address and some money in an envelope inside your bag; if we don't show up go to that address; you'll be safe there." Her grandmother's eyes were filled with tears as she spoke.

Sarah nodded, although her mind did not really understand what was going on. With these final words her grandmother pushed Sarah towards the ladder and handed her the rucksack. Carefully, Sarah climbed the ladder and as she reached the top, she glanced sideways down through the narrow glass panel above her bedroom door and caught a brief glimpse of her grandfather's silhouette still standing firmly in front of the house door. He looked younger than his seventy-one years: a strong, immovable object blocking the doorway, protecting them both from whatever waited outside. He was still arguing with the anonymous voices. She pulled her body into the attic and crouched on one of the great wooden joists that ran across the floor. The attic was only large enough for Sarah to stand in a stooped position. With a click, the loft hatch closed beneath her and plunged her into darkness, Sarah switched on the torch her grandmother had given her. She edged carefully along the wooden beam and fumbled awkwardly with the catch of the attic roof light; it was old, rusted and bent out of shape, but after several attempts it came free and Sarah pushed the window open. Despite the narrowness of the opening the rain flooded in.

At twelve years old, Sarah was slight for her age, so with a bit of wriggling she managed to push herself through the opening and reached back inside for her rucksack which she slung over her shoulder. As she lay face down on the wet roof, her arms outstretched and her body pressed against the cold slates, the rain continued to fall relentlessly. Sarah was aware that the pounding at the front door had stopped: the evening was silent except for the falling of the rain, but this silence was short lived. Suddenly, the night was filled with the explosive sound of splintering wood as the front door was ripped from its hinges. The violence of the noise made her jump and she lost her grip on the edge of the skylight. She slid down the roof; frantically trying to slow herself down as her hands grasped uselessly at the edge of the slates. With a jolt her feet hit the cast iron guttering at the bottom of the roof, which creaked noisily with the force of her landing.

Arms outstretched, she edged her way slowly to the gable end of the cottage and stepped down onto the flat roof of the outhouse. Sarah moved to the front of the outhouse roof and craned forward to peer round to the front of the building. She could hear shouting from within the house and the sound of breaking glass. The only other sound was the crackle of police radios. The three policemen were out of sight and the dark car remained motionless in the lay-by across the road. A young man emerged from the house and crossed to the car. He tapped on the window and it was lowered. He spoke quickly, but with an air of deference.

"She's not there - and they're being difficult. I know the type: threats or bribery won't work." A voice from within the car responded, but through the sound of the rain she could not make out the words; the tone carried an air of menace. The young man began to apologise in an urgent and pleading manner.

"I'll fix it; you know you can rely on me."

He turned and walked back to the house. Sarah could not see him clearly, but he had a strong profile, a straight nose and strong chin. He carried himself awkwardly, limping slightly.

She knew there was no time to waste; her grandparents were risking themselves to give her time to escape. Without looking back, she lowered herself over the edge of the outhouse and let go. There was a drop of about a metre and her feet thudded on the wet concrete slab below as she landed. She dashed across the open space and crouched behind the tool shed at the edge of the garden. Then, she climbed over the wooden fence and scrambled down the steep embankment to the garage. From here Sarah worked her way through the densely wooded verge along the side of the road. It provided cover until she reached the bridge at the bottom of the road, about a kilometre away. It took her longer as the undergrowth was thick and tangled and the ground underfoot was uneven, but she knew that she must not be seen.

The rain was still falling heavily and the trees overhead offered limited protection. Even with her waterproof jacket her trousers were already soaking, and despite wearing her winter boots, her feet were like lumps of ice. Her teeth were chattering uncontrollably as she reached the end of the wooded verge. It had only taken about twenty minutes, but it felt like hours since she had left the warmth of her bed. It was here that the road, which curved sharply to the left, formed a narrow stone bridge over the river below. At the edge of the bridge, on the other side of the road was a wooden ladder, which went up and over the wall, with three rungs on the roadside and six down to the field below. The ladder had been installed for holiday makers and hill walkers to cross into a large flat field which was skirted by the river. It formed part of a popular local walk that teemed with people in the summer months, but remained almost unused at this time of year. In the distance she could hear voices as the policemen shouted out for her asking her to come out. There was also the occasional glimpse of light from their torches, which they swung backwards and forwards, scanning the area surrounding the house.

Crossing the road would mean exposing herself, so she unhooked her rucksack and ran across the open space, throwing the bag over the wall and clambering over the ladder as quickly as possible. The wooden rungs were wet and slippery, causing her to lose her footing on the second last rung; she fell clumsily into the wet grass below. Although smarting from the fall she got to her feet, grabbed the rucksack and ran to the edge of the river. Carefully, and with some trepidation she lowered herself gently into the icy water, which swirled up around her legs. Cold and scared Sarah began to wade upstream through the freezing, fast-moving water.

The river was fiercer than she had imagined and soon her legs were completely soaked and numb. Progress was painfully slow as the stony riverbed made her slip and slide and on more than one occasion she nearly fell. In the hour since Sarah had fled her grandparents' home she had actually only travelled a few hundred metres having taken a circular path, completely doubling back on herself. She could still catch glimpses of the house through the trees: all the lights appeared to be on. She heard the police dog and saw the flashing of torches over on the road in front of the house. She waded upstream until she came to a fork in the river where it was joined by a narrow stream that flowed from the woods. By taking this route she could make it almost all the way to the tree house without leaving a trail.

Sarah was only a few hundred metres from her destination when she became aware of a bright light from the roadside, back towards her home. The light had an eerie glow, but the trees here were too dense for Sarah to get a good view of the source of this strange light. It would be easier to see from the tree house, she thought.

Her grandfather had built the tree house for her three years ago when they had first moved to the cottage. He loved to construct things and always had a 'project' on the go; either pieces of furniture for the house or items for her grandmother's garden. The tree house was made of old pieces of timber, which he had collected from the local farmer, and used to construct her very own house as a surprise for her ninth birthday. This had been her own private place, situated high up in the branches of a large oak tree in the densest part of the woods. Although she was not keen on heights, her grandfather had persuaded her to master the tricky climb. The lower part of the tree could be scaled by using the natural nooks and crannies and pulling herself up by the lowest branches. About four or five metres above ground level her grandfather had constructed a ladder made of two ropes and six wooden rungs, which hung down from the edge of the tree house. This meant that once inside, the ladder could be withdrawn and the house became impenetrable from the ground. Many happy summer days had been spent playing in the tree house when she was younger, but this last year Sarah thought she had outgrown such childhood games and her visits had become less frequent. She thought her grandfather had been upset that she no longer used it so frequently, but her grandmother had said he was just sad to see her growing up and not needing them as much anymore. Now Sarah felt she needed them more than ever.

Finally, Sarah had no choice but to leave the ever narrowing stream, which veered sharply to the right taking her away from her goal. She walked the last fifty metres to the bottom of the familiar oak tree. Her entire body ached with the cold, but she hauled herself up the tree and finally reached the top of the ladder. Once inside, she peered over towards the strange new light in the south-east: from here she could see over the top of many of the younger trees, and her view of her home, although still partially obscured, was recognisable. She was filled with horror, and her heart pounded so loudly it felt like it was going to burst as Sarah began to comprehend the source of this ghostly light: the cottage was engulfed in flames.

Lightning Source UK Ltd.
Milton Keynes UK
UKOW04f0729170316

270357UK00001B/5/P